Where Her

Lies

Where Her *Heart* Lies

CAROLYN TWEDE FRANK

Covenant

Covenant Communications, Inc.

Published by Covenant Communications, Inc.
American Fork, Utah

Printed in the United States of America
First Printing: January 2022

29 28 27 26 25 24 23 22   10 9 8 7 6 5 4 3 2 1

ISBN 978-1-52442-076-5

Praise for Carolyn Twede Frank

His Accidental Bride

It is well-paced, charming, and different enough to make it stand out from the usual romance, and its characters, finding their way in small-town Old West, remind us of the basic goodness of most people. The ending is to be expected, but it's a romance, after all, and there's plenty going on to keep the reader turning the pages with interest.

—Historical Novel Society

An impressively original and inherently entertaining novel that will hold particular interest for all dedicated romance fiction fans, *His Accidental Bride* by Carolyn Twede Frank is an extraordinarily well crafted story with many a reader-gripping plot twist and turn.

—Midwest Book Review

A quick, easy-to-read book set in the Old West with just enough romance, historical detail, and suspense to keep you turning the pages.

—Bookishwayfarer.com

"Celebration for Celia"
In *Heart of the Frontier* Anthology

I was amused that Frank's story acknowledges the existence of privies and chamber pots, topics usually skipped in historical romance. Overall, these four novellas are a quick, pleasant read for fans of sweet Western romance.

—Historical Novel Society

On a rare break from the constant work to establish their family's homestead, two sisters rescue a seriously wounded stranger. In the ensuing weeks, the older sister and the stranger develop strong feelings for each other, but she already has a commitment to someone else. Divided loyalties, honor, and gratitude lead to an unforgettable Fourth of July celebration. Readers will love this Western tale.

—Jennie Hansen, *When Tomorrow Comes*

I was immediately drawn into "Celebration for Celia." Carolyn crafts an engaging story with interesting tidbits keeping me reading until the very last page. She has an impressive grasp of the time period and characters of the western frontier.

—Jen Geigle Johnson, *A Torn Allegiance*

Carolyn Twede Frank took me back home as she described the areas of Idaho where I grew up. I could picture her characters visiting the City of Rocks just as I used to!

—Brittany Larsen, *The Matchmaker's Match*

Chapter 1

1910, Craig, Colorado

LOGAN COULDN'T HELP BUT STARE at the empty gallows. Any minute now, even more people would gather. Heavy boots would bump up those wooden stairs. By then, he'd be blocks away, busy at work, *inside* the livery stable—where he could neither see nor hear what all those onlookers would. The thought of watching while his brother was hanged turned his stomach.

Logan pulled his gaze away from the wooden scaffolding and focused on the crowd. These were his friends, townsfolk who gave him purpose. That's all he ever wanted, to live a quiet life amongst friends, helping them out, making them happy. But now his friends—men and women alike—gathered in groups of two or three, whispering behind their hands, their gazes skirting from the gallows to the jail as anticipation grew apparent in almost every set of eyes. A few caught sight of Logan and immediately looked away.

Did he begrudge them for being there?

No. He didn't blame them. He, more than anyone in Craig, knew firsthand that the prisoner about to meet his Maker was no saint. Yet Logan hadn't expected so many people to show up. His nose dripped, and he wiped his emotions away with the back of his sleeve.

It wasn't like there had been a public announcement telling every resident of Craig about this event. Logan swore, however, that everyone he knew in the northwest corner of Colorado was here. Perhaps it was because of the novelty. There hadn't been a hanging in town since 1889, nigh onto twenty years ago. They were now all done over in Canon City at the state penitentiary. Marshal Walker, however, had received special permission for this hanging, since he was fearful that his prisoner—with untold wealth to his name—could pay people off and get help to escape during transport to the opposite corner of the state. There would be a riot on the marshal's hands if that were to happen.

A heaviness in Logan's chest weighed him down. It seemed to hold his feet to the dusty road. He stared at his left leg, which was a full inch shorter than his right one, and his left foot, which constantly pointed inward no matter how hard he tried to straighten it. These were mere hiccups in his life compared to everything surrounding his brother. He needed to get out of here, but he couldn't help but stare at the gallows a minute longer and cry inside. His brother was not only guilty of being the meanest, most ornery, and most unlikeable son of a gun who'd ever lived in or around Craig, Colorado, he'd also shot a beloved member of the community, the owner of the mercantile, and a dear friend of Logan's—Sam Decker. In the back. In broad daylight. In front of multiple witnesses, including the victim's wife, Lavender Decker, who'd looked on, helpless and in horror.

All because of money.

Logan felt a hand on his shoulder as he readied himself to leave the crowd behind.

"Oh, I wasn't sure I'd see you come out to witness the hanging, Logan."

Logan turned to see Ned Clark, from the telegraph office. "Uh, I'm not here for that," Logan said, stating the truth, trying hard to come across as his usual friendly self. "I'm just heading down to the livery stable like I do every Tuesday about this time of day." He paused and gave Ned a questioning stare. "Say, who's tending the telegraph?"

Ned flicked his wrist over his shoulder in the direction of his office. "Pff! I closed up. I daresay Gus has already done the same with the livery stable too. He won't expect you there. Not today. Besides, everyone's here." He swept his hand across the unobstructed view of the gallows in front of him and then winced. "Sorry. But as long as you're here, you are welcome to join us."

Ned's wife, Constance, nodded at Logan. Both Joe the blacksmith and Stewart from the saddle shop tipped their hats at Logan while their wives waved. Then he spotted his good friend Ronald Smith half a block away. Ron stood next to Dorothy, his wife of twelve years now—oh, how time had flown. They waved at Logan too.

"Thanks, but I don't intend to watch." Logan lifted his hat momentarily. It was enough that he'd watched the men construct the gallows yesterday—and then adjust the trap door. They'd used only the best, freshly milled pine planks. Blasted all, it was an instrument of death; it didn't need such attention to detail.

No one cared that the hinges were the best money could buy. All that mattered was the noose, now swinging in the summer breeze, awaiting its victim.

He tore his eyes away from the noose and weaved through the crowd that clogged Yampa Avenue, wanting to make it to the livery stable before that rope saw any activity.

"Logan!"

He scanned the crowd, searching for who called him.

"Logan!" Gus called out again and waved his hands in the air, motioning for him to come his way.

Logan veered from his intended course and headed back into the crowd. "What do you need?" he hollered over the increasing noise of the crowd, hoping his boss *did* want him to open the livery stable. He hurried toward Gus as fast as his bum leg could walk, not caring to hide his limp. His leg had been crippled since birth, but he'd never let it stop him from doing what he'd wanted before—nor had he used it as an excuse to get out of anything. But at this moment, that might change if his boss wanted him to do something that would require he stay here in this crowd.

Gus latched onto Logan's shoulder the moment he arrived. "Where ya headed, boy?"

"The livery stable," Logan responded, expecting his boss to ask him something of more importance and thinking it'd been years since he was a boy. He did, however, smile inside at Gus's constant use of the inaccurate term. Logan stood half a foot taller than his short-statured boss. And in three months, September twenty-seventh, he would turn twenty-seven. "I'm due at work in ten minutes. I'm taking it you just left things unattended until I got there?"

"No. Locked things up tight. I figured ya'd either be out to your sister's place, you both consoling each other, or here watching, like ya are. Next to poor Sam Decker himself, yer probably the biggest victim of Stanley Jones's cruelty." Gus swatted the air in front of Logan. "So gracious be, don't be feeling like ya got to head on into work today. You've nary taken a day off the thirteen years ya worked for me. Besides, I made sure the horses were all fine before I left."

"Actually, I'd prefer going into work if that's okay." Logan thought about the affectionate animals he worked with. Yeah, he preferred being with horses right now. He didn't care to talk to anyone about Stanley, not even to his sister, Susannah.

"Honest?" Gus, with his brow wrinkled, stared at Logan.

"Honest." Logan sighed. "As tough as he's made my life, he's still my brother. And I don't care much to watch him die." That was the same reason he'd pulled his pa from their burning ranch house thirteen years earlier. His pa had died despite Logan's effort, but the pain Pa had left him with still lived on, haunting him from time to time.

Gus put his arm around Logan. "I understand, boy."

Logan doubted if Gus *really* understood, but for the portion that Gus did, he offered a sincere thank-you.

After a nod goodbye, Logan hurried on his way, wondering if anyone understood how he felt. He doubted it. His observations told him that most everyone thought the biggest crime inflicted upon him was the fact that Stanley got the entire Circle J Ranch and every dollar his pa had amassed. And since that awful day thirteen years ago when their pa died, Stanley had never given, loaned, or offered a red cent to Logan. Or his sister. But Susannah and her husband had discovered coal on their land, so they were set. The townspeople didn't worry about her finances, but they seemed to fret about Logan's.

He wished they wouldn't. He was doing just fine without making lots of money.

That familiar pain swelled at the back of his throat. It grew intense. Reaching down into his chest, it pressed against his heart. By concentrating on the positive things in life, he'd try again to bury the pain. He thought about horses—the nuzzle of thanks he'd received yesterday as he'd rubbed down a particularly friendly mare. It didn't help. The image wouldn't stay. There were too many other things on his mind.

He glanced over his shoulder at the noose that hung, still empty, above the anxious crowd. Finally, he felt it: anger toward his brother. Not for the crimes for which Stanley was about to die, but for digging up feelings that Logan had worked so hard to keep buried.

No, Gus *didn't* understand. Nor did anyone else. It wasn't Pa's or Stanley's money that Logan had been cheated out of. It was their love. And feeling worthwhile. That was all he'd ever wanted from them.

He glanced at the gallows once again. Anger was not what he wanted to be feeling for his brother right now.

Jerking his head back around, he focused on the near-empty end of Yampa Avenue and grappled for positive things to think about.

His mind gravitated to his efforts to connect with his seemingly lonely brother, a confirmed bachelor—not by choice. No decent woman wanted anything to do with Stanley. Logan had managed to visit his brother a few times before Stanley turned way bad. They'd talked about the weather and the price of beef, but that was about it. That served to remind Logan that it looked as though he was headed for bachelorhood himself. Again, not by choice. *No, these thoughts aren't positive enough.*

Yet there was a bright side to his bachelorhood. He was undesirable to the fairer sex because of a crippled leg, unrefined speech, and lack of money—not because he was manipulative, cruel, and egotistical like Stanley.

He sighed. There were other ways for him to stay happy besides the companionship of a wife and kids. One way would be to continue just being who he was. He enjoyed working at the livery stable part-time, and he enjoyed his new job as a postal carrier. Even though he'd been delivering the post for years, now he got paid for it. Not much, but that didn't matter to him. He liked doing it. He made sure he went out of his way to say hello to everyone he delivered the mail to and to those he saw on the streets of Craig.

The crowd thinned as he reached its edge. He stepped onto the empty, covered sidewalk. The shade felt good on his back. He took off his hat and fanned the sweat gathering on his forehead. Out of the corner of his eye, he noticed a wagon approach from the south end of town. It looked to be carrying a man, a woman, and two kids. They didn't appear to be in a hurry, so Logan doubted they were coming to see the hanging.

Keeping a brisk pace, he continued toward the livery stable. As the wagon moved toward him, he could see the horse more clearly and recognized it. The sable brown mare belonged to his friends, the McCurdys. Was Kate coming into town to do some doctoring? Or did Lucas need something for his sheep? Logan waved, glad to talk to someone about something other than the hanging. He broke into the lopsided run he'd worked hard to master. They met up just shy of the livery stable.

"Hey, Kate. Hey, Lucas, boys." Logan tipped his hat at each of them. "What brings you all to town?"

Lucas tilted his hat back, revealing his red hair, and wiped his forehead. He wrapped the reigns around a foot peg of the wagon and hopped down. "We're here to fetch Celeste." He pulled Logan into a half hug and slapped him on the back. "'Tis good to see you, lad."

Logan hugged him back. "Celeste?" he muttered, thinking back to when he'd first met Lucas's daughter. He'd been thirteen, and she'd been five. Lucas had gotten upset with her for pointing to Logan's legs and asking what was wrong with them. Logan smiled at the memory, having liked her pluck ever since the day he'd met her. He would take a child's honest curiosity over a grown-up's uncomfortable silence about his leg any day. "I thought she was away at some fancy boarding school or something." Logan wondered how Celeste's spunk had fared with her highfalutin education.

"She was." Kate, dressed in a tailored, dark-blue traveling dress, climbed down from the wagon with her husband's help.

"But she's done. 'Tis time now for her to come home for good." Lucas sported a wide grin. "She'll be here in five or ten minutes, on the twelve o'clock stage."

Little Lucas stood on the wagon seat, though he wasn't so little any more. He was thirteen now and almost as tall as his ma and had her dark-brown hair. He wrestled with his younger brother, Patrick, who had a hint of his pa's red hair, to get a good view of the crowd down the street. "Ma, can we get out?"

"Yes, you may," Kate said to them.

"Let's run down there and see what's going on," Patrick said mid-jump, landing on the ground, ready to take off.

Lucas stretched out an arm in front of both boys' chests. "Hold on." He glanced at Logan. "What *is* going on down there?"

"You mean you don't know?" Logan raised his eyebrows. "I thought everyone in Colorado this side of Steamboat Springs knew."

"Ah, 'tis the hangin', isn't it?" Lucas leaned and looked down the street.

"Stanley's?" Kate gasped. "That's dreadful. Oh, Logan, I am so sorry."

"I'd think he'd be relieved," Lucas said under his breath, and Kate elbowed him.

"When is the—" Kate cleared her throat "—hanging supposed to take place?"

"Noon." Logan glanced at the sun directly overhead and then toward the crowd, which stirred with even more clamor now. Had Stanley been brought out of the jail? He couldn't see, and that was good.

Kate grimaced. "What unfortunate timing."

"Don't fret, Kate." Lucas wrapped his arm around her and turned her away from the busy end of Yampa Avenue. "'Tis too far away for Celeste to see anyway. Even if she were to catch a wee glimpse, she's not all that frail—she won't faint."

"No, she will not." Kate turned toward the south end of the street. The stagecoach approached. "Because here she comes now. Lucas, you grab her bags the minute the stage stops. We are going to be back on the road before she has a chance to notice that awful gallows." She whipped her hand in the air. "Boys, back into the wagon. Now!"

"Well, I best be going. The horses are waiting for me," Logan said as an excuse as he waved goodbye.

"So . . . you're not going to watch?" Lucas asked.

"Nope. Don't care to."

Lucas nodded. "What's going to happen to the Circle J now? Are you finally going to get a piece of it?"

"Nope. Don't care to either. According to Pa's will, it's all going to my sister, Susannah." Logan honestly didn't want a cent of his pa's money. It represented too many painful memories. And those were something he'd rather not talk about. He quickly tipped his hat. "Gotta go," he said and hurried toward the livery stable.

A block to the south, the stagecoach kicked up a billow of dust in its wake. Two blocks to the north, the clamor of the crowd picked up. He would have liked to have waited for the stage with the McCurdys to say hello to Celeste. But under the circumstances . . . no.

As Logan turned the corner to head into the side door of the livery stable, he caught a glance of the gallows, the portion that rose above the crowd, which had now fallen deathly silent. Stanley was being led, and pushed, up the stairs. The handrail suddenly took on some purpose as it prevented his thrashing body from falling, or possibly leaping, over the side. From two blocks away, the string of curse words flying from Stanley's mouth reached Logan's ears with the same effect they always had. His skin crawled as his heart ached for his brother. That cursing had become worse as of late. As had all of his vices. Stanley had been spending money like it was as plentiful as horse manure, searching, Logan guessed, for ways to buy happiness.

Logan grabbed hold of the stable's door, his eyes fixed on his brother, who continued to yell obscenities, along with pleadings for release, he imagined. Logan could tell Stanley held no remorse for gunning down dear old Sam Decker. Apparently, his only remorse was for meeting an early death. *Oh, Stanley, how could you let money ruin you so?*

A hood went over Stanley's head, and he fell silent. Then went the noose.

Logan tore himself away. The *click* of the trap door opening and its *thud* as it hit the post below echoed down the street. Gasps, screams, and shouts immediately followed. Logan opened the stable door and ran inside. Backing up to a post, he hugged his arms to his chests and lowered himself onto the floor. Tears moistened his pinched-shut eyes. With each inch he sank, he muttered, "My brother, my brother, my brother."

Chapter 2

CELESTE COULDN'T HELP BUT LEAN to one side as the coach turned. A large stand of cottonwoods came into view. She stuck her head out the window to confirm her hope. *Yes!* The coach no longer traveled west. It had turned, and they headed north onto Yampa Avenue. She pulled her head in, leaned her back against the seat, and brushed a wealth of hair from her face. *Home!*

Relief engulfed almost every part of her. The worry in her gut, however, refused to quieten. Her parents were bound to find out sooner or later that she'd dropped out of school.

"That was quick," she said to Mr. and Mrs. Kirby, who sat across from her and would be continuing down to Meeker after this stop in Craig.

"I take it this journey is much nicer than it used to be?" Mr. Kirby asked.

"Yes, compared to before, this was delightful." Celeste scrambled to give a ladylike response. It wouldn't be proper for her to tell them she hated stagecoaches. After all, she had learned a few manners at school. "I remember the days before there was even a train to Steamboat Springs. When I first got shipped off to school it took two days by stagecoach to catch the train in Rawlins, Wyoming." She smoothed out her skirt, not that she cared about wrinkles, but she wanted to keep her hands busy. "This half-day stagecoach ride from Steamboat Springs is a vast improvement, to say the least."

"I hear Mr. Moffat has plans to extend the train on into Craig in the near future," Mr. Kirby said.

"That will improve your travel back and forth to New York even more," Mrs. Kirby added.

"I imagine that to be good news for most people in Craig, but I won't have further use for the train. I am finished with Bennett's School for Young Girls."

"Finished with finishing school, eh?" Mr. Kirby laughed.

"Yes, I am."

"So you've graduated with high marks, I presume." Mrs. Kirby gave her an approving nod. "Quite the lovely little lady you are."

Celeste felt the urge to laugh. "Far from it on both accounts," she said under her breath. Telling her parents she'd opted for an early graduation, which didn't exist, was hardly ladylike. Neither was concocting the story that her diploma was being sent in the mail, and when it didn't show up she'd remind them that letters get lost all the time.

Celeste squared her shoulders. "Truth be told, I was finished after my first year." Her voice wobbled, as did her nerves. "The only reason I stuck it out was for my grandmother's sake. Mother's too. It seemed to make them happy. My grandmother also paid for my schooling, and I wanted to make sure she got her money's worth. Things like that are important to her."

"She sounds like a wonderful grandmother," Mr. Kirby said.

"She's actually my step-grandmother." Celeste gazed out the window. "She reminded me of that a number of times while I was in New York. Oh, look, it appears we are here," she diverted their attention, not wanting to dwell on the subject.

Mr. Kirby stuck his head out the window as the coach slowed to a crawl. "There looks to be some sort of celebration in town. Perhaps they hold their Fourth of July a week early here?"

"No. No, they don't. It must be something else." From Celeste's vantage point, she saw only her parents and little brothers. "Wait, are those really my brothers?" She stared long and hard at them as the coach came to a complete stop.

The door flew open. Ma stuck her head inside the coach. "Ah, Celeste, it's wonderful to see you made it okay. Come now; get your things. We're in a bit of a hurry."

"What's the rush?" Celeste grabbed her handbag and let Mr. Kirby help her down. She offered him and his wife a fond farewell and then gazed at the whitewashed shops and dusty wooden sidewalks of Yampa Avenue, taking in a deep breath of the Colorado air. Things hadn't changed much. Then her eyes came to rest on her family. It was obvious her brothers had. Standing up in the bed of the wagon, Little Lucas appeared taller than she. Celeste was nineteen, so that meant he was nearly fourteen now, and Patrick was nine. She dropped her handbag and held out her hands. "Little Lucas, Patrick, come," she said, glancing at Ma. "Can't I enjoy a hug or two first? It's been four years since I've last seen you."

"But of course." Ma pulled her into an embrace. "We just need to be on our way before . . ." Ma released Celeste and rubbed her forehead. "Oh well, never mind the reason. We just need to—"

"Ma don't want us to see the hangin'," Little Lucas hollered and jumped from the wagon. Patrick hopped out after him. Both ran to Celeste and allowed her to gather them into her arms. Pa joined in.

"And rightfully so." Ma shooed the boys back into the bed of the wagon after their hug and after Pa stepped away. "No child of mine needs to witness such a thing." She motioned for Celeste to climb onto the bench.

"Who's the unlucky soul?" Celeste leaned around Ma. How often would a person get to see such a thing? Not that she wanted to see the actual act. Shivering at the thought, she told herself she wanted to get a look at just the noose itself.

In the distance, she could see it hanging from a scaffolding and swinging slightly in the summer breeze. It looked rather creepy. The setting was not exactly the kind of welcome home she'd anticipated. This epitome of the "Wild West" would certainly give the girls back at school even more reason to snub her. But they'd never know. She wasn't going back. Never again would she have to pretend to think like everyone else wanted her to.

She climbed onto the wagon's bench seat, stealing another glance down the street and quickly surveying the crowd. She gasped. "That man they're pulling up those stairs, is that who I think it is?"

Her pa nodded as he hefted her case into the back of the wagon. "Yep, Stanley Jones."

"Oh dear." Celeste brought her hand to her mouth, an acquired habit she'd finally managed to master this past school year—one of many habits Miss Bennett had attempted to force upon her. She looked around the empty end of the street for a moment or more. "No wonder I don't see Logan in the crowd." The scaffolding grabbed her attention once more. "What did Stanley do, finally kill somebody?"

"Yep," Pa said. "I'll tell you more later. Ahem." He cleared his throat and then spoke out of one side of his mouth. "If you want to hear."

"Of course I do." Celeste rushed her hand to her mouth. Ma glared at Pa and then at Celeste, reminding her that proper young ladies did *not* discuss such indelicate matters. This was exactly why she was here rather than in New York.

Her ears caught hold of a string of curse words from the direction of the gallows. She shook her head. "Stanley Jones never could curb his tongue. Even right before he's to meet his Maker."

Ma frantically motioned for Pa to climb aboard. "You've got her things loaded. Now hurry up. Get this wagon away from here."

"Calm down, Mother. I'm not going to watch them hang Stanley Jones." Celeste turned so she faced forward on the bench. She clasped her hands in her lap, squaring her back against the gallows. "Little Lucas, you and Patrick do the same, for Mother's sake."

Her brothers mumbled their complaints behind her.

"Thank you," Ma said and then held her breath.

Celeste had heard it too—the trap door releasing and the gasps of the crowd.

No one in the wagon said a word. The wheels rumbled forward in relative silence, except for the creak of their rims and murmurs of the crowd.

By the time their wagon passed the last house at the edge of town, Celeste still didn't feel like talking. A man was dead; Logan's brother, no less. What a horrible way to go. But the truth was Stanley Jones was a horrible person. She remembered how Logan used to suffer at the hand and mouth of his brother. At least, that's what she'd gathered back when Logan used to give her and her friend Bethany Tucker horseback rides while he delivered the mail. When she was thirteen, Logan talked to her all the time, talked to her like she was all grown up. He'd listen to her ideas too, not tell her she didn't know anything because she was "just a girl." She'd always appreciated that.

She hoped Logan was the same kindhearted soul as he'd been back then and would forgive her for not returning those letters he'd sent to her while at school. On the long trip from New York, she'd had lots of time to think. Her mind would drift to pondering on the kind of man she wanted to marry, a caring, thoughtful man. Not a superficial, self-serving young man like those she'd met in New York. Often, Logan pushed his way into her mind. He certainly was thoughtful. Heavens, he even cared about his good-for-nothing brother.

She wondered how he was taking the death of Stanley and hoped he was doing all right.

Ma took hold of her hand. "I'm sorry you had to hear that."

"Hear what? Oh." Celeste refocused. "Mother, it's okay. Don't worry."

Ma gave Celeste's hand a pat. "I fear it has brought you low—I can see it in your eyes."

"It is not the hanging." Celeste returned the pat. "It's just that . . . I'd hoped for a hearty welcome home . . . to help me move on with my life." *And forget school and New York and Charles.* "That's all." The pain of her first real love abandoning her, with hardly a word, still stung. Logan didn't count as her first love; he was merely a childhood swoon. Charles had been more than a suitor. Other than Reverend Francis, he'd been her only real friend while in New York.

Ma let go of her hand and pulled her into a hug. "Oh dear, and we swept you away from the coach in such a hurry."

"We'll fix that." Pa offered that warm smile Celeste always loved. "As soon as you feel settled, 'tis a party you shall have out at the ranch. And we'll invite all your old friends—and whoever else you want."

"Thanks, Father." She couldn't help but smile, partly because she found the picture forming in her head quite humorous: two lonely party guests, Logan and Bethany, sitting around listening to Pa's stories while feeling obligated to stuff themselves on mutton chops and nut bread. That was about all Ma could cook well, and of course, she would make more than enough. It actually sounded rather sad when she got right down to it. The girls back at school would certainly find such a party pathetically amusing and try once again to make her feel ashamed. Funny thing was, she'd never felt shamed by her humble Western upbringing before going to school, and she didn't want to now that she was home. Home here definitely appealed more than home there.

She chose not to dwell on those thoughts, and she let the humorous side of the situation draw her in another direction. "And thanks for adding the 'whomever else I want to invite' option. I've been gone so long I fear I haven't many, if any, friends in Craig." Her laugh sounded feeble even to herself. "Say, does Logan still live out of the back of Ronald Smith's law office?" she asked, more than curious. "And is Bethany still around?"

If she'd answered the letters Logan had written to her when she'd first arrived at school, more or less playing the role of a big brother, perhaps he would have continued to write. By the time she realized a big brother's words of encouragement would be nice, it was a full year later, and she was too embarrassed to reply to him. The same was true with Bethany's one letter. Putting off writing because of her melancholy had been a lousy choice. She knew that now. At least Ma and Pa had written to her. But then, she'd been forced to correspond with them as part of her etiquette training.

She hoped she hadn't offended Bethany and Logan. Miss Bennett was correct; Celeste was "hopelessly unrefinable."

Ma nodded. "Yes, Logan's not moved, and Bethany is still around. She married one of the McConnell boys over in Hayden. Did I not include that in one of my letters? Dear me, maybe I didn't. In any case, she lives there now, and I believe she is expecting her first child. Is that not right, Lucas?"

Pa shrugged.

"Don't worry about putting together a party. A big dinner with our family will be all the welcome home I need." Celeste looked over her shoulder at her brothers. "I'll show you all my stuff and give you some gifts then. Okay, Little Lucas? Patrick?"

Little Lucas cleared his throat. "Uh, Sis, I don't go by Little Lucas anymore."

"Yeah, it got confusing for Pa," Patrick said.

Little Lucas spoke up. "More like I didn't want to be called 'little' anymore. Would you?" He glared at Patrick.

"No." Patrick shook his head and grinned. "But at least when Ma yelled at me, Pa didn't keep worrying he was in trouble."

"So what do you go by these days?" Celeste chuckled and ruffled her brother's hair.

He swatted her hand away. "My middle name. Grandpa Donahue ain't around to make things confusing."

"So I call you Robert now?"

"Na, just Rob."

"All right then, Rob it is. But it might take some getting used to." She wondered how many other things had changed here in the last four years since she'd come home for her first and last visit. How many other things would she have to get used to? It didn't matter; it was so good to be home in Colorado, where no one expected her to be refined. Oops, except maybe Ma.

Patrick crawled close to the bench and tugged on Ma's arm "Can we have Celeste's party tonight?"

Ma turned and shook her head at him. "Not tonight. We'll get home too late for me to bake anything worthy of a party. How about tomorrow?" She turned to Celeste for her approval.

Celeste nodded. "That will be more than fine."

Pa leaned past Ma and looked at Celeste. "I could invite Logan to join us if you'd like. I know he's still around. In fact, we ran into him just before the stage arrived."

"You did?" Celeste felt a smile tug at her lips. "It's good to hear he is still in Craig. Is he working at the livery stable, same as always?"

"Yep, still there," Pa said. "Once he knew you were on that stage, though, I guess he would have liked to stay and say hello. But with the hanging and all, he was kind of jittery and seemed anxious to get away."

"He did?" Celeste's voice squeaked. "It's understandable that he didn't care to stay," she said, evening out her tone. She didn't want her family to know she had thought about Logan often during her trip home. She was still trying to sort out her feelings. And the ache she was feeling for Logan right now was simply her empathy for what he must be going through. "You really think he would like to have stayed to say hello—if it weren't for what happened to his brother, of course?"

"I am sure of it," Ma answered. "You know Logan."

"Yes, yes I do. He would have stayed around to say hello, even if I were a stranger," Celeste muttered. She *was* practically a stranger.

"So, do you want Pa to invite Logan?" Ma asked. "To supper tomorrow?"

"Yes, I suppose he would appreciate good company and a home-cooked meal. It would be good to invite him."

"Done," Pa said. "I'll ride into town tomorrow and ask him."

The wagon rolled down the dusty road at a slow pace. Celeste's thoughts gravitated to the hanging. Stanley was Logan's only brother. Thank heavens Logan at least had his sister, Susannah. Celeste envisioned him as a newborn baby, a deformed leg, mother dying, and his brother and father despising him for her death at his birth. What would have happened if not for his loving sister? She shuddered at the thought. Chances were that he would not have turned out to be the person he was today.

Celeste was certain of one thing: she was grateful Logan was not anything like his brother, Stanley.

Chapter 3

CELESTE SET A FORK ON top of the linen napkin to the left of each plate and stepped back to inspect the table. It certainly wasn't the kind of table Miss Bennett had taught her to present to dinner guests. Celeste, however, found it inviting.

"Grandmother Donahue might not be too thrilled that I'm using these napkins next to chipped dinner plates, but she need not ever know," she said to her brothers, who had just walked into the cabin from outside. She glanced at their worn-out overalls and messy hair and then around their tiny living area with its low ceiling and lack of a gas chandelier. Thankfully, the cabin did have three tiny bedrooms tucked behind this main room. It might take some time acclimating to the cramped space again, as well as the dry air and the outside privy. But here, people liked Celeste for herself, and money didn't determine who or what was important.

"What doesn't Grandma need to know?" Patrick spoke up.

"Oh, nothing. Never mind." Celeste flicked her wrist at her brothers. "Say, what are you two doing in here? Why are you not out helping Mother shell the peas?"

"She sent us inside to help you," Patrick said. "Rob was eating too many."

"Was not!" Rob slapped him. "You ate more than me."

Celeste smiled at the likelihood. "Unfortunately, there is not much more to be done in here before our dinner guest arrives, except finishing touches on the food. And perish the thought of you two helping with that. Mother's cooking is questionable enough as it is."

Rob wrinkled his brow. "Why do you call Ma Mother?"

"Because, Little Luc—I mean, Rob—she *is* our mother," Celeste said, stating the obvious.

"You talk too fancy," he shot back.

"Fine, do you want me to go back to calling you Little Lucas?" She'd never do it, but it was going to take some time to quit *thinking* of him as such.

"No."

Patrick pointed to the pale beige napkins beneath one of the forks. "What are those things, anyway?"

"They are napkins. Grandmother gave them to me for my trousseau." Celeste looked at her littlest brother and got his blank stare. "You use them to wipe your mouth and hands if and when they get soiled as you eat."

"Why would I want to use one of your fancy napkins?" Rob wiped his hands on his trousers. "It'd be easier to do this."

"Because that's bad manners." Celeste glared at his hands as he ran them down his thighs.

Patrick wrinkled his forehead. "What's a true-sew?"

"That's *trousseau*." Celeste pronounced it with the proper French accent. "It's a collection of items I will need when I get married, like household linens and wares."

Both of her brothers' eyes widened.

"Are you getting married?" Patrick said.

"No, I am not!" Celeste snapped. "I mean, sometime I surely will, but not right now."

"That's good," Little Lucas/Rob said. "We just got you home. We're not ready for you to up and leave again."

"Don't you worry. If and when I do get married, I plan on staying around here."

Ma walked in from outside carrying a bowl of fresh peas. "What's this? You are talking to your brothers about getting married, yet you have not said a word to me?"

"Oh, Mother." Celeste wagged the last napkin at her. "I was just educating Little—Rob and Patrick on the definition of a trousseau. Grandmother gave me these things to use with a future husband. Along with three tablecloths, a set of bed sheets, and a nightgown made from the scratchiest lace. I'd never want to sleep in it, even if it is pretty."

Ma quickly motioned the boys to the door. "You two go outside and keep an eye out for your father. Give us a holler when you see him coming."

The boys ran outside, and Ma carried the peas to the sink. She rinsed the peas in the sink, then dumped them into a pot on the stove.

As she placed the lid over the pot, she turned to Celeste. "My mother was really set on finding you a proper suitor, wasn't she?" Ma smiled.

"More like she was set on finding me a *husband!*" Celeste said, reliving the frustration. "One from New York. One from an *affluent* family. One who would marry me and keep me and her great-grandchildren close to her. And under her watchful eye and controlling hand."

"Sorry about that." Ma breathed deep as she stared off at nothing in particular. "I should have known. She tried to do the same with me, insisting on what I should do with my life and whom I should marry."

"Really?" Celeste suddenly saw Ma as a fellow victim. Appreciation for her stepmother grew that much more. "Is that why you ran away?" She'd always loved that story about Ma, how her parents and her fiancé didn't want her to become a doctor, even though she'd finished medical school, so she sneaked away and came out West.

"I wouldn't exactly call it running away." Ma opened the door to the stove and poked the fire. "It was more like following my heart."

"But didn't you fall in love with Pa *after* you got out here?"

"I didn't mean follow my heart in the romantic sense, but in what felt right—and true to myself."

"Oh," Celeste responded, wondering if her decision to come home early was as bold, wise, and true to herself as Ma's decision to come West. She could have likely stayed at school—even after being told she was "hopelessly un-refinable" and was asked to leave—if she had run to Grandma and begged her to use her influence with Miss Bennett. Perhaps if she had stayed, Charles Weathersby might have returned from wherever it was he had to go. As it was, she'd simply asked Miss Bennett to give her grandma the same story Celeste had given her parents: an early graduation.

"But I thought my mother had changed," Ma continued. "After she'd discovered she had grandchildren and she came crawling back to me to make amends, she acted differently."

"It is okay, Mother. I appreciate all the good things Grandmother did. Think about it; she paid out a lot of money for me, but after all was said and done, she didn't get her way." Celeste expected a victorious grin to pull at her lips, but it wasn't there. It was more like a pull of guilt mixed with pain. Maybe Grandma could have looked past his lack of money and approved of Charles—and everyone could have been happy. If he'd not left. Was he bothered by Celeste being "hopelessly unrefinable" too? She heaved a sigh. "Yet I got an education out of Grandmother's meddling. Albeit a lopsided one."

"I thought that was the one thing that the Bennett School for Girls prided itself on, giving its students a well-rounded education."

"That depends on one's point of view." Celeste straightened one of the napkins and the plate next to it. "If I cared about dinner parties, etiquette, and catching myself a husband, then it was well rounded. But since I care more about mathematics, science, and business, my education was much less so."

"You almost 'caught yourself a husband,' as you called it." Ma gave her a sideways glance. "Your grandmother was very disappointed when you called off your engagement with that one young man. Dustin, was it? You never wrote much about him."

"Oh, him. You mean Dudley Lester Probert?" Celeste said his name as if each word left a bad taste in her mouth. "And we were never officially engaged. I never said yes. His rich, egotistical, big head just assumed I would. So he told everyone, including Grandmother, that we were." She blew out a breath. "Do you think the table looks ridiculous? I mean, linen napkins, chipped stoneware, and roast mutton. Do they really go together?"

"I think it looks fine. Your brothers could stand to have some of your etiquette rub off on them. They certainly could learn how to use a napkin, at least." Ma laughed, and Celeste joined in.

"I wonder how long it will take for my brothers to rub off on me."

"Let's hope that's not the case." Ma took a taste of her gravy. "I'm afraid this needs something." She held out a spoon for Celeste to taste. "What do you think?"

Celeste took a sip and cringed. The flat-tasting, thin broth did not merit the name *gravy*. "It needs a little salt, maybe some herbs. And some thickener would help." She took the spoon from Ma. "Here, let me try a few tricks I've learned in one of my cooking classes. Besides, Father and Logan should be here anytime now, and you've still the potatoes to mash." She realized her heart was beating slightly faster than normal. Anticipation of a lovely evening surely contributed. But concern over how Logan would react, as a guest to a welcome-home party for a girl who rudely never answered his letters, was also a factor.

Rushing to the pantry, Celeste grabbed a sprig of dried sage and a clove of garlic, then returned to the pot of gravy. On the other half of the stove, Ma mashed the potatoes.

As Ma pounded the masher into the large pot, she looked at Celeste. "I hope you didn't break that poor boy's heart too badly."

"Whose?" Celeste feared in that moment that Ma had read her mind concerning Logan. She shook her head to dismiss the thought—that had been years ago, and she'd been a child. But why, then, did the mere mention of Logan make her stomach feel as though it were full of butterflies?

"That fellow your grandmother liked."

"Oh! You mean Dudley?" Celeste rolled her eyes. He was as flavorless as Ma's gravy.

"Yes." Ma nodded. "And those other young men. Your Grandmother told me you had more than your fair share of suitors this past year. She was surprised, and frankly your father and I were too, that you were not able to find at least one young man who caught your fancy."

"Oh, Mother, they were all very shallow. Either they liked me because they thought I had money, or they thought I should like them because they had money. None of them—from what I could tell—liked me for me. And there was not one of them who had any qualities I liked."

"Not a single one?" Ma looked her in the eye with disbelief.

"Okay, there was one." Celeste swallowed the pain at the back of her throat. "But for some reason, about the time we got along quite grand, he quit calling on me." She took another sip of the gravy. "Ooo, this tastes good now," she said, wanting to change the subject. "It's ready. How about those potatoes?"

"Almost done." Ma gave them a final stir, and they *looked* okay. "I wonder how long until they get here. I don't want the mutton to dry out."

"Yes, I do hope they hurry." Celeste envisioned Logan trotting his horse along next to Pa's at a good pace. His skills with a horse had always impressed her, even more so after she'd taken her first equestrian class at school.

"Well, if my roast does dry out," Ma continued, "at least Logan and your pa are not the kind who would complain about it."

"No, they wouldn't," Celeste said, and that set her to thinking.

Logan would make a good husband. He would always treat her well. He'd never expect her to be anything other than herself, and she had always felt at ease in his presence.

In that moment, she knew what she wanted. Actually, she could see now she'd wanted this ever since the long train ride from New York. She wanted Logan to court her and fall in love with her.

There was one problem with this idea: she was a woman. It wasn't her place to ask him. That meant she'd just have to convince him to do the asking. Her throat suddenly felt dry. A refined woman would never do such a thing.

She laughed inside. Well, it was a known fact that she wasn't refined.

U

Chapter 4

LOGAN ENJOYED THE SUMMER SUN as it warmed his back and lit the cottonwoods and pussy willows. "Isn't it a lovely day for a ride, Bootstrap?" He patted his stallion's neck and then turned to Lucas, who rode beside him on his old mare. "Thanks again for inviting me for supper. It's been a while since I've been out to your place, other than just delivering the mail. Sorry."

"No need to be, Logan. 'Tis me and Kate who should be apologizing." Lucas sighed. "Life gets so busy we forget what's important sometimes."

"Yep," Logan agreed. "But we can't let that happen, now, can we?"

"Nope."

"That's why I jumped at the invitation, Lucas. Thanks again."

"I don't take any credit. 'Twas Celeste who prompted the idea. She seems anxious to see you."

"Oh, really now." Logan found his voice rising in pitch. If that was indeed the case, why had she never returned his letters? When he wrote them, he imagined she'd be hurting, all alone back there in New York without her parents. As the months passed without a letter from her, it kind of hurt, but he figured she had her reasons. Most likely, she was stronger than he'd been when he'd first tried to survive without his parents. After all, she'd been a year older than he when he lost his pa. And her parents weren't really gone, just across the country. And she got to come home to visit at least once that he knew of. He'd seen her that one time after her first year of school at the ranch when he'd delivered the mail. She had waved. So had he. That was all. Nothing in the intervening four years.

"Is she home for good this time?" Logan asked, hoping, for Celeste's sake, that was the case.

"Yep." Lucas nodded. "Technically, she could have stayed one more year for what they called 'higher education,' but the school recommended that

Celeste be finished. The letter I got from the school," he held his hand up to his mouth, "which, by the way, I've not shown to Kate yet, said it more fancy-like though." He laughed. "Hah, finished with finishing school. 'Tis my guess Celeste didn't fit there and gave them fits with her stubbornness and her blunt tongue. Yep, that's my girl."

"Then why in Heaven's name did she keep going?"

"For her grandma's sake is my guess." Lucas had a faraway look in his eyes, one filled with adoration for his daughter. "Beneath Celeste's unbridled exterior, she has a kind heart."

"Yeah, I kind of could see that, you know, back when we'd go riding." Things made sense to Logan now. "No wonder she went and had you invite me out for supper. She's feeling sorry for me, having to cook for myself over that tiny little stove in Ronald's back room. Truth is, I don't cook for myself all that much. Folks like you invite me over for supper at least a couple times a week."

"You ever think of settling down? Finding yourself a wife and moving out of that place?"

"Sometimes," Logan said, careful to keep his voice steady and not reveal that lately he'd thought about it more than he used to. "But there's still three men to every woman out here. My chances ain't too good." He slapped his left leg as a reminder to Lucas that it was not gal-catching quality. "Leastwise at finding a wife. I could maybe move out of Ron's place now that I'm getting paid by the postal service, but the place ain't that bad." He prompted Bootstrap to trot ahead.

After an hour of riding, they turned off the main road onto the trail leading to the McCurdy homestead. The house was twice the size it used to be when Logan first started coming out here over fifteen years ago. He'd been eleven then. Lucas hadn't married Kate yet. In fact, he'd still been married to his first wife—who left Lucas soon after and went home to Boston, taking little three-year-old Celeste with her. Whoa, a lot had happened since then.

Once at the corral, Logan dismounted first. "Let me take care of the horses. You go tell Kate and Celeste I'll be in shortly."

Lucas nodded his appreciation and dismounted.

Logan liked how Lucas treated him like family. He set to work unsaddling the horses and rubbing them down, figuring he'd be here a good spell. Likely he'd spend the night in the McCurdys' barn, it being too far to head back to town by the time supper was finished and they played a hand or two of cards while they visited, like Lucas had mentioned.

With the horses taken care of, he swept the dust from his shirt, straightened his hat, and walked to the house. He knocked on the door.

Rob opened it and motioned him in. "Aw, come on, Logan. We knew you were here. You didn't need to knock."

"I haven't been here for a spell, so I thought I should anyway." Logan lifted his hat and stepped through the door. A wonderful, savory aroma filled his nose. His eyes met Kate's. "Smells awfully good."

"Thank you." Kate smiled. "It will be ready in just a minute. Please, take a seat at the table."

"Does it matter which one?" Logan looked around but didn't see Celeste.

"Nope," Lucas said as he sat at the head of the table so he was farthest from the kitchen. "Pick any one you want."

Logan walked toward the table with an easy stride, not worrying about hiding his limp—these were his friends. He eyed the chair on the other side of the table next to Rob, who was settling into his seat. He wanted to see if the boy would be interested in helping with the RFD mail delivery to this area of the valley, and he wanted to do it without his ma listening in. She might squash the idea before he had a chance to explain it right—so it wouldn't sound dangerous, because it wasn't.

The door to the addition swung inward. It caught his attention as he approached the table, and he looked over. He felt his jaw sag open as his eyes caught sight of Celeste. It had to be her. He recognized her chestnut-colored hair and vibrant green eyes. "C-Celeste?" he stammered. He removed his hat and gripped it tightly. "I should have known you wouldn't look like a kid anymore."

She paused in the doorway, rushing her hand to her mouth as if finding his statement funny. Then she stared at him, her eyes moving down the length of his body. Her eyes met his, and she swallowed noticeably hard. "You have changed too."

"I have?" Logan hadn't thought so. "Okay, maybe I've grown an inch or two up and an inch or two across. But it's the same ole me, I promise." He slapped his chest to bring home his point.

She walked toward him, gliding, it seemed, across the floor in one fluid motion that made her look as beautiful as a falcon swooping toward its prey. He could watch her do that again and again and not tire of it. She approached the table and placed a dainty hand on the back of the chair at her pa's right.

"Would you like to sit here next to me?" she said to Logan. "It's the best view of the window and the worst view of the sink full of pots." She smiled, and it reminded him of those times she made taking her for a ride sound like the exact thing he wanted to do at the moment, even though it wasn't.

"Sure, that would be nice." He walked over, pulled out the chair next to hers, and almost plopped down into it. Then he remembered gals liked their chairs pulled out for them—leastwise, that's what his sister had told him—not that he'd had much chance to do so. "Here you go."

"Thank you, Logan," she said as he pushed the chair and her toward the table.

Once everyone was seated, Lucas offered a prayer of thanks on the meal. Logan filled his plate from bowls of potatoes, peas, and sliced roast mutton passed around. He dug into his food, having had only a handful of dried apples since breakfast.

"This tastes really good," he said to Kate, making sure he'd swallowed beforehand. He didn't want to talk with his mouth full. Everyone around the table seemed to be on their best manners this evening, so he thought he'd better dust off what few he'd learned.

"Thank you, Logan." Kate gave a slight nod toward Celeste. "I had help."

"I made the gravy," Celeste said, "and assisted Mother with the potatoes."

"Those are my favorites, the spuds and gravy." Logan stuffed another spoonful of them into his mouth and nodded at Celeste.

"Really?"

"Um-huh." He nodded again at her, which seemed to delight her for some reason and made her smile.

"I helped shell the peas," Rob spoke up.

"Me too," added Patrick.

Celeste glared at her brothers. "May I remind both Patrick and you, Lucas Junior, that Mother was fortunate to save enough for this meal after you two *helped.*"

"There you go again," Rob said to Celeste. "Talking like you are from some other country."

"I am not," Celeste insisted.

"Okay, then at least too fancy for my taste. Lucas Junior. Hmph!" Rob left his meal untouched for a moment and folded his arms across his chest.

"You were the one who didn't wish for me to call you Little Lucas." Celeste's profile revealed a definite frown as she straightened her back nearly to the point where it arched toward her chair. "Can I help it you changed what you want to be called while I was gone?" She stabbed her meat with her fork and let it stand upright as she folded her hands in her lap and batted her eyelashes at Rob. "How about I just call you Mutton Head?"

Logan snickered behind his hand. This was more like the Celeste he knew. But with a twist.

"Now, Celeste, where are your manners?" Kate scolded.

"Oh, she's got them, all right." Rob chuckled as he added, "She's using them too—while callin' me names. That's some pretty funny stuff they taught you at school, Sis."

"Rob!" Kate quieted him with a glare.

No one spoke for a minute or two, except for Rob asking his ma to pass the potatoes.

At last, Lucas spoke to Celeste. "It's time you tell us a wee bit about school. Your brothers have been waiting to hear about it."

"I haven't," Rob mumbled with a mouth full of mutton.

"Well, I have," Lucas said. "And I'm sure Logan wouldn't mind hearing either."

"Sure, why not?" Logan said just before he took a bite of peas.

Celeste exhaled sharply. "What's to tell that I haven't already?" She glanced at her pa with a nervous look. Then she stared across the table at her brothers. "Or that they would care to hear. Besides, I'd rather not talk about school right now."

"Come on, lass." Lucas waved his fork "It couldn't have been all that bad. What about Dudley?"

Kate glared across the length of the table at Lucas, her eyes speaking volumes: his mouth was saying too much, and she wanted him to put a cork in it.

"Never mind." Lucas squirmed in his chair.

Logan sensed Celeste tensing up in her chair next to him. "Hey, pass me some more of those spuds and gravy." He glanced at her, hoping to ease things up. "You sure did a good job with that gravy."

She ducked her head and offered him a mighty pretty sideways glance. "Thank you."

The conversation around the table turned to the weather, how summer was officially here, and hopefully there would be rain this season to water the field enough to keep the sheep fed.

As soon as everyone was finished eating, Kate and Celeste stood from the table and began clearing off the dishes. Logan stood too, grabbing the empty gravy dish and the bowl of mashed potatoes that had about one bite left at the bottom of the bowl. He started carrying them over to the sink, and Celeste pulled them from his hands.

Celeste cleared her throat. "This is woman's work," she said, yet something in her eyes told Logan she appreciated his intention. She then motioned with her head toward the sofa on the other side of the room. "You go sit with my father and talk about . . . horses or something. Mother and I will be done shortly."

"We'll get the table cleared off," Kate said, "and the boys put to bed. Then the four of us can play cards."

"Bed!" Rob still sat at the table and grabbed hold of the seat of his chair like he wasn't going to move. "That's not fair! I wanna play cards."

"Me too." Patrick copied his brother.

Celeste looked at Kate. "Ma!"

It was the first time Logan had heard her call Kate *Ma*—at least since she was a kid. Then again, in that moment, it looked as though she'd reverted back to her childhood. If her skirt hadn't been high enough to expose her ankles, he might not have seen her foot stomping. But he did and found it humorous as he settled onto the couch.

Lucas stood from the armchair where he'd barely settled in and walked toward Rob. "Come on, boys. I'll read you a story and tuck you in bed."

"I'm too old for that," Rob whined.

"Me too," Patrick joined in.

Lucas stood between them, pulled their chairs out, and grabbed an arm of each boy. "No one's ever too old for a bedtime story." He looked to Logan for support as he passed by, dragging a boy in each hand. "Isn't that right, Logan?"

"Yep. I love to hear bedtime stories—anytime anyone's willing to tell me one," Logan said, feeling a pang in his heart that caused him to wince. Bedtime stories were not something he'd been accustomed to. His sister had so much on her plate when she'd raised him, having been just thirteen years older than he was. He could never have asked even more from her. "Take advantage of those stories while you can," he hollered into their bedroom.

Kate and Celeste made quick work of cleaning up the dishes. Celeste had the tablecloth removed—something Logan had never seen used before at the McCurdy table—and every crumb brushed free by the time Lucas emerged from the back rooms.

"Would you care to come over now?" Celeste said to Logan as she set a couple boxes of cards on the table.

"Uh, sure." Logan stood and walked to the table, feeling more inclined to hide his limp, wondering if it could be deemed as poor manners. He settled into the same chair he'd taken at supper.

Kate took Rob's chair next to Lucas. "Will you be staying the night then, Logan?"

Logan glanced out the window at the setting sun. "Uh . . ."

"Of course he will be staying, Mother. It'd be pitch dark before he got home as it is, and we haven't even had a chance to play a single hand."

"Yeah, it looks like I'm staying. The barn's fine."

"Wonderful," Celeste stated like she was checking off an order of business. "Now, would you rather play rummy," she asked Logan, "or pinochle?"

"It sounds to me like you've already got the evening mapped out in your mind. You choose."

Celeste stiffened. Her eyes skirted from Logan to her ma to a whole passel of spots around the room until they stared at her hands clasped together in her lap.

Logan chewed on his fingernail. Had he offended her? Or was she just using fancy manners to cover up her stubbornness?

"How about we play rummy." Kate opened one of the boxes of cards. "Would that be okay, Celeste?"

"Why are you asking me?" Celeste's back still looked stiff as a board, and her eyes remained on her folded hands. "Logan is our guest. It should be his choice."

"Don't matter to me. Rummy's fine," Logan said, thinking how Celeste had changed plenty in some ways, as in wanting everyone to be on their best behavior. But mostly in looking like a grown woman—all filled out and more than easy on the eyes. In some ways, however, she was that same headstrong child he'd gotten to know years ago. He was unsure which Celeste he liked better, not that it mattered.

"Okay, rummy it is." Kate shuffled the cards and dealt.

After the first round, which Celeste won, she appeared more relaxed, and so Logan relaxed. He won the next round by accident. On the third round, he held back, making sure he didn't win and hoping Celeste would. He wanted the happy mood around the table to remain. And it did. By the time the third round was over, everyone was laughing at how Lucas had come from behind and won.

"On that note, I think I'll quit." Lucas stretched his hands over his head and yawned. "'Tis late, and morning comes a wee bit early when you got a ranch to run."

"I'll fetch—" Celeste cleared her throat. "I mean, I'll go get you some bedding, Logan." She scurried out of the main room and seconds later returned with a fine-looking quilt and a pillow. Wagging her hand, she smiled and motioned for him to follow her to the door. "Come. I'll accompany you to the barn." She glanced at her ma. "With your permission, of course."

"I suppose." Kate nodded. "Just make it quick."

Logan stood and hobbled toward her, tired himself and not caring to hide his limp any longer. "I know the way," he blurted.

Celeste's smile fell away, and she shoved the bedding into his arms.

"But I'd love the company," he said quickly. That seemed to do the trick, because her smile returned.

"Wonderful." She motioned to the door "I'll open it. Your hands are full." Then she sucked in a breath like she'd said something wrong.

"Thanks." Logan walked outside, and Celeste fell in step next to him.

Slowing to a stop, she gazed at the night sky, and her shoulders relaxed. "It sure is beautiful, isn't it?"

Logan stopped and gazed too, but not at the sky. At her. Moonlight illuminated the soft curves of her face. "Yeah, sure is beautiful," he muttered. He shook his head to dislodge the impossible thoughts of him and her—together— forming inside his head. He resumed walking, leaving her standing there.

She scurried and caught up to him. "Don't you want to gaze at the stars?"

"Not right now." Logan kept walking. "Like your pa said, 'mornin' comes early.' I need to get my bed made and get some shut-eye, I suppose."

"Don't you want to stay up and talk?" She latched onto the crook in Logan's elbow as they walked into the barn.

He was acutely aware of her arm wrapped around his. He'd looped his arms with a few girls before, but none had left him feeling so peculiar. Juggling the bedding, he pulled his arm free and stepped away from her. "I don't know that I've got much more to say than what's already been said at the table."

"I could tell you the long, dark tale of my five years away from home." Her voice held a tone of sorrow that resonated with him.

"I'd love to hear it. We could pretend you're telling me a bedtime story." Why had he said that? He would be pining over his painful childhood while she told of hers. That didn't sound like a good way to end the evening. He kicked some loose straw into a flat pile, the reason dawning on him. It didn't matter what they talked about for the next little while; he just wanted to spend more time with her.

"Here, let me help you with that." Gently, she took the quilt from his arms and spread it over the straw. She straightened up and stood back. "I really like the idea of telling you a bedtime story. At least, telling you my story—telling someone my story." She heaved a sigh. "Ma and Pa . . . Well, they wouldn't understand. They thought they were doing what was best for me."

Logan tossed his pillow onto the quilt, lowered down, and sat cross-legged next to it. "Like I said, I'd love to hear your story." His eyes skirted around for a place where she could sit. Nothing suitable presented itself, except atop the quilt next to him. But that was unsuitable in a different way. At the beginning of the evening, he would have thought nothing of it. Not now; not with his feelings in such a jumble.

"Unfortunately," he looked around again, this time very noticeably for her sake, "there's no place for you to sit . . . except here." He patted the empty spot on the quilt next to him. "I'm not too schooled in etiquette, but I'm thinking this would not be a proper seat for me to offer you."

"I *am* schooled in etiquette, and you are correct. And at the moment, I don't care. I don't care that you are a handsome, eligible man of marrying age. You are you, Logan, my friend. And I need a friend to talk to." She moved toward the quilt like she was ready to sit down upon it.

"Well, thank you," Logan said, little else of his thoughts able to form into words.

Had she just said he was handsome? Did she consider him marriageable? Or was she thinking of him merely as a friend, one to whom she could open up to like she used to? That had to be the case. She was so refined, with years of schooling. He was as coarse and uneducated as a burlap sack, having had to pretty much raise and educate himself. She was young and pretty. He was old and—did she really consider him handsome? No, he shouldn't go down this trail of thinking. There was an eight-year difference in their ages. *That's nothing. Gus and his wife have twelve years between their ages.* She was merely a friend. *Friends make the best kinds of companions.* There was Dudley. *Yes, there is Dudley.* Why else would his name have been so obviously hushed at suppertime?

"Your ma said for you to be quick," he managed to say. He took a deep breath and felt his tongue loosen as he rose to his feet, which was a good thing. More than anything, he wanted her to stay; he wanted to hear her story, perhaps even help her by lending a listening ear. But he did have enough manners to know it wouldn't be proper. He gently grabbed her elbow. "I couldn't in good conscience have you sitting on my bed, telling me a bedtime story, no matter how much I'd like that. How about you come tell it to me in the morning while I'm saddling up Bootstrap. I'm sure he'd like to hear it too." He urged her toward the open barn door.

"Well!" She jerked her elbow from his hand. "I declare, Logan Jones, you are—! Never mind. Good night." She ran toward the house.

"I really do want to hear your story," Logan hollered to her back slipping out of sight, thinking school must have been hard on her. It was no wonder she hadn't written to him. "In the morning, I promise. I'll be waiting," he said to the darkness of the barnyard, hoping she would no longer be upset come sunrise. Hoping she'd spill a little more, enough for him to learn about Dudley—and determine if he, Logan Jones, had a chance in Hades to compete with the fellow.

Chapter 5

CELESTE FIGURED MISS BENNETT WOULD have a fainting spell if she discovered one of her students had tried to sit on a man's bed while alone with him in a barn. Well, Miss Bennett was long gone out of her life, and in all those insipid books Celeste had read on etiquette, not one mentioned the impropriety of sitting on a man's bed in a *barn*.

"So there," she mumbled as she walked outside carrying a plate of eggs and biscuits for Logan. He'd not joined them for breakfast. Pa had said Logan didn't want to put upon them for a second meal and would be saddling up and leaving as soon as he finished feeding and brushing down their three horses.

As she approached the barn, she hoped he'd meant what he'd said last night about wanting to hear her story. And that he'd be waiting. If so, it could provide a good opportunity to flirt with him. She was glad, however, that Logan had done the proper thing last night. After coming up with the idea of convincing Logan to court her, when he didn't respond exactly how she'd envisioned, frustration had gotten the best of her. But that did not excuse her poor choices.

"What's that?" Logan stepped out of the barn with saddle in hand and nodded to the dishcloth-covered plate she held.

"A spot of breakfast."

Logan hefted his saddle onto Bootstrap's back and proceeded to strap it in place. "It *is* a beautiful day. You going to eat your eggs out here then, are you?" He leaned back and peered into the barn. "The smell of manure ain't the best thing to make one's breakfast taste good. Your eyes tell me that's where you were headed. Bad idea. Don't you think those stumps would be a better place to sit down and eat?" He nodded to a pile of wood next to the barn waiting to be chopped.

"I made this plate up for you," Celeste said, trying to keep her voice steady and ladylike. She was unsure if he was teasing her or if he really had no clue that she was being nice to him.

"I told your pa I didn't need breakfast. I ate more than my share of food last night at supper."

"Ma made plenty." Celeste removed the cloth and held out the plate toward Logan. "This will go to the pigs if you don't eat it."

Logan's eyes lit up. He hesitated and then reached out for the eggs and biscuits. "Well, we wouldn't want that to happen, now, would we?"

Celeste felt a bit of a lump form in her throat as she watched him dig into the eggs like he couldn't believe his luck. Going without breakfast was probably a common occurrence in Logan's life. Bringing him this plate of food took on a new purpose. Her desire to tell Logan her story became unimportant. Her selfish need to unload her penned-up emotions, or to bat her eyes at him, paled in comparison to the problem of Logan often going hungry. Here was yet another time Reverend Francis was right. "Put others first; you'll be happier," he'd said.

That second year at Bennett's had been particularly hard. The taunts about her humble, Colorado upbringing had grown worse. Then she found a friend in Reverend Francis at the church across the street from the school. He certainly didn't care that her father was a rancher without a lot of money.

"Celeste, my child," he'd said with notable concern in his voice on one of her darker days. "We are molded by the things we love. If we love good things, then we are free. If we love the wrong things, we are enslaved by them." Then he read to her from the Bible in Timothy about how money was *the root of all evil* and how those who covet it *pierce themselves through with many sorrows.* "Your classmates love money," he continued. "They are enslaved by all the luxuries their parents' wealth heaps upon them. Always thirsting for more, they are never satisfied with what God has given them, and they become unhappy. Then they see you and how you love your family and your humble ranch in Colorado and how the simple things in life bring you happiness—and they can't comprehend it. So they taunt you."

At that time, she certainly didn't need to add to her sorrows, so she'd learned to look at life through a different lens than her schoolmates, and her melancholy became manageable.

Now, through that lens, she could see Logan's circumstances were more dire than hers. The desire to help him burned strong. She sighed, breathed in a little too deeply, and coughed from the smell of manure wafting out of the barn door. "You're right," she said. "Those stumps outside would be a more fitting place to eat your breakfast."

"Would you care to join me?" Logan pointed with his plate to the logs leaning against the side of the barn. "Then you can tell me your bedtime story."

He gathered his horse's reins with his free hand. "Come on, Bootstrap. You can listen too. I've been waiting all night to hear it."

"Really?"

"Yep. Leastwise, while I was awake." His gaze held a peculiar look.

His eyes betrayed that he'd been awake a good portion of the night, but he wasn't sorry for it. Could he possibly have been thinking about her?

"I hope that you didn't lie awake too long," Celeste said, contrary to her feelings. She settled onto one of the stumps and smoothed out her skirt to cover her ankles as best she could. "Okay, my story, where should I start?"

"How about at the beginning?" Logan smiled that smile she liked, the one where one side of his lips curved up higher than the other.

"Are you sure you have time? I no longer feel the need to unload it, like I did last night."

"Don't worry, the mail can wait a few extra minutes before I deliver it. And I'd love to hear the story." Logan let go of his reins, leaving the homely looking horse standing patiently at his side, and lowered himself onto a large, upturned log.

"The beginning, huh." Celeste took a deep breath of the fresh air, realizing the desire to share her woes was still there. "You already know I was shipped out five years ago come September. Three months before I turned fourteen."

"Yeah, I remembered that much." He nodded for her to continue before he took another bite of eggs.

"Well, the first year wasn't so bad. All the other girls my age were just as awkward and homesick as I was, so I got along with them—somewhat. I got to come home the following June for summer holiday."

"Yeah, that's when I saw you last," Logan said. "How come you didn't come home the next summer? Or did you, and I just didn't notice you was home?"

"Grandma refused to pay for my train ticket home."

Logan's eyes widened. "What about your ma and pa?"

"They couldn't afford to pay for it. Grandma made up some excuse and pulled the wool over their eyes somehow, because that time you saw me was the last time I've been home until now."

"Whoa."

"Yes, *whoa* sums it up quite nicely. You see, Grandma didn't want me to go home during the summer holidays because she was afraid I wouldn't return in the fall. I didn't realize this was the case until just two weeks ago when the summer holiday started after my recently completed school year. Grandma let it slip out one afternoon when she had me down to her mansion—yes, I said *mansion*. She and Grandpa are loaded." Celeste wagged her hand at her rambling. "That's beside the point. Anyway, when I found out that Grandma had kept me there at her place for the past four summers because she wanted to keep an eye on me—and guarantee I'd return next fall—I loaded up my things and demanded Grandpa take me to the train station."

"Did she oblige you?"

"Not at first. She forbade Grandpa to do anything." Celeste felt a smile form. "But then I told her if Grandpa didn't take me, I'd go anyway and dig up the money for my fare however I had to. When her eyes widened in fear, I went in for the kill. I could have told her something worse but kept it mild by saying I would consider working as a scullery maid for the first person who would hire me."

"You really meant to do that?" Logan's eyes widened now, almost as much as her grandmother's had. "Not that I know what a scullery maid is, but it don't sound good."

"No, I just led her to believe that." Celeste chewed on the corner of her lip.

"And so I take it your grandpa took you to the train station and paid for your ticket." Logan's eyes didn't move from her face. "This is a right good story, by the way."

"Thanks," Celeste nodded to herself as much as for Logan.

"So are you going back next fall?" Logan asked. His voice held a hint of disappointment, and that made Celeste glad.

"Not on your life!" Celeste's jaw tightened at the thought. "Here is the irony: I was trying to decide how to tell Grandma that I would not be able to enroll this fall for my final year when I learned about her meddling."

"Why couldn't you go?"

"Miss Bennett approached me personally and told me—" Celeste paused. This knowledge would ruin her chances for sure with any fellow in New York. Would it do the same with Logan? The need to get this off her chest pushed her to continue. "How do I say this without making me look . . . well, bad?"

"Just tell me already." Logan picked a piece of straw off his shirt and tossed it at her. "You're not gonna look bad. Maybe a little silly—but not bad. Not you."

"Thanks—I guess." Celeste was not sure how to take that at all.

"Keep going. I'm enjoying this."

"Okay, so Miss Bennett told me that I was a hopeless case when it came to . . ." She mimicked the old woman's nasally voice as best she could and said, "'Becoming a polished young woman that my school can be proud of.'"

"She actually said that?" Logan's eyebrow lifted, and he stuffed his last bite of biscuit in his mouth.

"Yes and more."

"Maybe I should go back there and take a few of her classes, and then she'd for sure see that you were plenty polished up."

"Thank you, Logan." She placed her hand on his, sincerely appreciating his words. "Unfortunately, I hate to admit it, but Miss Bennett might be correct."

"Come again?"

"Miss Bennett hit the nail on the head about me. I didn't belong there. Oh, I could act polished, act like I enjoyed socializing—until someone said the wrong thing."

"Wrong thing?"

"Something I didn't agree with. Or, in their uppity way, bad-mouthed someone or something I cared for. Then I let them have it—with my words. Of course, I'd never throw a punch. Though I was tempted a few times. I'm afraid I was like a lump of coal attempting to be turned into a diamond in five years."

"Oh, come on, Miss Celeste. As far as I'm concerned, you are the most refined, finished young woman this side of Denver."

"That's not saying much." Celeste laughed. "And please," she continued to chuckle, "do not call me Miss Celeste. That only serves to remind me of the mindless young men who insisted on calling upon me. I had to accept each call in front of Miss Bennett and act all prim and proper and polished for her sake. Every time. It was grueling."

"Grueling, huh?" Logan didn't smile.

"Okay, *grueling* was a poor choice of words. I'll go with *unpleasant.*" Celeste blew out a breath. "Speaking of unpleasant, let me hurry and finish telling this tale. I have yet to get to the part I had actually intended to tell."

Logan's back stiffened. "I've been finding this morning bedtime story of yours rather pleasant. But if you don't want to, please, don't feel like you gotta continue."

"No, no, that's not what I meant at all. It's the remainder of my story that's unpleasant."

Logan relaxed. "Oh."

Celeste leaned forward and looked to the right, then the left of the barnyard. "But it's the part that weighs the heaviest on me." She glanced down at his hand, now holding on to the empty plate. It was mere inches from hers. She wished he'd set the plate down and reach over and take her hand in his. She'd been in much less private situations as this with Dudley, and he'd more than taken her hand. Dudley had wrapped his hands around her waist and stolen a kiss . . . or ten. When she hadn't wanted to give him one. She wanted to give her hand to

Logan though. "You're such a gentleman." She whispered her thoughts without realizing it.

"I'm sorry. I couldn't hear that." Logan leaned in and looked at her to repeat it.

"I was mumbling, sorry. See, a real, refined woman does not mumble." She rolled her eyes. "Back to my story. For five years, I suffered through Miss Bennett's school alone. I had my parents' letters, and the reverend at the church across the street from the school, but they were no substitute for friends."

"Are you saying you had no friends?"

Celeste nodded.

"Not a single one?" Logan sounded like this was hard to believe.

"Oh, I guess I could say I had *friends*, but of the male gender—just another reason to make the girls in my dormitory dislike me." Celeste rubbed her forehead to ease the painful memories. "But none of those young men liked me for the right reason—except for one fellow. And all of the girls disliked me for the wrong reasons. Except for acting sociable, I refused to pretend to be someone I wasn't. I couldn't lie and tell my roommate that it was okay to cheat on a test or say something mean about one girl to gain the friendship of another or value money more than anything else." She brought her other hand to her face and covered it. "I am sorry. I never intended on this story turning into a complaint session. Yet again, I would be giving Miss Bennett cause to dismiss me."

Logan peeled her hands away from her face. "You're not complaining. You're sharing your sorrows with a friend. And thanks for thinking of me as such." He lowered her hands into her lap and let go. "And you're not giving that ole school teacher cause to do nothing. You up and left that place because it sounds like you were the smartest one there."

At that moment, Celeste wanted more than anything to wrap her arms around Logan's waist like when they'd shared the saddle. She longed for that comfort he'd always seemed to give her years ago. "Thank you, Logan," she said and looked away.

"So is my bedtime story over?" Logan smiled and tossed another piece of straw at her.

"At least for today." Celeste stood and brushed the pieces of straw from her skirt. "I just want to add that even though I'd learned to act refined on the outside, the polish never penetrated far enough inside me to change who I actually was. And I'm not sorry about that. I like who I am. Most of the time."

"And who are you?" Logan asked.

"Someone who likes to think for myself." She touched his arm. "Good day, Logan. And thank you for coming to my welcome-home party. I'm glad you came."

She strolled toward the house, taking her time getting back to the kitchen and her chores, waiting to hear Logan mount up and ride away. As she moved past the opened barn door, she caught sight of her pa. He walked toward her as Logan rode past.

"Bye, Lucas. Bye, Celeste. I had a grand time." Logan waved and rode off.

Celeste's throat tightened. Her pa got Logan's first notice. She sucked in a breath—it didn't matter. She was determined to stick to her idea of pursuing Logan as a husband. He was kind, accepting, and a good listener. He was also more of a gentleman than any of those supposed well-bred fellows she'd met back East.

"Celeste." Pa's voice held that serious tone of wanting to have a talk with her.

"Yes?" Celeste shuffled her feet to a stop. Then her heart sank to her stomach. Had he overheard what she'd told Logan?

"We need to talk." Pa took her by the arm and gently turned her to face him.

"You heard us, didn't you?"

Pa nodded. "Everything—with not even a wee bit of effort."

"I can explain." Celeste swallowed hard. "I should have told you earlier, I know, but I was hoping it would get easier. I really tried my hardest to fit in at Miss Bennett's school, I promise, but—"

"Worry not." Pa pulled her into an embrace. "I already knew about your dismissal from school. 'Tis not what I wish to talk about."

"So, you're not upset with me being expelled, more or less, from finishing school?" Celeste held her breath.

"Not I." Pa hugged her tighter. "I already knew—got a letter from your school. But perhaps t'would be best to wait a bit longer 'til we tell your ma. What do you say?"

"I'd say that would be nice. Thank you, Pa." She tried to pull away, thinking that was all, but he held on.

"I've more to say, Celeste." He released his embrace and held her at arm's length so as to look her in the eye. "It's great to be a free thinker, but to *think* your ideas are always the best will lead you to be anything but free. Remember that. Will you m'dear?"

She nodded at Pa, and he walked away. She remained standing in front of the barn, staring into its dark interior. For some reason, Pa's words reminded her of Reverend Francis's: "When we love good things, we are free, and when we love bad things, we are enslaved by them." Was her pa referring to her idea to convince Logan to court her and hopefully marry her? How could that be seen by anyone—especially her pa, who liked Logan—as anything other than a good thing?

Chapter 6

LOGAN DRAPED HIS OLD SADDLEBAGS over the back of Bootstrap and led him out of the livery stable. He glanced at Gus on his way out and smiled his appreciation to the old man. Being able to keep Bootstrap there for free really helped out. There certainly wasn't a place for a horse over at the law office where Logan lived. And Logan couldn't afford the rates his boss normally charged.

"Off to deliver the mail, I see?" Gus said.

"Yep. With Sam gone . . ." Logan paused for a moment to let the pain work its way out, trying yet again to fathom how his brother could shoot the man, such a right nice man, in the back. "Lavender needs more help with the mail. Her daughter, Rosie, has stepped up to help, but it's not enough."

"You delivering mail in town now?"

"Sometimes. But mostly just the RFD routes."

"You need more time off?" Gus winced as he smiled.

"That would be nice." Logan felt his shoulders relax at the thought. "At least until they get that new post office finished. The postal service is going to hire themselves a man to run it. Imagine that; it's all the man does, take care of the mail and boss us mail carriers around. No running a mercantile on the side for him."

"If the mail service has all that money, maybe you could hit them up to buy you a new set of these." Gus slapped Logan's worn-out saddlebags. "Heck, they should be supplying you with an official-like set, with some sort of fancy seal on it anyway—not making you use your own."

"Aw, I don't mind none," Logan said, feeling good about being able to save people money whenever he could, even the government. "Well, I'd better get going. The mail's waiting."

"I might be cutting my own throat here." Gus rubbed the stubble on his chin. "But why don't you go apply for that job at the new post office? Sure as shootin', the government can afford to pay you more than I do."

"Nah." Logan swept a hand at Gus and resumed leading Bootstrap out of the stable. "I've thought about it once or twice, but sitting inside at a desk all day ain't for me," he said over his shoulder.

He took a deep breath of the warm morning air, mounted up, and adjusted his hat against the rising sun. "Come on, Bootstrap. Let's get going." He prompted his pal into a brisk walk in the direction of the mercantile.

Rosie greeted him with a smile the moment she let him into the store. "Always on time; that's our Logan." She motioned for him to follow her through the empty store and to the back room where the mail was sorted.

"Say, how's your ma doing?" Logan draped the saddlebags over his shoulder, noticing the *clomp* of his boots on the floor seemed to echo more than usual. He glanced around, realizing it wasn't just because the store had yet to open for the day, but also because the shelves were half bare. It'd been two months since Sam died and over a week since Stanley was hanged. A stifling sense of forlorn seemed to fill the half-empty store. He wondered if Lavender would ever feel happy again and the mercantile get back to where it used to be.

"As good as could be expected under the circumstances." Rosie led him into the back room.

"I am so sorry about my brother." Logan removed his hat. He wished he could do more.

"You're not responsible for your brother." She pulled the saddlebags off his shoulder and laid them on the table. "Stanley was his own man." She stuffed bundles of mail into each pouch. "I'm just grateful you're not like him."

Logan grabbed a bundle and shoved it into the biggest pouch with force. "Oh, believe me, *I* am glad for that too!"

"Save room in that big one for this." Rosie handed Logan a package wrapped in brown paper and tied off with a white string. It was about the size of a book but felt much softer.

"Ah, a package. They're always fun to deliver. Makes folks feel like it's Christmas when it's not." Logan felt himself smile. "Where's it going?"

"Out to the McCurdys'." Rosie glanced up at Logan. "It's for their daughter, Celeste. You heard she was home now, haven't ya?"

"Yeah, I've heard." Memories of his time out there a few days ago filled his thoughts with fondness. He liked how he was able to lend the listening ear Celeste seemed to need.

"Five years at a fancy finishing school!" Rosie pulled a face. "Oh, please, God have mercy on the poor child. I hope she survived. I'm afraid I'd have shot myself in the foot the first year so I could come home and stay if it had been me."

"She survived without too much damage."

"That's good." Rosie chuckled. "So I take it you've seen her? Has she changed much?"

"Yeah, I've seen her," Logan said in a wispy tone, visualizing Celeste's flawless face. "In some ways, she's changed. And in some ways, she ain't changed at all." He scratched his head. "It's all good."

"Nice to hear pleasant news for a change." Rosie pulled the loaded saddlebags from the table and handed them to Logan. "You better get going so you can get back before dark. Oh, and thank Gus for lettin' us borrow you more than usual."

"I already have." Logan draped the bags over his shoulder once again. He hurried toward the front door, meeting Stuart Hoy on his way.

"Is the place open?" Stuart asked. "The door was open."

"You'll have to ask Rosie." Logan cupped his hands around his mouth and yelled toward the back. "Rosie, you got a customer."

"Dang it all!" came Rosie's reply.

"Have a good day, Stuart." Logan tipped his hat and rushed outside.

On his way out of town, Logan's mind drifted to the package he'd be delivering to Celeste. He hadn't looked at the return address. Curiosity niggled his insides. He lifted the reigns, ready to slow Bootstrap to a crawl so he could turn in the saddle and pull that package out. Instead, the reigns got a good flick. There wasn't time for such nonsense. Besides, it was probably from one of Celeste's many suitors. It'd sounded like she had plenty of them. When he delivered the package, he'd be careful not to look at the return address. It wouldn't sit well with his gut anyway to see the name Dudley scrolled across the upper left-hand corner in fancy, highfalutin handwriting.

He stared at the dusty road ahead, keeping Bootstrap at a good pace and concentrating on the list of names Rosie had given him. He appreciated how she wrote down which homestead had mail each time and which didn't.

But he didn't appreciate how Celeste kept creeping into his thoughts. It wasn't like he was planning on courting her.

Or was he?

No, I can't—I've nothing to offer a wife.

True, Celeste had done a thing or two that led him to believe she was interested in him. Like touching his arm when she'd said goodbye the other morning. But she had been pouring out her sorrows, and that was her way of saying thanks for him listening. He shouldn't be reading more into it than there was, especially since she'd mentioned more things that pointed the other way. She had suitors galore: ones with the means to support a family; ones who were polished; ones who were closer to her age; one who was named Dudley. Logan and Celeste's friendship was one forged years ago. That was something perhaps he had over all those other fellows. And as such, he meant to keep it that way—for Celeste's sake. Friends, nothing more.

Logan concentrated on his job, delivering mail to five different ranches and two homesteads before he reached the turnoff to the McCurdy place.

"Friends," he muttered as Bootstrap brought him closer to Celeste. "We're just friends."

The whitewashed cabin came into view. He saw Rob out front, chopping wood. Patrick could be seen in the side yard working in the garden, and Celeste knelt on the ground by her brother's side.

Logan's heart slipped in an extra beat. He'd feared he might have to deliver the McCurdys' mail without seeing her. But there she was, looking as lovely as ever, even in a pair of men's trousers. She looked up. Did she recognize him? Maybe—she jumped to her feet, dusting off her knees, keeping her eyes on him.

She ran toward him. "Logan!"

Was she possibly excited to see him? Logan waved back. "Hello there. I got mail. Come and get it."

Patrick made it to Logan's side before Celeste. "Anything for me?"

"Afraid not." Logan reached into his bag for the bundle holding the McCurdys' mail. He undid the string, sorted through it, and pulled out a letter for Lucas. "But I got one for your pa. Can I trust you to deliver it to him?" Logan winked.

"Of course." Patrick snatched it from Logan's outstretched hand and then ran into the house.

Celeste stood a few feet away now. The noonday sun lit her face and high-lighted flecks of gold in the mossy green of her eyes. She shielded her face as she gazed at him. "Is that all?"

"Why do you ask?" Logan said in his teasing voice. "Are you expecting something?" Why had he done that? He really didn't care to hear she was waiting for a package from Dudley.

"No, not really," she responded. "I had hoped maybe you'd—" She sounded disappointed before she cut her words short and stared at the ground. "Ah, never mind."

Logan couldn't stand to pain her like that, knowing she was prone to melancholy now and again. At least, she had been before going away to school. That's why he'd taken her with him to deliver the mail at times. It had always put a smile on her face. And from her morning "bedtime" story, it sounded like school hadn't helped her bouts of sadness. "Sorry, I didn't mean to tease." He reached into the big pouch and pulled out the package. "I do have something else," he said, handing it to her. "It's addressed to you."

"Me?" Celeste perked up. She examined the package while a skeptical expression contorted her face, and then she shook it. "I wonder what it could be."

Rob was by her side now, reaching for the package. "Let me see. Who's it from?"

"Probably Dudley," Logan mumbled. He held his breath. Why had he said that? He'd delivered the mail and needed to get going. No sense waiting around to hear the man's name uttered by her lips.

Celeste shot him a sidewise glance and then examined the package. "It's from Grandma Donahue." She pulled the package in close, away from her brother's reach.

Logan exhaled. "Your grandma? Like the one who held you hostage in New York all those years?" He winked at her, and she smiled. His heart warmed from her reaction and her news. Since it wasn't from Dudley, and from the way she ran to meet him just now, maybe there was a chance they could be more than friends after all.

Rob turned away from the package and stared at Logan. "Grandma did what?"

"Nothing." Celeste dismissed her brother's question with a brush of her hand and proceeded to open the package. She ran her fingers across something made of white fabric, not seeming to care that they left a smudge of dirt.

"What is it?" Rob helped her tear the paper further.

"Looks like pillow cases for me to embroider." Celeste stopped her brother from tearing the paper away entirely.

"Why?" Rob's eyebrows bunched up.

"I'm sure she sent them for my trousseau." Celeste moved the package around to her back and out of sight. "I'll read her letter later." She gazed at Logan. "How much more mail do you have left to deliver?"

"Most of it. Three bundles, if that helps answer your question." Logan patted his saddlebags. "My turn. What's a trousseau?"

"Stupid napkins and things for when Celeste gets married," Rob spoke up, and Celeste glared at him.

Logan blew out a breath. So much for hoping Dudley was out of the picture. "Are-are you getting married?" The question stumbled out of his mouth.

"Eventually. I hope." She batted her eyelashes.

"You got something in your eye?" Logan asked. He didn't care to hear more about her marriage plans. "I know the cotton from the cottonwoods can get right-down annoying this time of year."

"There's nothing in my eye," Celeste stated in a firm voice.

"I should be getting on now." Logan patted his saddlebags to hopefully let Celeste know he wasn't trying to be rude, but he really did need to go. Not so much because of the mail, but because he didn't care to linger and have his feelings strengthen for Celeste. Especially when it appeared he should suppress them. "Good seeing you." He tipped his hat.

"Do you really mean that?" she said, like she didn't believe him.

"Of course," Logan said. Sometimes she asked the dangdest things.

She looked off into the distance, as if she was thinking about something. Her eyes lit up as she turned and looked at him. "Where's your next delivery?"

"The Thompsons', about five miles from here."

"I know how far away they are," she said. "Perfect distance for a horseback ride. It'll be like when I used to come with you to deliver the mail."

"You want to come with me?" Logan asked, tempted to dig the wax from his ears. He must have misunderstood her. Or maybe she just needed a bit of cheering up, like when she was a kid. But could he handle having her ride behind him while trying to suppress his growing feelings for her?

"Yes, but of course."

Logan turned and glanced at Bootstrap's back. "This here's a new horse since last time. I don't know if he'll let you. He's not used to anybody but me on his back. I daresay you're a lot heavier than last time."

"Well! I never!" Celeste turned her back on Logan.

Rob laughed. "I don't think you're supposed to tell girls that you think they are heavy. Leastwise, that's what Ma told me."

"Sorry, Celeste." Logan laughed this time. "I didn't mean nothing by what I said. Promise. Of course, you're heavier than last time we rode. You were nothing but a kid then. Now you're all grown up and pretty as the day is long."

"Really?" Celeste's cheeks took on a lovely shade of pink. "You're not just saying that . . . to make me feel good?"

"Of course I mean it." Logan motioned to Rob. "Go fetch me a saddle blanket for you sister to sit on." Then he smiled at Celeste. "If you want to ride with me over to the Thompsons', I'm sure Bootstrap can handle that just fine. I was just teasing you before."

While Rob ran into the barn, Logan thought about how he really didn't have time for this, and it would be a challenge to keep his feelings in check. But what was life all about if you couldn't help another person be happy when you got the chance?

After Rob returned and laid the blanket behind the saddle, Celeste handed her package to her brother. Logan pulled his boot from the stirrup so Celeste could mount.

"It'll be just to the Thompsons'," Celeste said as she grabbed Logan's hand and let him help her mount. "I don't want to keep you from your work, so I'll walk home from there."

"Nonsense." Logan scooted a tad forward in the saddle, and she settled in behind him. "I have to backtrack somewhat anyway. I'll bring you back. I've got time."

She wrapped her arms around his waist, and he was tempted to say he had all the time in the world—so long as she continued to hold on to him like that.

Logan turned the horse around and headed back down the McCurdys' road, and Celeste hollered to her brother, "Rob, tell Mother I went for a ride with Logan."

Celeste didn't let go of Logan as Bootstrap walked down the road. Logan liked that she didn't hold on to the back of the saddle like she used to do when they took things at a leisurely pace.

"Sure is a nice day for a ride," he said as they turned onto the main road.

"Yes, it is." Her hold around his waist tightened.

It caused him to smile, and he got to thinking that being more than just friends would be mighty nice. "It was handy you were wearing trousers."

"They're Rob's. He's grown out of them, and they don't fit Patrick yet. They're more practical to wear than a dress when weeding the garden. I know Miss Bennett wouldn't approve. Ma wasn't too keen on it either, but I don't care."

"Well, you look right nice in them." He wanted to make up for calling her heavy. "Not many a gal could wear 'em and still look so pretty."

"Thank you." Her arms gave his waist a squeeze.

He was careful not to shift much in the saddle or do anything that would force her to let go as they continued down the road.

"I like your new horse," Celeste spoke up after a minute or two of silence.

"Thank you. Bootstrap will be glad to hear that. I realize he's not the most handsome of mounts, what with his splotchy coat and gray-and-dirt-brown mane, but I got him awfully cheap, and me and him are best friends now."

"I'll bet it's nice to have such a good friend," Celeste said.

"Yep."

"Why is it that you are so easy to talk to, Logan Jones?" Celeste leaned her head against his back.

"I don't know." Logan could definitely grow accustomed to having Celeste next to him for more than this single horseback ride. It was likely he was playing with fire, with his feelings and Dudley and all. But he'd enjoy it for just a moment, or two, or three, then he'd try to keep his distance.

Chapter 7

WHEN THEY REACHED THE THOMPSON place, Celeste got down from the saddle to rest her behind while Logan visited with Mrs. Thompson for several minutes. Logan was definitely the same as he was five years ago, unwilling to deliver mail without saying a lengthy hello and goodbye to each recipient. He was much better at that kind of thing than Celeste.

Celeste stayed in the background, not really knowing Mrs. Thompson. The family had moved in about the same time Celeste had been first shipped off to school. Perhaps she should go and introduce herself? Maybe she could take a lesson from Logan and make a friend.

She chewed on her lip and stayed near the horse, telling herself it wasn't necessary. From what Ma had said, Mrs. Thompson rarely left her homestead. Even if Logan were to court her, she wouldn't be riding with him to deliver the mail all that often, if at all. So why go through the awkward how-do-you-do's if she'd probably never see Mrs. Thompson again? Besides, she was through pretending to enjoy talking to strangers.

Logan finally said goodbye and hobbled at a quick stride toward the horse. He mounted and then helped her up. Once on the road, he turned his head to speak to her. "You should have come and said hello."

"Sorry." Celeste stared at his profile, finding the gentle point of his nose and his tanned skin very pleasing to her eyes.

"Mrs. Thompson probably thought you were unfriendly, which I know ain't right. You're plenty friendly."

"Around you," Celeste admitted. "The truth is, I have a hard time making friends. The other day, when I was complaining about all the girls at school, I didn't tell you the whole story. I didn't try very hard to make friends. Because that is *hard* for me. So I'm just as much to blame as anyone."

"Aw, come on now." Logan shook his head. "That can't be true. You were the one who kept bugging me to take you along on my mail trips."

"I was a kid looking to get out of chores." Celeste let out a laugh. Then she became somber. "And you were easy to talk to. I suppose that's why I bugged you so much."

"What about Bethany? You made friends with her, didn't you?"

"She did all the work."

"Aw, I think you're being too hard on yourself."

Celeste swore the horse clipped along at a faster pace than it had on their way out. Was that because Logan was truly concerned about delivering all the mail before it got too late? Or because he'd had enough of her?

As Logan rambled on about the Thompsons' new foal that had just been born, Celeste got to thinking. Just because she felt more comfortable around Logan than any other fellow she'd ever met, did that necessarily mean they were right for each other? If it bothered Logan that she hadn't tried to visit Mrs. Thompson now, how would he react once they were married if Celeste struggled to visit their next-door neighbors wherever it was that they lived?

That brought up another question. Where would they live? The back of the law office? It was barely big enough to fit his narrow cot. And would two part-time jobs provide enough to support a family? True, she didn't love money like her roommates back at school did, but a married couple needed enough of life's means to take care of themselves.

Why was she having such thoughts already? What if they didn't end up together at all?

She thought about Logan skipping breakfast the other morning when he was at their place. Even if she didn't marry him, she was still worried about his circumstances.

An idea came to her.

"Logan," Celeste said softly when he'd finished about the foal. "Father says the postal service is building one of those post offices in town. And they're planning on hiring what's known as a postmaster. Have you ever thought about applying for the position? You'd be perfect for the job."

"I beg to differ."

"What do you mean?" Celeste leaned to get a view of his face. Was he kidding?

"I'd no more be perfect for that job as you would be at taking on your Miss Bennett's job back at that fancy school."

"Wh-what?" Celeste huffed. "I might have been asked to leave early, but I learned everything I was taught and could act the part of a finished young lady very well, thank you very much!"

"I don't doubt that a bit." Logan sounded apologetic. "What I'm trying to say is that though you'd be good at it, you'd hate every minute of your job."

"Oh." Celeste bit her lip. "So you're saying you would hate being the postmaster."

"Pretty much."

Their conversation moved on to the weather and how Logan thought that was part of the fun of being a mail carrier, enjoying the different seasons.

When they got to the turnoff to her parents' homestead, Logan brought Bootstrap to a stop.

"I'm running a bit late," Logan said. "Do you mind if I let you off here and you walk the rest of the way home?"

"Uh, no," Celeste responded, a little taken by surprise.

"Great," Logan said. "Hop off."

Celeste frowned. "What? You're not going to help be down?"

He hesitated. "Of course I will," he said in his usual, cheerful voice and dismounted. He reached up to assist her. "Not that you need my help. You're almost as at home on a horse as Rosie."

"Thanks." Celeste was certain he meant that as a compliment, but she hardly wanted to be compared to a woman everyone this side of Denver knew as the roughest, toughest cowgirl God ever made. She slipped off the back of Bootstrap, adding, "I think," under her breath as her feet touched the ground. Logan let go of her, and she turned toward home and took a small step or two.

"Goodbye, Celeste." Logan's voice rang out behind her, as did the sound of him mounting up.

Then she heard the sprint of horse hooves. She'd expected him to keep talking, to beg her to turn around and linger a minute or two longer. He could have at least been more reluctant to leave.

"Oh!" Celeste fisted her hands and held them straight down at her sides. "Sometimes that Logan Jones can be so sweet, and sometimes he can be so infuriating."

She kicked a clod of dirt out of her path, thinking how she'd gone out of her way to try to get Logan to notice her—as a woman, not as that moody little girl he used to be nice to five years ago. She'd used every trick her five years of learning manners and proper flirting had taught her. But it wasn't working.

"Maybe it's time I forget about being subtle!" she yelled at the sagebrush. "Maybe it's time I quit hinting at what I want and just flat-out tell him to court me."

That's what she would do the next time she saw Logan. She didn't know when that would be . . . and that left a pit in her stomach. Maybe she could ride with Ma next time she went into town to tend to patients at her doctor's office. Ma had said she was planning on going in more often now that Celeste was home. But that was because Celeste could stay home and help tend to the boys and the meals.

She slowed her steps to a near crawl. Perhaps it would be best if she stayed at home. What had started out as a wonderful-sounding solution to her future was ending up as a mess. Now that she was here, face-to-face with the "man of her dreams," the man who would want her for who she was, she wasn't so sure he was the perfect match for her.

Chapter 8

LOGAN WALKED OUT OF THE mercantile with a load of mail packed in his saddlebags, ready to ride out and start on Thursday's RFD deliveries. At this point, he was grateful he only did the RFD routes twice a week. Running into Celeste left him such that his head and his heart didn't know right side up from wrong. One moment, she acted like she was fond of him, and the next moment, she talked about a whole passel of fellows who were sweet on her, and in another moment yet, she acted disgusted with him. Add to that her noticeable disappointment in him for not taking the postmaster position, as if she had some say in the matter. He obviously didn't have the ability to put a smile on her face like he used to when she was a kid. And then there was Dudley. It'd be best for both him and Celeste if he avoided her place. Maybe he could merely leave the mail on the McCurdys' doorstep and then hop back on Bootstrap and get the heck out of there.

Out of the corner of his eye, he saw someone waving at him. He turned and recognized good ole Ronald Smith walking toward him. Even though Logan slept in the back room of Ron's law office, he rarely saw Ron nowadays. Logan left for the stable or to deliver mail, depending on the day, long before Ron made it to the office. And now that Ron was married and he and Dorothy had four kids, nighttime visits rarely happened either. Ron's family came first, as it should. Just like Logan's sister, Susannah, put her husband and three children before Logan. He was doing just fine, visiting folks while taking care of their horses or delivering mail. The occasional supper invitation helped fill those lonely evening hours. As for nighttime, when he retired to that tiny back room with its narrow cot, a single chair to sit on while he pulled his boots off and on, and a coal-oil lamp set on a sturdy crate to light up the place, well, he had a whole stack of books to keep him company then.

He waved at Ron and walked toward him. "Good morning. What brings you this way?"

Ron met up with him and pulled him into a manly hug. "I came looking for you. You are a difficult person to track down, believe it or not."

"No, I don't believe it." Logan smiled. "I'd never hide from you or anyone else." Then again, wasn't that kind of what he was planning on doing with Celeste?

"I've been trying to meet up with you for two days now." Ronald released Logan and stepped back.

"Well," Logan said, "we're meeting up now. What can I do for you?"

"I've got some good news." Ron looked up Yampa Avenue to the north, then down to the south. "I would prefer speaking with you in my office, if you wouldn't mind."

"I was on my way to deliver the rural mail. Can it wait?" Logan gazed at the sun quickly rising above the eastern hills. "I'd rather not ride in the heat of the afternoon if I don't have to. This last week of June is ending up being a hot one."

"But of course." Ron nodded. "Can you stop by my office somewhere between four and five o'clock?"

"Be there with bells on my toes." Logan slapped Ron on the shoulder.

As he headed south out of town, he spotted a familiar horse and rider heading toward him. Kate McCurdy, what luck! He slowed Bootstrap and waved as they met up in the middle of the street.

"Good morning, Logan." Kate pulled her mount to a stop.

"It's good to see you, Kate. What brings you to town on a Thursday?"

"Mrs. Brown is in labor. Her oldest boy came out early this morning to fetch me. So I can't talk long. What can I do for you?"

"I got lots of mail to deliver today. Got three letters for your place alone. Would you mind if I just passed your mail on to you right now?" Logan saw this meeting as fortunate indeed. Not only would he avoid seeing Celeste, but he could cut some time from his route. He couldn't imagine what kind of good news Ron had for him, and he didn't want to be late. "That'll save me from veering off the main road apiece to get to your place."

"I would be happy to take it." Kate held out her hand.

"Hold on. Let me get it." Logan rummaged through his saddlebags, located the correct envelopes, and passed them to Kate. "Thanks." He tipped his hat. "I appreciate this more than you know."

U

Logan guessed it was close to five o'clock by the way the sun hung in the sky. Another mile or so lay between him and Craig and some good news. He clicked his heals into Bootstrap and galloped the rest of the way into town, hoping he could make it to the office before Ron headed home to his family.

He slowed Bootstrap as they turned onto Yampa Avenue at the south end of town, continuing to rack his brain, trying to imagine what kind of "good news" awaited him. Maybe Ron was going to move into a bigger office, one with a bigger back room? No, Ron could have told him that this morning on the street. Was it possible that Dorothy was expecting another child? No, again, Ron could have told him that easily enough that morning.

He went straight to the law office, not bothering to stable Bootstrap for the night—he'd do that later. As he wrapped Bootstrap's reins around the hitching post, Ron walked out of his office backwards, locking the door behind him. He turned around, and his eyes met Logan's.

"Ah, you're here. I'm so glad." Ron turned and unlocked the door again. "Come inside. This won't take long." He glanced over his shoulder at Logan. "I hope."

"You hope?" Logan fell in step behind Ron. "What's that supposed to mean?"

"Just what it sounds like," Ron said as his feet clapped a rhythm on the tile floor. He rounded the partition that separated the entry from his desk space. "I hope this won't take long, because it's little Delphi's birthday today."

"Heck, why didn't you say something about it being your little girl's birthday?" Logan followed Ron around the end of the partition. He stood in front of the desk, not wanting to take a chair like Ron motioned for him to do. "I can come in tomorrow at . . ." He thought about when he was done for the day at the livery stable. ". . . at five o'clock."

"You, Logan, are as busy a man as I am." Ron pointed at the chair at Logan's side with more force. "Sit. It's best we take care of this right now before it drags on any further. The Circle J is in, what one might say, limbo."

"Limbo?" Logan muttered as he sat down. What really had him concerned was Ron's mention of the Circle J. "What are you trying to tell me, Ron? I had the idea you were going to give me good news."

"To ninety-nine percent of the human population, this would be good news." Ron pulled out a folder. He opened it, shuffled through it, and scooted a sheet of paper that held a type-written paragraph with a couple of signatures below it. "But to you, Logan Jones, I know you enough to have my doubts. Nonetheless, the Circle J Ranch and all of Stanley's holdings are now yours."

"What?" Logan felt numb everywhere but his head. It ached. "Nonsense. That can't be right!"

"What I state is correct." Ron looked Logan in the eye. "Whether you wish to believe it or not."

"No, no, it should all go to Susannah—now that Stanley's gone." Logan took off his hat and raked his fingers through his hair. "I've seen Pa's old will. In fact, you're the one who showed it to me years ago, and it didn't surprise me one bit. It said if something were to happen to Stanley, Susannah got everything."

"Yes, you are correct on that point." Ronald growled under his breath. "This will has never been fair."

"And I never cared." Logan folded his arms across his chest and leaned back in the chair. "About the money," he added under his breath.

"Fortunately, your sister, Susannah, did. And does." Ron tapped the paper sitting on the end of his desk, the one he'd just set there. "This is a sworn, legal statement made by Susannah and her husband, Joseph. They are turning every bit of Stanley's holdings, along with the ranch, over to you."

"Why?" Logan shook his head. "Why would she do that? That's crazy."

"Logan," Ron said his name in a gentle voice. "Listen to me. Susannah and Joseph do not need the money or the ranch. The coal mine on their land has made them very well off. They both want you to have what should have rightfully been yours from the very beginning."

"Why didn't Susannah tell me this herself? Why is she going through a lawyer?" Logan's throat tightened with pain. He hadn't seen his sister in weeks. Was she going to end up being like Stanley, never finding the time to talk to him either? "Is she too highfalutin now," he continued, even though his throat choked on the words, "that she can't come and talk to her dirt-poor brother— who's doing just fine—but she's got to hire someone to do it for her?"

"Logan." Again, Ron said his name with such compassion that it helped ease the ache in his throat. "You know Susannah is nothing like your brother. She and I only want what is best for you. The only reason she didn't tell you about this," he pointed to the signed paper, "is because she was afraid she'd be unable to stand up to you and insist you take it when you said no." Ron gave him a sideways glance. "She asked me to take on that difficult task."

"I don't want it." Logan pushed the paper toward Ron—it represented too much pain. "Tell Susannah to keep it."

"It's too late." Ron pushed it back. "It's not hers anymore. All you have to do is add your signature at the bottom of this page, and it is yours. Just take it, gosh darn it all! Buy yourself a house in town and then give it all away after that—if that's what you want. Not that I care if you stay here, but, Logan, can't you see? You can't live in my back room forever. Your ship has come in. You'll be set for life." Ron ran both hands through his thinning hair.

"I said I don't want it, and I mean it."

"Why not? Tell me one good reason."

"I don't know." Logan couldn't boil it down to one reason. He only knew that it hurt. For years he didn't want it because Pa hadn't wanted him. But that wasn't the feeling rolling around inside him right now. The fact that it wasn't Pa who was giving it to him made him want to push that paper back across the desk and clean across western Colorado for that matter. He'd never pictured his sister giving him the ranch. It was not the way he'd wanted it to happen. "I just don't want it."

"Could it be that you just don't want what it represents?"

"Huh?" Logan wrinkled his brow down to where it closed half an eye.

Ron held his hands out to Logan. "My conjecture is that because your pa and your brother never believed you would amount to anything, you want to prove them wrong."

"Uh . . ." Logan couldn't find his voice. Ron had a point. He'd had a constant yearn to succeed on his own, without a stitch of help from Pa or his brother. His voice found him. "You might be right."

"I'm glad you agree. Besides, your pa and brother are gone, so proving something to them is no longer relevant." Ron pulled a pen from his desk drawer.

"Thanks for setting me to thinking." Logan held his palm up to refuse the pen. "I've got to noodle on this for a while, if you don't mind."

"Sure, sure, take the time that you need." Ron grinned with one side of his mouth. "As long as it's not more than a week or so. Legal matters like these can become problematic if not taken care of in a timely fashion. Understand?"

"No, I don't." Logan pushed his chair back and stood. "And I haven't said I was going to sign that blasted paper, only think on it." He hobbled away from Ron's desk and scrambled for the door.

Once outside, he mounted Bootstrap and headed for the river where he could think without pressuring voices, only the tumble of water against stone to aid his thoughts.

Was Ron right? Was the real reason Logan didn't want his pa's money or the ranch just so that Stanley could look down from heaven, or more likely gaze up from down below, and Logan could prove he *was* worth something by surviving plenty fine without Pa's or Stanley's attention or stinking money?

Chapter 9

"Get up, Celeste. It's the Fourth of July!"

"I don't want to." Celeste jerked her shoulder away from whoever was shaking it. How dare they wake her at this moment? She had been enjoying the most wonderful dream. Logan, dressed in a dapper suit and tie with his long hair parted down the middle and combed neatly to each side so as to bend up at his ears, was walking toward her with his arms outstretched. He wasn't hiding his limp or his thick cowboy drawl. He was being his regular self, only cleaned up. With his always-cheerful smile spreading across his face, he reached out to her with both hands and said, "Come here, Celeste. I've been waiting my whole dang life for a gal like you to love me." Then he pulled her into his arms and kissed her.

And then Patrick woke her up!

She opened her eyes and glared at her little brother. "Why'd you have to do that?"

"Pa says we can go into town as soon as we get our chores all done. So hurry and get dressed. I don't want to miss the parade because of you."

"Parade?" Celeste sat up in her bed. "Since when does Craig have a parade?" She had hoped to spend this holiday morning reading a book in her favorite spot under the cottonwood tree after she'd completed her chores.

"Since two years ago." Patrick pulled on her arm. "And we didn't get to go to those neither, so come on. I've never seen a parade before."

"I can't imagine it's very grand." Celeste thought about the parades down crowded streets she'd been invited to go to while back East. Even they weren't worth getting up early for.

"I don't care." Patrick furrowed his eyebrows. "It'll be plenty grand to me. Pa says it's going to march all the way from the south end of Yampa Avenue to the north end. And that we should be there early enough to get a good spot to watch."

Celeste immediately visualized the spot she wanted to claim . . . if she went. "Will it go past the livery stable?"

"I imagine. It's on Yampa, isn't it?" Patrick tugged some more. "And what does that matter?"

"A lot," Celeste said under her breath. She peeled back the covers, swung her bare feet onto the floor, and flicked her hand at Patrick. "Skedaddle so I can get dressed."

Patrick ran from her room, yelling, "Celeste is coming!"

Celeste pulled off her nightgown, thinking if this had been a week earlier, she wouldn't have been coming, infuriated at Logan like she'd been. But then she'd softened, thinking about how kind he was underneath all those worn-out clothes—not that his clothes mattered to her. As for his blindness to her flirtations, she'd forgiven him. Then with that dream . . . It was definitely worth going into town early for a parade. Her book could wait.

While she got dressed, she envisioned standing next to him as the floats passed by, chatting about the nice weather and some new horse that just got born out on a homestead or something like that. It didn't matter what; she'd be talking to him and he to her, both feeling at ease in each other's company.

Yes, she definitely needed to go to the parade. She and her family had been planning on going into town for part of the Fourth of July celebration anyway. But only for the rodeo this afternoon. Ma had volunteered to be the doctor on call. If Celeste knew Logan, he'd be one of the participants standing in line to wrestle a bull or something else just as ridiculous. She shook her head at the thought. Like it or not, her schooling *had* rubbed off on her. It didn't matter; it'd been a week and a half since they were together, and she wanted to see him. She'd make sure to do so during the parade.

She was glad she'd taken over for Ma yesterday and made the apple pie for the pie-eating contest in the park after the rodeo. Hopefully Logan would participate in that too and taste her pie and determine she was a pretty good cook. Heavens, the man had the kind of appetite to easily compete in such an activity—one viewed as uncivil at the Bennett School for Girls. Celeste smiled, glad once again to be free of that school, or at least part of it. She'd learned much that she wanted to keep, feeling she'd become a better person by refining her rough edges. But she was grateful to be shed of all the judgement and importance of wealth. It was no wonder she liked Logan.

U

Pa slowed the wagon as they approached Craig. "It looks like they've already got Yampa Avenue blocked off for the parade." Pa pointed to a field of pasture grass where several wagons were parked. "We'll just pull over there and walk, if that's okay."

"That will be fine, dear." Ma touched his arm as he commanded the horse to an open spot.

Rob and Patrick jumped out of the wagon before it came to a stop and broke into a sprint toward Yampa Avenue. "Hold on there, boys," Pa yelled. "Wait for your ma and your sister."

"Aw, Pa," they said together.

"You two can help me unhitch the horse and put him with the others while you wait." Pa motioned with his eyes to the fenced area provided for everyone's horses.

"What do I do with this pie?" Celeste lifted it from her lap and held it toward Ma. She feared it would look a mess by the time Logan got to taste it. "I don't care to carry it around all morning. That will be difficult at best with this." She extracted her parasol from beneath her seat with one hand.

"Put it under there where your parasol was. Keep it covered with that dish cloth, and I'll add my shawl for extra shade," Ma said. "Heaven knows I don't need it today."

"Are you sure it will be okay?" Celeste set down her parasol and slipped the pie beneath the shade of the wagon's bench.

"'Tis a pie, not a wee babe." Pa raised his eyebrow.

"Well . . . oh, never mind!" Celeste took hold of Ma's shawl, certain that neither Ma nor Pa—or her brothers—understood.

She'd just spent five years of her life at a school whose sole mission was to prepare girls for marriage and then see them successfully married off. And she'd more or less been expelled. Miss Bennett might not believe in her ability to catch a "proper" young man, but Celeste did. And she was going to see to it. Determination was one thing she did learn from school. True, Logan was more proper than most every young man she'd ever courted. But she feared he wasn't that interested in her. He was merely being nice because that was his nature. If that was indeed the case, she didn't want her family to know she had hopes of marrying Logan.

Her ma still didn't know she'd been asked to leave school. Perhaps Celeste should tell her. After all, Pa didn't seem to care. But she wouldn't do it today and take the chance of ruining what she hoped would be a wonderful Fourth of July.

Celeste carefully draped the shawl over the seat to form a spot of shade for the pie regardless of the shift of the sun. "That will have to do," she said as she hopped out of the wagon. She walked side by side with Ma toward the clamor of voices.

As they turned the corner onto Yampa Avenue, Pa and the boys joined them. He pointed to a barber shop Celeste hadn't seen before. There was an empty spot in front of its red-and-white striped pole. "How about there?" Pa said.

"Yes, that's got some good shade—for the moment," Ma said.

Celeste looked down a block at the livery stable. She held out her hand and motioned down the street. "There is even more space over there, in front of the livery stable."

"Why would I want to go over there when I got a shady spot over here?" Rob asked.

"I'm with your brother. That spot's in the sun," Pa said, and Ma nodded in agreement.

Celeste looked at Patrick. "What about you? Would you like to watch the parade over there with me? There's even a bench in front of the livery stable if your legs get tired from standing."

"Nope."

"Well, I wish to *sit* over there, if it's okay." She looked at her parents.

Ma inclined her head. "Suit yourself."

"'Tis your choice." Pa smiled.

Celeste walked away, hoping Ma and her brothers wouldn't deduce her reason. Pa, she feared, already suspected she had her sights pinned on Logan. She looked over her shoulder at them. "I quite like the sun and the lack of a crowd." That bit of truth pulled her across the street almost as much as her desire to meet up with Logan. Looking for Logan, she scanned the myriad faces. Hopefully, he was still working inside the livery stable. He probably wouldn't venture out until the parade passed by.

The sound of trumpets and trombones drew her eyes up the street. Musicians in blue-and-gold uniforms marched her way. She hurried the rest of the way across the street and planted herself directly in front of the smaller, man-sized door of the livery stable.

The sun beat upon her face. Grateful she'd brought it, she opened her parasol. She looked over the crowd gathering on her side of the street, not seeing a single other parasol. Suddenly, she felt out of place. A nervous laugh escaped her lips. Where *did* she fit in? Apparently not here in Craig any more than she fit in at Miss Bennett's school.

"That's nonsense, and you know it," she whispered to herself. Parasols were handy. Maybe she could start a new trend. She belonged here in Craig, Colorado. This was home. And she was going to be happy here.

The urge to burst into the livery stable and find Logan burned strong inside her. She wanted to see his friendly smile and hear his voice. That would calm her nerves. She shuffled toward the double-wide doors and leaned her ear against the slit where they met. Maybe she could hear Logan in there tending to the horses or pitching hay around—anything, any sign that he was inside. A neigh, then a whinny was all she heard.

Her heart sank.

The smaller door to the right opened, and her heart lifted again.

Logan strolled outside, chewing on a piece of hay. Celeste straightened and hurried away from the double doors and, as demurely as possible, gazed up the street at the oncoming parade while twirling her parasol over her shoulder. She tried to appear aloof and not to notice Logan, but her eyes refused to quit sneaking a look his way.

He caught sight of her, their eyes meeting for a split second. Celeste looked straight ahead, expecting him to hobble over and say, "Good day." Instead, he dashed back toward the door. What? She couldn't let him slip away. She needed him to notice her, to lend her confidence amidst this crowd.

"Logan," she called out and set off after him.

He stopped with his hand on the doorknob. Taking a deep breath, he slowly turned toward her. "Oh, Celeste." He hesitated. "What're you doing here?"

"Watching the parade of course." She sensed he wanted to head back into the stable, and she panicked. Her demure hints and batting of eyes obviously didn't work with Logan like it had with other fellows. She held her hand out toward the spot where she'd been standing. "I wanted to watch it with you. I even saved us a spot."

"Uh . . ." He stared off to one side—at the ground.

Did he not want to watch the parade? Or just not with her? Celeste choked down the ache at the back of her throat, telling herself at least he wasn't like the men back East who only wanted her for her "pretty face." But it appeared Logan didn't want her at all. The ache refused to subside. Rather, it swelled to where it reached into her eyes and made them water.

She wiped away a tear with the back of her hand. "Please, Logan," she said, hoping the old Logan she knew five years ago would shine forth. Her voice surprised her with how shaky and insecure it sounded. She glanced at the daunting crowd, then at her family gazing at the oncoming parade, oblivious of her. Just as they had been for the last five years. Shaky or not, she had to continue. "I do not care for large crowds, yet I don't want to be alone. But I do want to see the parade. Please, I need you to stand by me."

Logan shifted his gaze to her face. He peered into her eyes with such tenderness that her throat took on a more pleasant sort of ache. "Of course I will," he said softly. He offered her a pinch-lipped smile and walked toward her. Placing his hand on the small of her back, he guided her to the open spot in the crowd lining the street.

His gentle touch upon her back was like a blanket of comfort. It enveloped her with tingles.

"Thank you," she murmured. She turned her head and looked at him. "I mean that sincerely."

Logan kept his eyes forward. "You're welcome. Nice day for a parade, ain't it? If I was working the ranch, I wouldn't get to see it."

Celeste didn't know what he meant by that, but she didn't care. He was by her side now; the scores of people no longer felt daunting.

He leaned out past the crowd and looked up the street. "The school band sure looks smart in their new uniforms. Three years ago, they didn't even have a band."

"Really?" Celeste observed the band as it marched closer. "Then again, I wouldn't know. I never attended the town's school." She gave up talking for the moment.

The horns blared much too loudly, and numerous misplayed notes made her wince. Logan, too, appeared content just to watch, never leaning close to attempt a word or two or even giving her a glance as the band marched by. The band consisted of four trumpets, three trombones, one tuba, two clarinets, and two drummers forming three rows of four. All wore dark trousers in varying shades, tall, dark-blue hats with visors trimmed in gold, and gold sashes across their mix-and-match white shirts. If Celeste stretched her imagination, she could see how Logan could call their attire "uniforms." She smiled. It felt good after her panic of a few minutes earlier. This band was delightful in its own simple way. Back in New York, people would have scoffed at it, perhaps even lifted their noses in the air at these school kids playing their hearts out.

"I'm glad the school has a band," she said after the blare of the horns moved on sufficiently to hear herself speak. "And that the parade has a band."

"Yeah, that is something to make one feel good." Logan nodded. He turned and looked at her. "That's a smart idea, bringing that pretty umbrella of yours to keep out the sun. I hope you are enjoying yourself okay in this spot."

"Yes, yes, I am. Thank you."

"Now, that's something you don't see every day." Logan pointed to an automobile with shiny red fenders coming toward them.

"I've seen my share of them back East, but I never figured I'd see one this far west." Celeste twirled her parasol.

Logan leaned into the road, apparently to get a better view. "Well, if that don't beat all. It's Mr. Hoy driving the thing. His wife's in the seat next to him."

"Who is Mr. Hoy?" Celeste wondered who out here could afford, or want, an automobile. "Does he have lots of money?"

"Next to Stan—I mean, next to the Circle J Ranch," Logan took a noticeable breath, "his ranch is the biggest." His eyes appeared glued to the hand-painted sign attached to the side of the car.

Celeste swore she detected a trace of fear. Or was it dread clouding Logan's eyes? She read the sign to try to make sense of it. *The AUTOMOBILE: soon to be the popular means of travel. No horses required.*

Logan rubbed his forehead and dragged his hand down his face. He pointed up the street. "Now, there's a fine-looking horse if I've ever seen one," he said, noticeably switching his attention to the next entry in the parade.

Pulled by a huge white horse, a wagon rolled by, decked out in red, white, and blue banners. A sign in the middle had words painted in black: *A.S. Robinson, Craig City Mayor.* A round-bellied gentleman dressed in a pin-striped suit sat up front on the seat next to the driver, waving first at one side of the road and then the other. As the mayor rolled past them, Celeste saw the back of the wagon. It held another sign: *Craig City, Founded 1908.*

Grateful for an excuse to do so, Celeste reached over and touched Logan on the forearm. "But Craig has been around since just before my Pa moved here. That's what he told me."

"It was 1889 when the first folks, like your pa, moved here to homestead. Investors followed and laid out the streets of Craig and started selling off building lots. Two years ago is when the town got made official by becoming incorporated with the state."

"Oh, okay," Celeste said as a group of young children marched by pulling their decorated toy wagons. Wanting to keep him talking, she asked the first pertinent-sounding thing that came to mind. "I wonder how Craig came to be called Craig. I knew a Craig Bradford back in New York. Every time I saw him, it always made me think that Craig was a fine-sounding first name for a fellow but a peculiar-sounding name for a town."

Logan moved the piece of straw to the other side of his mouth. "Craig ain't a first name in this case. The town was named after Reverend William Byard Craig. He don't live here no more, but he was one of the men who invested money into the place—you know, hoping to make a nice town to draw businesses here to serve all the homesteaders flocking in."

"That's interesting." Celeste grinned at a little girl pulling a lamb, wearing a pink ribbon, inside her wagon. "How'd you come to know so much about this town?"

"Talking to people." He took the piece of straw from his mouth, tossed it on the ground, and turned toward her. "You really don't like talking to people?" His voice sounded slightly higher.

Celeste nodded.

"You talk to me plenty fine." He sounded confused.

"That's because you're easy to talk to."

"Aw." He flicked a hand at her. "Not any more so than anyone else."

"That's not true. There've been very few people, besides my family, who I can talk with and feel totally at ease. Usually when I talk to people, my insides make me feel like I want to go run and hide."

"That's only 'cause you know me." Logan wagged a finger at her. "If you got to know those other folks just as good as you know your family—or even me—you'd do just fine talking to them."

"Perhaps you are correct." Celeste pulled her eyes from Logan's and stared at an approaching wagon that held a woman dressed in a blue satin saloon-type dress playing a honkytonk song on a piano. A single banner decorated her float, which read: *Sunny Saloon and Sunny's Place: Everything from Bourbon to Braised Beef.* "But getting to know them is just as frightening as talking to them," she admitted.

"That's just because you've been stuck talking to snobby people for the past five years. Stick with me today, and I'll show you that the people of this here horse town are a heck of a lot easier to talk to than those folks back East."

Celeste's heart lifted nearly into her throat. She coughed. "You really mean that?"

"Sure. It's nice to feel needed." Logan gazed at her. His countenance had changed somehow. Was it his warm, brown eyes that held a bit more spark, or his lopsided grin? Or both. "I'd consider it a privilege to accompany you. At least until the rodeo at four o'clock. I entered a passel of different events. They wouldn't exactly let me take you with me down into the chutes, now, would they?"

"No, no, I don't think so." She didn't exactly know what he meant by the *shoots*, having never seen a rodeo before. But she'd make sure she watched this one come four o'clock. For now, she was watching a parade. With Logan. Like she'd envisioned. Four riders on four almost-identical horses trotted by, each carrying a flag with words printed across: Craig, Colorado Rodeo. "Is the rodeo new, like the parade? I don't recall hearing about it before now, even when I was a little kid."

"Yes and no." Logan stared at the horses, now crisscrossing from one side of the road to the other while prancing with high steps and moving forward.

"Yes and no!" Celeste braved a sidestep that took her right next to Logan. "It's got to be one or the other. It can't be both."

"Well," Logan said, not moving away, not even leaning away, but standing firm even when she brushed her arm, holding her parasol, against his arm. "The rodeo's not new. The hands over at the Hoy ranch have been holding rodeos for years." He paused and, wincing ever so slightly, added, "Even my brother let them hold one or two down at the Circle J. Then two years ago, when the city became official and they started the parade, the ranchers were asked to put together a rodeo for the townsfolk. It's gotten right popular in those two years." He offered a slight smile. "I know I like 'em—rodeos, that is." The smile widened. "You might too. I think you should come watch. Maybe even cheer me on when I'm about ready to let go and fly off that darn bull. Hearing your voice will help me hang on tighter. It might even make you speak up in a crowd without realizing it."

"I'll be there. Ma's volunteered to be the doctor." She cringed as the purpose dawned on her. "Why does there need to be a doctor at the rodeo? Are you telling me what you and those other cowboys do is dangerous?"

"Aw, quit your worrying. Life *is* dangerous—and not just from things that draw blood. So what we going to do about it? I say, let's watch the parade." He looked up the street. "It looks like it's going to be over within about two floats and another bunch of horseback riders."

Celeste didn't think a wagon with a banner and a pretty girl showing off a brood of piglets should be considered a float, but she was in Craig now. And she liked being here. Especially standing next to Logan. Unfortunately, as Logan had said, the parade was about finished.

"What are your plans for after the parade?" She held her breath.

"I was going to go to the new park and have myself a free lunch." A spark lit his eye, like he thought he was clever. "I entered myself in the pie-eating contest. I can't think of a better meal than some fresh pie that I didn't have to cook myself." He held his hand to the side of his mouth like he wanted to shield others from hearing—not that he needed to, because of the noisy crowd. "If they had a contest for the world's worst cook, I'd win."

Celeste laughed. "I'm sure you would not. Besides, it's not like you've got a family to cook for." She chuckled softer. "Now, my ma, maybe she should enter that contest."

"Oh, come on now. Your ma ain't *that* bad. I've eaten her meals a number of times and lived to eat another one."

"You're right. She's not that bad," Celeste said. "But she's not that good either. That's why I offered to bake the pie Ma volunteered to bring for the contest."

Logan stepped back and looked at her with his head cocked to one side. "You don't say." He turned his focus to the tail end of the parade. "What kind did you make?"

"Apple."

"Mmm. My favorite."

"Really?" Celeste's insides danced. "Try to get a piece of mine. I think you'll really like it. At least, Mrs. Shuler liked my pies—I did fine in *some* of my classes."

"How will I know it's yours?"

Celeste noticed the road in front of them was filled with people now, not floats. "I'll go get it right now. You can come with me while I take it over to the park. It's out in our wagon in the shade."

"Lead the way." Logan stretched his arm out and motioned for Celeste to start walking.

She didn't lead but stayed by his side as she walked to the wagon. Every other step, she debated whether she should slip her arm around the crook of his elbow. She dared not be too forward and decided against it. The last thing she wanted was to undo the progress she and Logan had made, during a short parade, no less.

"What time is the pie-eating contest? Do you know, by chance?" she asked, anxious for him to taste her pie.

"Twelve noon." Logan looked at the sky. "Which is in fifteen or twenty minutes, so we'd better hurry."

They made it to the wagon in good time. She reached under the seat and, to her delight, found the pie had weathered well in her makeshift shade. She pulled it out and held it up for Logan to see. "What do you think? Will you be able to remember this pie once they slice it up?"

"Slice it up?" Logan laughed loud. "They don't slice it and serve us a dainty piece all pretty like. Heck, anyone could enter and win that kind of contest."

"W-what do they do, then?"

"We race to eat the whole pie. Heck, we don't even get a chance to taste it or enjoy it; we're so busy chomping and swallowing." Logan surveyed her pie. "Sure is a pretty-looking one. I'll make sure I park myself in front of it."

"So, you'll not even taste it? Because you'll be eating so fast?" Celeste chewed on a fingernail. "Oh dear," she muttered quietly, reminding herself that she chose to be here in Craig, not in New York.

Chapter 10

LOGAN STEPPED BACK FROM HIS pie the moment the whistle blew to stop the contest, licking his lips and grinning. He glanced at the table where his half-eaten pie sat, knowing darn well he could have won. But heck, that new homesteader, Cliff Harper, needed the prize money more than he did. Plus, that pie was so dang good he hated to spoil it by eating it so fast.

He wiped his face with the napkin provided, then glanced at Celeste, who stood several feet away in the shade of an old cottonwood tree. She wasn't looking at him for the moment, so he dared to stare at her—trying to figure her out and trying to figure himself out. This morning when he'd stepped out of the livery stable and spotted Celeste standing only spitting distance away, he'd tried to hightail it back inside before she saw him. But she'd seen him, and he couldn't be rude. He hadn't been in the mood for a repeat of the other day, with her being all fickle-like and confusing. Then she'd gone and tugged on his heartstrings. When she'd shared with him how hard it was for her to talk with people and be in crowds, he couldn't move. His feet felt nailed to the road—with one of those nails poking all the way up into his heart. He could see the anxiety in her eyes. How could he abandon her then? Especially when she said please like she really meant it.

It was hard for him to understand how someone could be afraid of talking to people. That's what made the happiest. It made him ache for her all the more. What started out as a bit of a service project—keeping Celeste company during the parade when he'd wanted to run back into the livery stable—was ending up with him being the one benefiting now.

She turned and looked his way. He held her gaze momentarily and then looked away himself. He really shouldn't be letting himself desire to be with her for the remainder of the day. She had Dudley. *So what? Dudley isn't here.* And if and when Dudley did show up? Logan clenched his fists. He'd rarely used them to fight, but by gum, maybe it was time to start.

Or maybe he should just content himself with keeping her company until Dudley returned—if that was what Celeste needed.

He was at least going to enjoy this day with her. He walked briskly to where she stood, trying his best to hide his limp. Holding out his hands toward her, he said, "That was the best apple pie I've ever eaten."

She grasped his hands and pulled him next to her. "But you only ate half of it." A slight frown appeared on her face.

Logan let go of one hand, relishing the smoothness of her fingers intertwined with his. He pointed to his partially eaten pie. "That's mine, and I'm taking it with me as my prize. I'm going to eat it real slow and savor every bite."

"So you liked it?" Her face beamed, and he couldn't help but smile.

"Liked it? Heck, I liked it so much I lost on purpose. I wanted some time to taste it." He kept hold of her one hand and pulled her away from the pie-eating table. "I'm going to eat the rest of it later." He pointed back to Lavender Decker, who was wrapping Celeste's pie in its dish towel. "I asked her to save it for me. Right now, I want to take you to meet folks so you can see that it can be a right enjoyable thing to do." He gave her hand a squeeze. "Don't worry. I'm going to be by your side every step of the way."

"Can't we just sit under a tree somewhere and enjoy the shade by ourselves?"

"I'll help you know what to say. But only if you need me to 'cause I know you'll do fine."

"You really think so?"

"Yep, I do. Just think of them all as family, and it'll be easy. And you'll find yourself enjoying the day more than if we kept to ourselves."

"Thank you, Logan. I'll try." She squeezed his hand.

Tingles ran up the length of his arm. He definitely wanted to spend the rest of the afternoon with her. "How about we start over there." He pointed to where Ethyl Hoy laid out gunny sacks in a row on the ground.

Hand in hand, they walked over. Logan tipped his hat. "Afternoon, Mrs. Hoy. What you got going here?"

"We're getting ready for the gunny-sack races." Ethyl smiled, and the wrinkles by her eyes looked like crows' feet. "You want to sign up? It's not too late."

"No, thanks. I don't hop too good," Logan said. He then motioned with his free hand to Celeste.

"Would you like to, dear?" Ethyl asked Celeste, who shook her head emphatically.

Logan laughed. "I wasn't pointing to her for that. I just wanted you to meet Celeste here and say howdy. I know you haven't seen her for a while."

"Celeste McCurdy?" Ethyl shook her head like Logan had told her a lie. "Lands, girl, I didn't recognize you. Last time I saw you, you were nothing but a child."

"I've been away at school for five years."

Ethyl reached out to Celeste for a hug. "I know. Your ma told me all about it. Come here. Give me a proper hello."

Celeste hesitated, then let go of Logan and wrapped her arms around Ethyl. "It's good to see you again," she said, hugging the middle-aged woman. She let go and stepped back to Logan's side. "So you think I've changed, do you?" she asked Ethyl.

"Yes, you've grown from a skinny little thing into a beautiful woman, dear Celeste. And you're all calm and mannerly. I remember your ma coming in to the saddle shop before heading upstairs to her office, all frazzled some days, saying she didn't know what to do with you. She thought it was all on account of her being your stepmother, not your real ma."

"That—that's just not true," Celeste stammered.

Logan nodded in agreement. Celeste had never treated Kate as anything but her own ma. It was something he'd always admired about her.

"Exactly what I told your ma." Ethyl glanced at Logan and looked back at Celeste. "It looks as though your schooling did you good in other ways too. You couldn't make a better choice than Logan." She took Celeste's hand in hers and patted it. "It does me good to see the two of you together."

Logan hiccupped. Just once. He'd not thought about others looking at him and Celeste holding hands and what that said to folks' imaginations. He only knew that he enjoyed the feeling of her hand in his. He didn't rightly care what others thought of him, but if and when that Dudley fellow showed up in town and swept Celeste back off her feet, they might judge her as being fickle. The thought of that did not appeal to him, for they didn't understand. He was spending the day with her to lift her spirits and help her adjust. And keep her company until Dudley returned. That was all.

"Celeste! Logan!" Rob's voice rang out.

Logan turned to see Celeste's brothers running toward them. "Hey, Rob. Hey, Patrick," he yelled as they approached, letting go of her hand.

"Are you two going to do the sack race too?" Patrick stared at Celeste with amazement.

"No, not at all," Celeste said firmly.

"We're just here visiting with Mrs. Hoy, waiting for you and the others to show up so we can watch." Logan lifted his left leg. "This fellow here doesn't cotton much to hoppin'."

Patrick laughed. "Hey, that rhymes."

"I know. That's why I said it." Logan shooed him toward the other boys lining up where the gunny sacks had been laid out. "You better get going, or they'll start without you."

He and Celeste watched four rounds of gunny-sack races until the final winner was announced. Rob beamed as he accepted a blue ribbon with *first prize* printed on it in gold lettering. All through the races Logan kept his arms folded to avoid the temptation to take Celeste's hand in his. He didn't think that would be a good thing to do in front of her brothers, not now that he was aware of people's impressions.

As he strolled side by side with Celeste with his hands clasped behind his back, away from the sack races and the eyes of her brothers, he wondered if there would ever come a day when he could hold her hand in public because Celeste no longer cared for Dudley. Had he made a mistake earlier? Had more than just Ethyl Hoy noticed Celeste's hand in his?

Logan unclasped his sweating hands and swept one of them across the park. "Who would you like to visit with next?"

"Could we simply get some ice cream and take a stroll down to the river by ourselves?" She hung back and pulled on his arm a little.

"But you did so good back there. You were talking up a storm with Ethyl."

"That's because I know her. Ma's doctor's office is right above their saddle shop."

"Exactly, you just need to get to know all these folks." Logan pointed to Mrs. Brown serving up chili at one table and Mrs. Clark churning ice cream at another. Then at the host of other folks walking around seeing what the activities of the day had to offer. "You got to know all those fellows who courted you back East, didn't you?"

Celeste's eyes widened like she'd seen a snake, and Logan knew he'd gone and put his foot in his mouth—his bad one.

"I didn't really get to know them," Celeste said. "It was more like I endured their company for the most part. Batting my eyelashes and feigning polite conversations, like I was taught to, helped me get by. I never actually got to know most of those fellows. And most never got to know the real me. It was totally an act on both sides. One I didn't care for."

"I'm sorry. I didn't mean to dig up painful memories." Logan rubbed the back of his neck, finding it interesting how she'd said *most* of them. His mind raced to Dudley. Then he forced his thoughts elsewhere. "I promise you, getting acquainted with these folks will be different. I know 'cause I know them. They're genuine."

"I believe you." Celeste blew out a breath. "Let's start with the woman making ice cream. Isn't she the telegraph operator's wife?"

"Yep. See, you know these people more than you thought. Come on. We'll get some ice cream while we're at it, if it's ready." Logan shoved his hands into his pockets and fingered his change. He hoped he had enough, not having planned on buying Celeste ice cream when he left his place this morning. Or chili. He'd probably need to do that too, because he certainly wasn't going to eat a bowl alone in front of her. He needed something in his stomach besides that half a pie if he was going to wrestle bulls later this afternoon. Would it be possible to run back home and fetch some more money? Celeste would likely be willing to take that stroll with him, for it looked as if the whole town was in the park and that would leave the streets pretty much empty. No, it wouldn't do him any good. He only had a few cents left at home.

Normally he didn't fret when money got scarce between paydays, but at the moment, his stomach felt sour at the thought of being near penniless. It was like the grim reality of his finances punched him in the gut.

As they strolled toward Mrs. Clark and the ice cream, Logan spotted a banner spanning the six-foot space between two trees. It announced the dance tonight. He had planned on sitting home and reading a book during the whole thing.

Celeste gasped, her eyes noticeably focused on the banner. "A dance? I didn't know they had dances here." She grabbed Logan's arm and pulled him to a stop.

He stiffened. "Yep." It was all he cared to say.

"How delightful!" She gazed into the distance. "That was one thing I did enjoy at school, the dances. Music soothes my fear of being around strangers."

"Most likely 'cause you had all those suitors clamoring to dance with you." Logan let his thoughts tumble out without thinking.

She batted her hand at him. "Oh gracious, there weren't all that many. I merely went to all the dances because I like to dance. You don't have to talk to someone while you dance with them."

"Does that mean you won't say a word to me if we dance? I don't know if I'd like that."

"Oh, Logan." She laughed in a cheerful tone. "You are delightful. Of course I would talk to *you*." Her hands latched onto his and pulled them to just under her chin. "Oh, it would make me so very happy if you would take me to the dance this evening."

Logan swallowed the wad of nerves gathering in his throat. "But don't you and your family need to get going after the rodeo? I've been on the road to your place after dark. It ain't too pleasurable."

"Ma packed the wagon with bedding. She and Pa decided we'd camp out in her office and leave at the crack of dawn."

"Oh." He stared down at his shorter left leg. Kate McCurdy had shown him exercises to do years ago, and they had helped him gain strength in his leg and straighten his foot out a bit, but no amount of working with his muscles would lengthen the bone. He would always be inferior to other men when it came to his legs. And he'd learned to deal with it.

Celeste's hands flew to her mouth. "Dear me, I am so sorry." Her head shook from side to side, then she placed her palms together in front of her heart. "Please forgive me. I totally forgot about your legs. How thoughtless of me, wanting you to take me to a dance."

Logan reached out and pulled her hands out of their begging pose. He loved that she'd forgotten. "You don't need to apologize. I would be more than willing to clomp out a few dance steps with my clumsy feet if you're willing to put up with them this evening," he said, letting his heart speak the truth, though his feet didn't agree. Today he would live for the moment, enjoying Celeste's company while he could. And when Dudley came to town, he'd deal with that. Even if it meant stepping out of the picture and letting Celeste have the man she deserved. "Notice I said 'join you.' It'll be best if we meet there. A rodeo can make a man awfully dirty, and not just from dust, if you know what I mean." He smiled and rubbed the stubble on his chin, hoping she wouldn't make him talk about manure in her presence. "I don't think you'd let me get near you if I didn't clean up first."

"Oh, yes!" Her eyes lit up. She kept her hands in his. "Meeting you there would be plenty fine. And I don't care if you are not the best dancer. We don't have to dance all that often. Just to be with you and know you want to be there with me will be like the icing on the cake of this already-beautiful day." She reached up with both hands, pulled his face toward her, and kissed him on the cheek. "Thank you."

Logan's head felt as though it would float away. No girl had ever kissed him like that. His sister and little old ladies didn't count.

"Are you ready for some ice cream?" He barely managed to talk straight. "We need to mosey along 'cause I've got to get over to the south end of town real soon. That's where the rodeo's going to be."

"Yes, I'm ready for ice cream, Mister Logan Jones." She winked. "And everything else this day has to offer."

Chapter 11

CELESTE HELPED HER MA SPREAD the old quilt out in the shade of one of the park's large cottonwoods.

"We were fortunate to find this spot," Celeste said as Pa hefted the picnic basket onto the center of the quilt. She glanced around the park at all the other families eating their supper in similar fashion.

Rob stood at one corner of the quilt, jutting his chest out. "That's only because me and Patrick snagged this spot as soon the Browns finished up with their picnic."

"And stood here with our picnic basket and saved it while you were off wandering around," Patrick added.

"I was not 'wandering off,' as you put it." Celeste stood upright and placed her hands on her hips. "I went with Ma and Pa to take our bedding over to Ma's office and to clean up after the rodeo."

"Why did you need to clean up?" Patrick smirked. "You didn't patch any of those cowboys up."

"Because there's going to be a street dance right there come 7:00."

"How do you know?" Rob jutted his chin out at Celeste as she lowered herself onto the quilt.

"Because I can read." Celeste caught Ma's warning glance and softened her jab. "A banner—the one hanging over there." She pointed to the far end of the park where it was barely visible between the people. "Can I help it if you're not as observant as I?"

"That's enough!" Ma knelt beside the basket and opened its lid. "Who's ready for supper?" She pulled out a loaf of bread and sliced it into pieces.

"I am!" Patrick sat down next to Celeste and pulled a face at her. "I saw the banner but didn't think nothing of it. A dance sounds about as fun as catching a finger in the sheep shears."

"Don't worry. You won't have to go to the dance tonight." Ma glanced at Pa. "While we were at the office, we got all of our bedding laid out so you children can fall asleep before your Pa and I get back from the dance."

"You and Pa are going to the dance?" Celeste dreaded the possibility of them remaining by her side all night.

"Yes, we are." Ma placed slices of cold lamb and cheese on the bread.

"What about Rob and Patrick? Who is going to stay with them back at your office?"

"We had hoped you would, Celeste." Ma handed Pa a sandwich and then looked at Celeste with pleading in her eyes. "It's been so long since we've had a night out together. Alone."

"But, but—" Celeste's frustration choked off her words. She had to meet Logan.

"I think Celeste wants to go too." Patrick looked Ma in the eyes as she handed him a sandwich. "I'm nearly ten. Rob's thirteen. We don't need to be babysat no more. We'll be fine over there by ourselves."

"Heck, I'm not going to sit over at Ma's office with Patrick," Rob spoke up. "Not while everyone's still at the park."

Pa swallowed a sizeable bite of sandwich and looked at Ma. "Well, dear, the vote is in—we're all going to the dance." He looked at Celeste and smiled. "'Tis what you wanted, aye?"

Celeste lowered her sandwich and stared at it resting there in her hands. "Well, yes."

"Ahhh." Rob gave her a coy grin. "I get it now. You're wanting to dance with Logan tonight, aren't you? I saw you standing next to him during the parade. And the way you screamed when he got bucked off that bull at the rodeo."

"Who wouldn't have screamed?" Celeste said, trying to change the subject. "People here call that entertainment?" She shuddered. "I call it ghastly, watching a man's leg be impaled by a bull horn. Or seeing that poor fellow getting bucked of his horse, then see his horse come down on his arm. I shan't be going to the rodeo next year."

"Aw, come on, Celeste. It looked like fun to me." Rob tossed a stick at her across the quilt. "Besides, Ma patched them up good. Give them a few weeks, and they'll be right back at it. I don't think it scared them half as much as it scared you."

"I don't care. I still didn't like it." Celeste supposed if Logan hadn't been out in that arena, then it might not have affected her so adversely. If she and Logan were to get married, she'd definitely have to talk to him about participating in such nonsense. *If* they got married. The possibility that they might not sank her heart down into her gut.

She heaved out a sigh. Logan *had* agreed to accompany her at the dance. He could have made an excuse to get out of it tonight. That's what she kept telling herself over and over as their shade shifted away from the quilt and the picnic drew to an end.

Celeste kept an eye on Patrick and Rob while her parents took the basket with the leftover food back to Ma's office. The sun, though dipping lower in the sky, beat upon her back and made her perspire.

"I'm going to find some shade," she hollered to her brothers, who were playing tag with a group of boys. They might not care if they got all sweaty, but she did.

Strolling from tree to tree and staying to the shade, she observed the families still picnicking in the park and the couples gathering near where the dance was to be held. Happy faces showed on all the women serving their families or walking arm in arm with their men. Those women obviously felt like they belonged. That's what Celeste wanted. To belong somewhere. And to someone.

Both sides of the street soon filled with people: some old, some young, some by themselves, but mostly hand in hand as couples. Of those standing alone, the number of men far outnumbered the women. It appeared the complete opposite from Miss Bennett's dances. Probably another reason her dormmates didn't care for her. She'd rarely sat out a dance.

She scanned the faces of all the young men she could see, catching the eye of many of them. A lot of them smiled back. One with a particularly large moustache and a white hat walked toward her. Panicked, she looked away, searching for Logan. What if he was too exhausted and sore from the rodeo? Or worse—had he decided to avoid showing her any further interest and stayed home?

In her searching, she caught a bothersome glimpse. The man in the white hat was in the middle of the road now, beelining it toward her. "Logan," she muttered quietly, desperately.

"How'd you know I was right behind you?" Logan's voice sounded like an angel's from heaven.

She turned her back to the approaching fellow and wrapped her arms around Logan. "Thank heavens!" She hugged him and did not wish to let go.

"Whoa there." Logan stumbled back a step. "You afraid I wasn't going to come?"

"I'm just glad you're here." She let go of him and looped her arm with his before she faced the man in the white hat.

The man stood about three feet away when she looked up. Taking a wide stance, he surveyed Celeste and Logan from head to toe. "This gal's with *you?*" The man's deep voice came out laced with disbelief.

Logan straightened his back. "Yes, Tom, she is," he said with a noticeable tone of pride. "For the entire dance."

The man called Tom glared at Logan. And then he laughed. "Just 'cause you take a bath and put on clean duds, you think a girl as pretty as her is going to stick with you, huh?" He turned to Celeste. His mustache tilted to one side, and she guessed he was smiling out of half his mouth. "A gal like you doesn't need to waste your time with the likes of him." He poked his elbow in Logan's direction. "I got a real job. Pays awful good. I could buy a pretty little thing like you all the pretty little things you could ever want. Think about that. And if'n you change your mind or he steps on your pretty little toes one too many times," he laughed, "I'll be saving a dance, or two or three, for you."

"Goodbye, Tom," Logan said firmly.

"Yes, goodbye, Tom, whoever you are," Celeste repeated, grasping Logan's arm with her other hand too.

"Tell her who I am, Mr. Logan Jones." Tom stared at Logan. "Tell her how I got the job that should have been yours."

"You mean the job I never wanted—even if it had been offered to me?"

"I can't help that." Tom straightened his white hat as he jutted out his chest.

Celeste looked to Logan. "What job is he talking about?" It was the first she'd really set her eyes on him since that annoying man in the white hat showed up. Logan *had* cleaned up nice. He wore a freshly pressed blue shirt that appeared stretched to its limits across his upper arms and chest but gathered nicely where it narrowed dramatically and was tucked into trousers at his waist. His freshly shaven face showed off his smile. She liked how he never hid it behind one of those annoying moustaches. And his dark-brown hair, still damp from a good washing, hung down to the collar of his shirt, curling at the ends. Her heart did a little flip as she realized how appealing he appeared.

"I'm talking about the head manager of the Circle J Ranch," Tom said, every word loud and succinct.

"Since Stanley Jones, uh, got sent to jail, and then . . ." Celeste didn't finish. The band started to play, and she wished this Tom fellow would go find himself a partner and dance. On the other side of the park.

"No, since four years ago when Stanley hired himself a manager 'cause he had so much money he didn't need to work no more at running his ranch. I did all the work, keeping the ranch going while he spent a good share of the profits. It's a real nice job." Tom smirked. "One you would have thought his kid brother would have been a good fit for. After all, everyone knows ole Logan here didn't inherit a dime from his Pa. The least his brother could have done was pay him the obscene wage I'm getting and let him help run the place. That would have gotten around the inheritance part quite nicely. But no, Logan wouldn't take the job." He laughed, leaning his head back and holding a hand to his belly.

Celeste looked at Logan. "Is that true, Logan?"

Logan's jaw clenched, and he didn't meet her gaze. "No." His voice was flat. "Tom, I said goodbye. I'd be much obliged if you'd say your goodbye now and be on your way."

"Fine." Tom lifted his hat at Celeste. "Goodbye for now, pretty lady. You know where to find me if you change your mind." Ignoring Logan, he walked into the crowd.

When he was out of sight, Celeste released her pent up breath and her grip on Logan's arm. "Sorry," she said and tried to smooth out the spots where she'd wrinkled his shirt. "Your shirt looked so nice . . . on you. Now I've made a mess of it."

"Nonsense." His smile calmed her. "Besides, I'm used to wrinkled shirts." He bent his brow into a sheepish expression that made *her* smile. "It was Dorothy Smith, Ronald's wife, who washed and ironed this shirt up all nice for me. And then threatened to scrub me down herself if I didn't get down to Porter's bathhouse before I put that shirt on."

Celeste ran her fingertips along his clean-shaven jawline. Its strong, square outline set her fingers to tingle. "I'm glad you did. You clean up nice."

Logan gulped. "Really?"

"Yes." She ran her fingers over his shoulders and down his arm, feeling the firm dips and rise of his muscular frame. "You know what else I'm glad of?"

"What's that?" Logan gulped again.

"That awful man named Tom is gone." She clasped her hands together in front of her and looked to her right, then her left to make sure.

"I'm glad of that too." Logan appeared more relaxed. He tapped his foot to the fiddle playing a catchy polka tune. "Walt and his buddies out at the Double Bar Ranch make quite the band."

"You've been to other dances where they've played?"

"No—barn raisings."

Celeste inched closer to Logan. Their arms brushed up against each other. She stared at the banjo player, afraid to look at Logan lest her eyes would give away her racing heart. "Why would that Tom fellow say such things about you that weren't true?"

Logan stiffened slightly. "Well, he wasn't totally telling a fib."

"What do you mean?"

"The truth is, Stanley asked me once, and only once, if I'd come live out at the Circle J and help him run the place for pay." Logan's eyes seemed to beg her to listen to the rest of what he had to say before she passed judgment. "That was four and a half years ago when Stanley's manager up and quit on him for being nigh onto impossible to work for—him being gone all the time and then drunk when he was home. Stanley was in a pickle, desperate for help. No one for miles would come to work for him because of the things the old manager spread around the county. That's the only reason Stanley asked me. He was desperate, nothing else."

"And you told him . . . what?" She looked at him now.

"No." Logan's eyes held a faraway look, one laden with sadness. "If he would have asked at any other time, I would have jumped right in and helped him. Especially if he'd just said four little words: 'Please, I need you.'"

"And he didn't?" Celeste noticed more couples fill the street with the snappy steps and twirls. The desire to join them wasn't there. Theirs was an unfamiliar dance, nothing like the quadrille and waltz taught at her school. Logan's heartfelt story pulled her attention to him with much more draw.

"Not even close. He came to me on his high horse. I don't mean one of God's gentle creatures He's sent to soothe me over the years. Stanley marched into the livery stable while I was helping a fellow saddle his horse and demanded I leave Gus high and dry that very minute and come out to the Circle J and take on my rightful responsibility at the ranch."

"He didn't!" Celeste knew little of Stanley, and at that moment, she wished she knew even less.

"Yeah, he did."

She placed her hand on Logan's bare forearm just below where he'd rolled up his sleeve, catching her breath as she felt his skin against her fingers. Gazing into his eyes, she wondered how he'd managed to stay cheerful all these years. She heard much of what he'd been through from her parents, enough to bring her to tears at their telling. How did he survive? Her trials had been nothing compared to his. Yet at times she wanted to curl up in a corner and not go on. "What did you say?"

"I told him that he and Pa took no responsibility to take care of me when I needed them, so now that he needed me, I didn't see that it was my problem."

"Bravo." She slid her hand down his arm, slipped her hand into his, then squeezed. "I imagine that took some courage."

"Yeah, especially when he exploded with a barrage of cursing the likes of which I'd never heard before and don't care to ever again." His hand responded to her touch, caressing her fingers and making her feel like he enjoyed holding her hand, that he wasn't merely doing it to be kind.

At least, she hoped he felt something like the tingles she had running up her arm. "I take it shortly after that is when Stanley hired Tom."

"Yep. Two peas in a pod they were." Logan took a deep breath. "I rarely went down to the ranch after that, not even to look in on my favorite horses."

The music stopped, and the man with the harmonica stepped to the front of the band. "Okay folks, time for a little square dancin'. Who's up for it?"

A roar of approval rose from the crowd, causing Celeste to cover her ears.

She leaned toward Logan's ear and smelled a hint of sage and cedar on his neck. Breathing it in, she almost forgot what she was about to say. Regaining her wit, she whispered, "Miss Bennett would be fainting about now."

"Then it's a good thing she's not here." His grin looked especially charming as the setting sun cast an orange glow upon it.

"Gather yourself into groups of four for this first one," the harmonica player yelled out.

Logan leaned close this time. "Did she by chance teach you how to square dance back at that fancy school?"

"Not hardly. I doubt she even considered that a dance." Celeste laughed. It felt good.

"So you don't know how to square dance?"

Celeste shook her head.

"Good, 'cause I don't know how either." He swept his hand toward the five different groups of four forming in the middle of the street. "How about we just watch?"

"Sounds lovely."

The music started back up. She and Logan watched without talking, listening to the music as people danced.

"Okay, here's your last chance for joining in with us on a square dance," the harmonica player yelled out. "After this, we're goin' for some more good ole-fashioned polka again."

While the last square dance got underway, she watched the dancers with a bit of envy, especially when the men wrapped their arms around the women's waists and swung them into a wagon-wheel-like formation. "Have you ever danced the polka?" she asked Logan, aching to have him wrap his arm around her waist. Though she had never danced the polka herself, she'd watched enough at the beginning of the evening to give her the confidence that she could easily pick it up once they got started. *If* he was willing.

"A few times. My sister Susannah taught me."

"Wonderful."

"I gotta warn you—I'm not very good."

"So are you saying you're willing to give it a try with me?" She looked at him straight on and let her eyes beg. My, but the shade of his eyes was striking, like caramel and chocolate mixed together. "Because I've never really learned that particular dance, only observed."

"If you're willing to do so with me." His lips pinched together into a straight line.

Her heart softened to where she felt tempted to cry. He was doing this difficult thing for her. He didn't have to do it, but he was. "I am."

The squares had broken up, and a polka-sounding song blared from the instruments now. She pulled him away from the main body of dancers and the two electric light posts that lit up the dirt dance floor. "How about we dance out here where we have plenty of room to work with?"

"Or do you mean where it's darker and there's not many eyes to look at us?"

They laughed together.

When they got to a nice spot of their own, far enough away from the crowd to have some space and close enough to hear the music, she cupped his face in her hands. "I don't care if anyone sees us stepping on each other's feet. And I don't care that you have one leg that's different from the other." She glanced down at his left leg. There was enough twilight to tell the difference between his legs, how the right pant leg fit tightly around his thigh while the left one hung loosely, and how his belt and buckle cut across his slim waistline at a slight angle because of the different length of his legs. "That's never bothered me."

"I know," he whispered. So humbly did his voice tumble from his lips that Celeste wanted to scoop him into a hug like she would a small child. "Thank you," he said and wrapped his arm around her waist and took her hand in his.

As Celeste placed her hand on his shoulder, anticipating the quick steps of the polka, she sensed his eyes on her. She looked up and gazed at his face. He leaned close to her. She'd seen that look before in other men. Was he going to kiss her? She closed her eyes and held her breath. Nothing would end this day better than that.

Chapter 12

Logan held Celeste in his arms—actually held her! And her body complied as he took her hand and pulled her next to him, as if she wanted what he wanted: to be close, to be caressed, to be loved. He gazed into her face at her beauty, both inside and out. The desire to kiss her consumed him. She looked so beautiful, so willing. He leaned his head downward for the briefest moment before rational thought punched him in the gut. His head came up, fighting the urge.

He had never kissed a woman on the lips. Now was not the time and place to attempt his first try. A hundred sets of eyes could be on them in a flash, watching him stumble through that milestone in his life. A milestone that he was unsure was his to take. Celeste had been home for not quite three weeks. He'd only seen her a few times since then. That hardly gave him call to consider her his girl, especially when she had another suitor in the wings. Just this morning, he'd wanted to hightail it away from her. Funny how differently he felt now.

Her eyes were closed, perhaps dreading the polka as much as he. Light spilled over from the distant streetlamp. It cast shadows on her face, accentuating her high cheek bones and dainty nose.

"Hold on," he said in warning and swept her into a polka.

"Oh!" Her eyes popped open in obvious surprise.

"Did you not want to dance?" he said over the music, his legs stepping lively. "We can stop if you want."

"No, no, I wanted to dance," she said with a bit of hesitation. "I just thought you were—never mind." A hint of a grin surfaced on her lips, the kind that came from frustration. "Yes, let's dance. Or at least try to dance."

Ignoring the strain it put on his short leg, Logan concentrated on matching the steps Susannah had taught him to the beat of the music. After a minute or so and a bit of stepping on her feet and she on his, and a round of laughter with each blunder, he swore Celeste and he were moving somewhat as one. "Hey, this is kind of fun."

"Yes, I am quite enjoying myself," she said.

The music stopped. The banjo player let his banjo hang loose from the strap around his shoulder and neck and brought both hands to his mouth. "Okay, all you fine folks out there. It's good to see you enjoying yourselves, but it's time for the band to take a break. Don't worry none. We'll be back in a quarter hour."

"And just when we were getting the hang of it." Logan snapped his fingers and flicked his wrist.

"If you can call what we were doing 'the hang of it,' then sure." She smiled at him.

Logan kept his hand around her waist. "Yeah, I want to call it that." Instinct wanted to pull her back into his arms and spend the next fifteen minutes pretending to dance with everything but their feet and his throbbing left leg. He would even hold her a little closer. Arm's length might be good for dancing the polka, but in his pretend dance, that would not be the style.

Out of the corner of his eye, he saw Lucas and Kate approach. He immediately let go of Celeste's waist, unsure if they would approve of his advances. Though he was their friend, matters of courting one's daughter needed to proceed all proper like.

Had he just admitted he wanted to court Celeste?

Yes, he had. *What about Dudley?*

Maybe he was worrying about Dudley for nothing. Chances were the man would never show up. In the meantime, Logan wanted to follow where his heart was leading him.

"Aye, there's our Celeste." Lucas's Irish brogue was easy to pick out from the clamor of the crowd, now chatting instead of dancing.

Celeste jerked toward the voice. "Oh, Father, Mother. Have you been enjoying the dance?"

"We were going to ask you the same," Kate said, holding her hands out.

Celeste glanced at Logan before answering. "I can't answer for Logan, but yes, I have enjoyed myself immensely this evening. All day, in fact."

All eyes were on Logan now. He couldn't rightly tell them exactly how he felt. Lucas and Kate would whisk Celeste away quicker than the shake of a stick. But he could still speak the truth. "Yep, I've had a grand time. Celeste is quite the dancer." He winked at her.

"Oh, really now?" Lucas appeared skeptical. Most likely he was as baffled as Logan was that a man with a bum leg could enjoy dancing.

"You have yet to answer me," Celeste said to her parents.

"Ah, 'tis exactly why we're here, intruding on you young-uns' privacy." Lucas rubbed the small of his back. "This ole man's had enough dancing for tonight."

"I'm in agreement with your pa." Kate nodded. "Plus, I need to get the boys to bed. Morning comes early when one wants to be on the road at the crack of dawn." She gazed at Celeste. "I am assuming you do not wish to come back to the office with us right now?"

"Yes, Mother, you are correct. I will be fine." Celeste looked at Logan. "I imagine I can get Logan to accompany me safely home."

Lucas and Kate turned their heads toward him at the same time, as if waiting for his response.

"Absolutely." He could feel himself smile. He'd like nothing more. Okay, he'd like lots more, but at the moment, he was perfectly content with ending this day by walking Celeste back to her ma's office.

"Wonderful," Kate said. "We'll leave you two alone, and we'll be on our way. Lucas, round up the boys."

Lucas allowed Kate to walk on ahead, then motioned with a wag of his finger for Logan to come hither. Logan left Celeste's side and hobbled over.

"What?" His gut tightened. "Have I done something wrong?" he asked quietly so Celeste couldn't hear.

"Quite the opposite," Lucas whispered. "I just wanted to say thank you." He placed a hand on Logan's shoulder. "I've never seen my lass so happy. Ever since she came to live with me and Kate when she was five, it's been a struggle to get her to smile when she's away from us. 'Twas part of the reason I agreed to send her away to school—to wean her off needing us so much. Unfortunately, I had my fears that only made her melancholy worse. But today, practically every time I spied her with you, she was a smiling." He slapped Logan's back and hurried toward Kate.

Logan returned to Celeste's side, pondering what Lucas had said. Was it true? Rough-as-burlap Logan Jones, who'd spent less time in school than a fish, actually made Celeste happy? The possibility made *him* happy. He was also anxious to spend the rest of the evening with this lovely person, and with her parents' blessing, no less.

"What did Father say to you?" Celeste asked the moment he drew near.

"He just thanked me for making you smile." The background behind Lucas's words dawned on him and tore at his heart. "He made it sound like you've been sad a heap of times."

Celeste nodded. "But mostly when I'm away from my family." She reached for his hand and wrapped both of her hands around it. She brought it to her mouth and kissed his fingers. "Except for the times I'm with you. You seem to have this uncanny ability to lift me from my sadness."

Logan's fingers thought they'd died and gone to heaven. "Really?" he muttered. She could kiss them all night, and he'd not stop her. Even if she went on into the morning and he had to give up eating breakfast so she could continue.

"Yes, Logan." She let go of his hand and gazed down to the other end of the street at the band. Only the streetlamps provided light now, the sun having long since slipped away. "It appears the band is getting ready to play again. Do you want to keep dancing? Or just listen to their music?"

"A little of both, I suppose." He really did like holding on to her, so a dance or two would be worth it. "But maybe something besides the polka."

"I would like that too."

The music started up. For the first two songs, they stood side by side listening to the catchy polka tunes, Logan tapping his bad foot, resting his weight on his good one.

On the third song, they braved the Virginia reel. They returned to the edge of the street dance floor when that ended, both admitting that was enough dancing for the evening and just watching the others swing their partners around the street. Then the night air sent in a bit of chill with a breeze that kicked up.

Celeste rubbed her arms. "Who'd have thought July could be cold?"

"You've forgotten Craig sits a lot higher up on God's good earth than New York. Here, I'm used to it." He wrapped his arm around her and pulled her close, shielding her outside arm with his hand.

She gazed into his face. He wondered if she could see much, for her features appeared not much more than shadows to him. But he could feel her expression as she murmured, "Thank you," and it warmed him plenty against the chill of the air.

He pulled her closer, loving the idea of shielding her from the unpleasant wind. Up until today, he didn't realize that she had struggled so much with sadness. The desire to help her battle this plague swelled inside him. He wanted nothing more than to help her, protect her, and shield her any way he could. Such purpose felt as satisfying as each breath of air he breathed and each bond a horse formed with him.

"Okay, folks," the banjo player announced. "This is our final song. If you haven't had a chance to dance with that gal you wanted to, now's your chance. Tap that fellow on the shoulder who's been hoggin' her all evening, and tell him it's your turn."

Logan's eyes gravitated to the remaining crowd, searching for Tom's face, hoping beyond hope that he'd gone home.

Tom hadn't. He emerged from the crowd and strutted toward them.

Logan stiffened.

Celeste gasped. "I'm ready for you to take me home now. I don't care to stay for this last song."

"Me neither." Unfortunately, the most efficient and safest way to Kate's office was to walk past the band and continue on to Fifth Street. Keeping his arm around her, Logan took a deep breath and forged toward the crowd, keeping to the rocky fringes of the street.

"Hey," Tom yelled out. He rushed toward Logan and Celeste at a frightening pace. "You heard the man. Time to stop hogging that gal and give me a chance at her."

"Sorry, Tom. We're leaving," Logan said. He kept walking, corralling Celeste in with his arm. "She's wanting to go home."

"I'd be more than happy to take her." Tom was five feet away now and closing in quickly. "Stop! You hear me, Logan, you good-for-nothing piece of flesh." He reached out and pounded Logan on the shoulder. "I'm tapping you, just like old Clem said. I say it's my turn with her."

"I'd hardly call that a tap." Logan stopped. He had to. He had to bring this matter to a close. Celeste's eyes shone with fear. He knew how she struggled to speak to amiable people she did know, but here, standing in front of her, was the meanest dang man—next to Stanley himself. A man she didn't know from Adam and one who most likely cared little for propriety. Logan stood four inches taller than Tom and that much wider in the shoulders. Good chances he could win in a fair fight. But in all Logan's days, he'd observed that a fist fight never solved anything. If he had plans to protect Celeste, he'd better start now. He turned and faced Tom, whose breath smelled of whiskey. Releasing Celeste, he moved her behind him.

"Tom, you're drunk. Go home."

"No, I say it's my turn with the little lady."

"I don't care what you say, Celeste chooses to be with me tonight."

Celeste nodded emphatically.

"Well, I don't care what *you* say!" Tom stepped around Logan, his arms outstretched toward Celeste.

Logan stuck out his bad leg, tripping up Tom.

Tom fell facedown in the dirt.

"Run!" Logan grabbed Celeste's hand and ran, panic fueling his legs to where he kept up with Celeste. He glanced over his shoulder and saw Tom struggling to stand. Some of the other dancers gathered around him, holding him down. *Thank you, Dear Lord, for the good folks of Craig.*

They stopped running when they made it to Yampa Avenue. Logan wished they had a streetlamp over here. The moonlight was sufficient to find their way but not to make him feel safe. He wondered how Celeste felt. He looked over his shoulder again. No one was following them.

"Are you doing all right?" he asked when they slowed their pace to a brisk walk.

"Yes, I'm fine." She latched onto his arm. "Thank you for protecting me. I shudder to think what would have happened if you were not here beside me."

"But I am here." He squeezed her arm against him.

"I hate for this night to end," she said as they walked across Yampa Avenue. "I'm afraid I might not see you for some time. Ma comes into town twice a week, but I fear I shall not always be free to come with her."

"Would you like for me to come out to your pa's ranch . . ." He took a breath and ventured the words. "And call on you?"

"Yes, I would like that."

Logan's mind raced to figure out a time he could come. He rarely took days off. Working two jobs hardly allowed for that. And before now, he had no need for spare time. It just served to set him to thinking about his lonely future. "I'll be delivering mail tomorrow. I could hurry things up and stop by your place at the end of my rounds."

"That would be lovely."

"Dang it!" He clenched his fist. "I forgot I was planning on going out to Susannah's place tomorrow after my rounds and staying the night. I need to talk to her about something. Plus, it's been way too long since I've been there, and it's the only good opportunity I have to squeeze in the trip. My sister and my niece and nephews will think I've forgotten them if I don't go."

"I understand." Celeste looked at the ground.

"How about Sunday? There's no mail, and Gus's place is usually quite slow. I'm sure he wouldn't mind if I locked up the place and moseyed on over to the church. We could meet up there." Logan hadn't been for ages, not caring to sit alone while everyone else sat as families.

"My parents rarely make it in to worship, what with all the work to be done on the ranch and how far it is to come. Father says he prays to God every day anyway, each time he looks over the flocks at how well they've provided for his family and then at the grass-covered hills and willow-lined riverbed that runs through his land."

"Ah, good ole Lucas. I always have liked your pa. He's a good man." Logan found himself at the foot of the stairs leading to Kate's office.

"But I'd love to go to church with you. It's one thing I've missed from New York." Celeste stopped and turned to Logan. She released her hold on his arm and reached up with one hand to his cheek. "You don't need to accompany me up the stairs. Thanks for a wonderful day." She stood on her tiptoes, pulled his head toward her lips, and kissed him on the cheek. "Good night, Logan," she said and scurried up the steps.

Logan stood unmoving, planted there like a tree. Her lips had obviously missed their mark, for they had brushed the corner of his mouth. By what that tiny bit of his lips experienced in the way of sparks tingling his body, he could barely imagine what it would feel like if the whole of his lips were to meet with hers.

Chapter 13

THE JOSTLE OF THE WAGON lulled Celeste into drowsiness. She nodded in and out of sleep. Last night, sleep had been slow in coming, her mind whirling as it had. The image of Logan, in his freshly starched shirt stretched tight across his shoulders, refused to slip from her thoughts. Her heart sped each time she considered how much she enjoyed his company. And how handsome he had looked. Then came the other thoughts, the ones that had kept her awake with worry. Miss Bennett's school had taught her a few things she saw of value, one of those being that a husband needed to be able to provide for his family, no matter how comely his appearance or how kind his heart. That variable could prove to be problematic with Logan. But by the wee hours of the morning, she'd convinced herself that together they could work through that problem.

The sun peeked above the eastern mountains about the time Pa turned the wagon from the main road and onto the rutted lane that led to their ranch.

"Mother, when do you plan on going into town next?" Celeste asked, wanting to see Logan.

"Next Tuesday, a week from today. I have no Thursday appointments," Ma said. "Why do you ask?"

Celeste shrugged. "No reason, really. It just gets a little lonely out on the ranch. I was getting used to being around people back at school." She cringed inside at the lie. "And town seems like the next best thing."

Rob laughed and then slapped Celeste on the back from the bed of the wagon. "Are you sure it's not 'cause you want to see Logan?"

She turned her head. "Excuse me, I was speaking to Mother and Father. If I had wanted your input, I would have asked."

"Ah, go easy on him." Pa chuckled. "He's just as excited to see his sister hitch up with a nice young man as we are." He reached over and patted Ma on the wrist. "Right, Ma?"

"That's correct." Ma smiled at Celeste. "They don't come much nicer than Logan."

"Now, Mother, you talk like you've got my future husband chosen and all wrapped up into a neat parcel ready for me to marry. Logan and I are friends. We may choose to court each other, or we may not. These things take time," Celeste said with a firm jaw, still unsure about Logan. Despite how much he appeared to like being with her, a few memories weighed on her mind. Him rushing back into the livery stable when he first saw her yesterday, for one. And his unwillingness to kiss her, for another. Then there was the matter of the Circle J. That weighed on her in another way. It plain and simple wasn't fair to Logan, yet he didn't seem to care.

"Father?" Celeste spoke back up.

"Yes, Lass."

"What's going to happen to the Circle J Ranch now that Stanley's dead?"

Pa blew out a breath. "I don't rightly know. From what I understand, the ranch is Susannah's now."

"I think it's an awful shame that Logan's pa left him nothing. What kind of father does that?" Celeste clenched her fists as they rested at her sides on the wagon bench, thinking of how Logan often went without meals. "Are you sure there's no chance of him getting something? I mean, it's hardly fair, given the circumstances."

Ma nodded. "I agree with you, dear," she said in a voice heavy with hope. "After all, Logan's sister and brother-in-law are some of the richest folks in the county."

"Yes, they are." Celeste's hands gripped the edge of the wagon's bench, and she dug her fingernails into the wood. Not entirely because of the unfairness of the Circle J, but now she worried Ma wanted to see Logan come into that wealth. Was that so he would be a more suitable husband for her now-prim-and-proper daughter who'd just graduated from finishing school?

"All's I can say to that, dear Celeste," Pa said, "is that life doesn't always *appear* fair. That's because what's important to us and what's important to the Good Lord are not always the same thing."

"That don't make no sense, Pa," Rob spoke up from behind.

Celeste agreed with her brother. Yet she knew it was true. It appeared she and Logan would just have to work harder than most if they were to marry and make a home together. She was okay with that. Perhaps she should persuade Logan to take that postmaster position if for no other reason than to keep himself fed right now. Strangely, just thinking about how unfair life had been for Logan made her want to see him sooner. Perhaps because he took it in stride so eloquently. She'd take that kind of eloquence over some guy's educated tongue any day.

Celeste looked at her ma. "So next Tuesday is the soonest, then?" Her stomach tightened. She really needed to tell Ma the truth about school before it came out on its own. Especially, if by chance, Ma pushed the issue of Logan needing his rightful inheritance.

Pa turned to her with that loving look in his eyes "I think I might need to come back into town on Friday. Pick up a few supplies. I could use some company."

"Oh, Pa, I'll come with you. How long do you think you'll stay?"

"Maybe an hour. But if you care to stay a wee longer, I bet I could find you someone to bring you back home." Pa smiled his crooked smile. "My good friend Logan Jones is always one to help out when I need a hand."

"Oh, thank you, Pa." Celeste could hear her little brothers snickering, but she didn't care.

Pa winked at her. "What happened to 'Father'?"

"Oh, Pa, I'm tired of pretending I'm someone I'm not." Celeste clasped her hands together and let them drop into her lap, determined to take control of her life. "I'm not a prissy girl with more manners than a dog has fleas. I never cared for those fancy parties Grandma made me go to or those etiquette classes I failed in school." She glanced at her ma. "Yes, I failed a number of my classes. But I'm in Craig now, in the Wild West, as some past acquaintances might call it. And I like it here."

"Really, now?" Ma's brow lifted.

"Yes," Celeste responded, tired of pretending altogether. "It's time I told you the truth, Ma. I didn't graduate early. There will be no diploma coming in the mail. Miss Bennett asked me to leave. I failed school. There, I'm glad that's out. I'm sorry if I've disappointed you. But I had to be true to myself, and I couldn't be myself at that school." She chewed on her lip while she awaited her ma's response. The creak of the wagon's wheels sounded extra loud during the long moment of silence that followed.

"Oh, sweetie." Ma finally turned on the bench and looked Celeste in the eye. "I wouldn't say you failed school. You've grown; you've learned so much, both from books and from life. I don't need you to present me with a diploma to see that." Ma gave her a hug. "I'm not disappointed with you; I'm proud of you."

Celeste hugged her back. "Thank you, Ma. I'm only sorry I didn't tell you earlier."

"It's all right." Ma patted her back. "Sometimes good things take time."

Pa leaned forward and caught Celeste's eye with his mischievous grin. "Don't feel like you need to tell your grandma about this though."

"I quite agree with your pa on this." Ma chuckled quietly.

"Don't worry. I don't feel that need," Celeste responded. "I'm never going back to New York. I appreciate what Grandma has given me but plan on staying in Craig and settling down here." And if she married a man with no money, they'd make do, and they'd be happy. As long as they loved each other unconditionally, nothing else mattered.

Chapter 14

LOGAN DELIVERED HIS LAST BIT of mail at the Clifton place and then pressed his heels into Bootstrap's flanks in the way that meant, "We need to hurry now." He patted Bootstrap's neck, glad he and his horse could work as a team and that he didn't have to resort to hurting the animal like some owners did to get them to respond. "Good boy. I want to get to Susannah's before supper time. Okay?"

Bootstrap seemed to understand from those words alone, for he broke into a gallop.

On top of a horse, with the rushing air brushing the hair from his face, the freedom to move unfettered, and the sense of control restored to his legs, Logan felt whole. If he could live on a horse, he would.

He laughed into the wind. Of course that would be impractical, all his hours spent in the saddle. How could he ever hold Celeste in his arms if he did? Last night had changed him. Life held new meaning. She didn't judge him, and she made him feel like he could do anything. He wanted Celeste to be part of his life. Forever.

And he had to tell someone.

Susannah was the best one to share his good news with—the only one he had to share such news with—the sum of his family, but hopefully not for long. What had started out as a dutiful visit to his sister was quickly turning into one of a different purpose.

The scaffolds looming above the entrance to the coal mine came into view first, poking their blackened wood above the sage-covered hills like a skeleton of some unearthly creature. It didn't belong here, disrupting the grassland where the mine cut into the hillside. Logan had never spoken those feelings to his sister. The coal had been good to her and Joseph when they'd been forgotten from Pa's will as well. For that, Logan had been happy, even though he'd not been so fortunate. Still, he'd survived just fine.

The white farmhouse came into view next as he and Bootstrap rode past the hill that tucked the Iversons and their coal mine away from the neighboring homestead. Logan chuckled at the memory of Joseph telling him about the first day he'd seen his homestead after paying out his $160 for this land he'd never laid eyes on before. Only a fraction had been worthy to farm. Most was made up of rocky hills, a fact Joseph had cursed the first four years of homesteading the land, until they discovered coal. Then the man who'd sold Joseph the land cursed.

The blue trim of Susannah's house was now discernable. His two nephews, Alvin and Joey, played in the yard. He wondered if little Clara was inside with her mother. Seeing his nephews and niece always brightened his day. "Come on, Bootstrap. Daylight's a burning."

Logan rode into the yard to cheers from Alvin and Joey. "Hello, boys." He removed his hat and hurled it toward them like he always did. Joey caught it this time.

"You wanna sleep outside with us?" Alvin said the moment Logan dismounted. "Pa made us a tent out of Ma's clothesline."

"Yeah," Joey chimed in. "And it's a lot more cooler outside than inside at night."

"Count on me," Logan said. "I'd love to camp out with my two favorite nephews."

Joey clamped his hands on his hips. "I thought we was your only nephews."

"Yep, that's right." Logan ruffled Joey's red hair. "And you're my favorites too." He ruffled Alvin's hair next. It reminded Logan of his own dark and curly locks. "Where's your little sister? And where's your ma?"

Both boys shrugged at the same time.

The screen door at the front of the two-story house flew open. Susannah ran out with three-year-old Clara on her hip. "Logan!" She reached out with her free arm and pulled him into a hug. "What brings you out this way?"

"You." Logan hugged her back. "I haven't seen you in a long time, way too long of a time."

"I know, I know. I really should get into town more often." Susannah let go of Logan and hefted Clara up further on her hip. "But with the children and all . . . it's hard."

"What about coming in for supplies?" Logan remembered the days when she'd make a point of seeing him at least those times.

Susannah waved her hand at a new building in between the house and the barn. Logan had seen it only as a shell of a structure the last time he'd stopped by. "We've got servants for that now. You can reacquaint yourself with them at suppertime. You are staying the night, I hope?"

Logan looked at the sun in the west. "Yeah, of course. I don't care much for camping out on the trail. Especially when I can camp with my nephews in their tent on the clothesline." He sent a sidewise glance to Alvin and Joey, who now stood a few feet away.

"Nonsense. There's a bed for you in the extra bedroom. Come." Susannah motioned for him to follow her into the house. "I bet you could use a cold glass of sarsaparilla right about now."

"Sounds awfully good." Logan's dry throat agreed. He glanced at the new building before stepping into the house. It didn't look much like another shed, like he'd assumed it would be. It had two windows on each side of a yellow door, and behind the glass hung what appeared to be lace curtains. "Tell me about your new shed."

Susannah grinned. "It's not a shed." She motioned for Logan to sit in a fancy new wingback chair while she settled on to the couch with Clara. "It's a cottage. We built it for Willow and her husband, Barry, in exchange for their help around here. Plus, we pay them a good wage. They're the ones who go into town for us now."

Logan caught a glimpse of a woman in the kitchen. "You mean Willow Tree and Runnin' Bear?" He remembered them well from when he lived near here in that cabin that got burnt down when Susannah first married Joseph.

"Life on the reservation is getting harder, Logan. It was the least we could do for our friends. Plus, I really needed the help. Joseph and I thought of offering the cottage and the job to you, but, well, I really needed a couple, two people who could help both me and Joseph."

"I understand," Logan said. Even a week ago, he wouldn't have wanted the job. His sister's place was too far from town and other people. But if he were married, he could handle being way out here. "If you could've just waited a bit longer, maybe you would've been able to hire me on—with a wife, to boot."

"Logan!" Susannah slapped her hands to her cheeks. "Are you telling me you are sweet on someone?"

Logan nodded, trying hard to hold back his smile. He was doing a lousy job at it.

"Willow, bring my brother a drink!" Susannah hollered into the kitchen and then focused on Logan. "Tell me all about her. How'd you meet? How long have you been courting her? Do I know her?"

"Which one of those do you want me to answer first?"

"Doesn't matter." Susannah bounced on the edge of the couch. "Just tell me about her."

"First off, we're not officially courting, so don't go blabbin' any of this to Joseph or anybody else, for that matter. I don't want word getting back to her and maybe scaring her away. You got that?"

Susannah held up her hand, palm outward. "Not a word."

"As for how we met, I've known her since she was five and moved out here just after her ma died."

"Celeste McCurdy!" Susannah's eyes widened to near twice their normal size. "But she's just a girl."

Logan grinned at the image continually hovering in his mind. "Oh, believe me, she's not a little girl anymore. She'll be twenty years old come this December."

"Twenty, you say?" Susannah clapped her hands together and brought her fingertips up to rest under her chin. "This is perfect. She's more than old enough to get married." She rubbed her palms together. "Oh, Logan, I'm so excited for you. And what perfect timing, what with you inheriting the Circle J and all."

"Well, now . . ." Logan hesitated, not looking forward to bringing up this subject. But it had been bothering him like a burr in his trousers ever since Ron had talked to him two weeks ago. "This here's another reason I wanted to pay you a visit."

Willow Tree entered the room holding a glass of sarsaparilla. "Logan, it be good to see you."

He wiped his sweaty hands on his trousers and accepted the cold glass. "Thanks so much. It's good to see you too."

The older woman, who had a lot more wrinkles than the last time he'd seen her, smiled and nodded at him. "You most welcome." She hurried back into the kitchen as Logan thought out his next words.

"We need to discuss something." He took in a deep breath and pushed it out, wishing he could push out all the emotional pain with it. "Neither Pa nor Stanley ever intended for me to have the Circle J. They say people don't change just because they die and pass on to the other side. So Pa's probably up there right now, looking down from heaven on us as we speak. Or maybe he's looking up from down there with the devil and Stanley. It don't matter where he's watching from; I'm not going to let him see me take on the ranch like it was mine and without a lick of work to have earned it. Nope, I don't care to be like Stanley, the spoiled child who never really worked a day in his life and never lifted a finger to help his neighbor. Or his brother. They didn't need me, and I don't need them. So keep Pa's money—if there's anything left of it now after Stanley's had his hands on it. And keep the Ranch too. There's too many painful memories there for me. It's yours. Pa gave it to you."

"But I gave it to you." Susannah's face drooped. "Didn't Ronald Smith get in touch with you?"

"Yeah, he did. But I didn't sign that dang paper. It's still yours."

"Logan, me and Joseph don't need it. But you do!"

"Who says? I'm doing fine without it. If Pa'd just take an extra minute to look down here, or up, he'd see that I'm the son worth being proud of. I'm the one who works my fingers to the bone supporting myself, not living on the coattails of someone else's hard work. I'm the one who can be happy without a red cent of that money!" He rose to his feet. "Now if you don't mind, I'm going to go play with my nephews. Call me in when supper's ready." He lumbered toward the door.

"Logan, you're being ridiculous," Susannah hollered at his back. "Let's say things do work out for you and Celeste. How are you going to support her and your children when they come? Have you thought about that?"

Logan stiffened. He had thought about that. More times than he cared to admit. "I'll work something out. With the new post office going in, they're looking to hire on a postmaster. I was thinking about applying for that position." He stepped outside and hurried down the porch steps. So much for convincing his sister as to whom Circle J belonged. And so much for being excited about sharing his good news with her. Wanting to marry Celeste didn't even feel like good news to him anymore. It felt like a path with a giant mountain sitting smack dab in the middle of it.

"Alvin, Joey," he yelled. The boys came running around the house. "Come show me where we're sleeping tonight."

U

The road back into town felt longer than the one he'd taken going out to Susannah's, even with all the stops he'd taken to deliver mail on his way yesterday morning. Maybe because he wasn't in a hurry to get back to Craig and back to the problem he needed to face sooner or later. He was dirt poor. Even Celeste had hinted about him finding different employment. His plan had been to ask Celeste if he could officially court her the moment he came back from his sister's. Would Celeste turn him down because he could not support a family? Obviously, it was a concern of hers. That made it a concern of his.

He heaved a sigh and prompted Bootstrap to walk faster. "Perhaps Dudley is the best man for Celeste after all," he muttered. Bootstrap flicked his ears. "You heard me. I gotta let her go, Bootstrap. She's used to fancy things and fancy men with fancy manners. Who was I to think she wanted someone like me?"

Bootstrap reared up on his hind legs, catching Logan off guard and nearly tossing him to the ground. "Whoa, hold on there, boy." He soothed Bootstrap down. "What just got into you? That's not like you."

Bootstrap sputtered his horse lips.

"Trying to tell me something, ay?"

Bootstrap sputtered again.

"You're right, you're right. I'll quit being so hard on myself." Logan sighed inside where Bootstrap wouldn't hear him. He was afraid that loving himself, like he'd always tried to do when he got down, wasn't going to help here.

Logan's stomach was rumbling by the time he rode into town. Sunny's Place sounded good, but he didn't have enough money for a sit-down meal at a restaurant. He'd mosey on over to the mercantile and buy himself a box of crackers and a wedge of cheese, his usual meal when left to himself to prepare it.

"Mornin'." Lavender Decker glanced up from the cash register as he walked in. "Be with you in a minute, Logan." Her usual smile and cheery voice were gone, even though she was ringing up a lady with loads of fabric—Lavender's favorite thing to sell.

"Morning to you," Logan responded. "If Rosie's in the back sorting the mail, I'll go talk to her 'til you're done." Things certainly had changed since Stanley shot Sam Decker. How could his brother ever become so selfish?

"Yep, she's there."

Logan strolled past the stack of crackers, figuring he'd pick a box up on his way out. He opened the back door and peeked in. "Rosie, you here?"

"Sure as shootin'." Rosie emerged from behind a set of storage shelves. "Logan! You delivered the RFDs yesterday. What you doing here today?"

"Can't a friend come and say howdy?"

"Yeah, but is that why you're really here?"

"No. You got me there." Logan scuffed his boot across the wood floor, brushing a scrap of paper out of the way. Did he really want to do this? Be cooped up inside working behind a desk? "I wanted to ask if you still have the address where I send to apply for the postmaster position. Do you know if it's still available?"

"I haven't heard yet if they've picked someone for the job. I do have the address though. It can never hurt to try. But you'd better hurry. I know they're deciding soon." Rosie thumbed through some papers and then scribbled down an address on a piece of paper. "The new post office will be opening in a month. I can't wait. I wanted to be shed of this job long before now." She handed it to Logan. "I sure hope they pick you. You'd be perfect for the position."

He might be perfect for the position, but was the position right for him? Yet he was willing to take it over the ranch. Why?

Because Pa and Stanley had nothing to do with the post office.

"Thank you kindly, Rosie." Logan tipped his hat and hurried back into the store, needing to go write that letter before his resolve to do so slipped away.

Lavender was busy now with another customer.

"Bye." He waved at Lavender on his way out. Crackers didn't sound that good anyway. Once home, he'd see how much beef jerky he had left. If he remembered right, there should be half a bag of dried apricots too.

Halfway across Yampa Avenue, on his way to his room at the back of the law office, he looked up the street and noticed the stage coming in, a cloud of dust in its wake. Not due at the livery stable for another two hours, Logan thought he'd stroll past the town hall where the stagecoach stopped. It wouldn't take long to apply to that postmaster job, so why not? He made it to the town hall about the same time as the stagecoach. Leaning against the wall to stay in the shade of the covered sidewalk, he quietly observed the new driver slow the team down and bring them to a stop.

He thought this new driver's name was Theron, but he wasn't sure, only that he wasn't as good with those horses as John Mills used to be. Craig *was* changing. Lots of new people were moving in—more than Logan could keep up on. And there was the matter of those new-fangled automobiles like he'd seen in the parade. If they really did end up being popular, there wouldn't be much need for Gus to have another hand at the livery stable. Then Logan might be out of his main job.

Logan leaned away from the town hall, ready to write that letter for the postmaster position. The door to the coach swung open, and a young man in a snappy suit hopped out. He quickly pulled the box down for the others to step out on and then assisted Mr. and Mrs. Wilson out of the coach and then a woman and a child Logan guessed to be Mr. and Mrs. Wilson's daughter and granddaughter.

"Thanks for such delightful conversation," the man in the suit said with a bow to the Wilsons.

Logan knew the Wilsons, knew that *delightful* and *conversation* were rarely included in the same phrase with those folks. Perhaps it was their daughter he was speaking to.

"Good day." The man tipped his hat at the daughter and child. "It was more than a delight to share the coach with you as well."

The Wilsons waved goodbye to the man and left him standing there on the wooden sidewalk, less than a stone's throw from Logan. The man's suit, though fancy and finer than anything sold in Craig, was wrinkled. Obviously the man had been traveling for some time. He placed his new-fangled white skimmer hat back on his sandy-brown hair and looked first to the north and then south along Yampa Avenue. His skirting glances told Logan the man was at a loss as to what to do now that he'd finished his stagecoach ride.

The man had a face that was not necessarily striking, but his smile lines were well defined and his eyes friendly. He stood somewhat shorter than Logan and much narrower through the chest and shoulders. Logan guessed his age to be a few years younger than himself.

"Howdy," Logan said, sensing the fellow could use a friendly greeting about now. "Welcome to Craig. I'm guessing you've never been here before."

"That would be correct." The young man's voice had a cheerful sound to it. "Would you be so kind as to help a fellow out?" His face lit up with a smile that bore appreciation.

Logan couldn't help but smile back. "Certainly, what can I do for you?"

"First of all, if you could point me in the direction of your best restaurant, I'd be much obliged. I didn't eat enough on the train, and I was unaware the stagecoach ride didn't include dinner, so I'm rather famished."

"You're not from around here, are you?" Logan asked, chuckling inside. *Dinner served on a stagecoach? Hardly!*

"That's right. I hail from New York."

"Ah, East Coast fellow." Logan smiled and held out his hand for the man to shake. "I won't hold that against you though. The name's Logan." In that instant, a buried fear reared its ugly head. *What if this is Dudley?*

The man shook his hand. "I'm Charles."

Logan exhaled rather loudly. "Charles, eh? Nice to meet you." He looked south, down Yampa. "As for fine dining, I'm afraid the best place Craig has to offer is Sunny's Place. Come on. I'll show you the way." Logan hid his limp and walked down the south side of Yampa, keeping to the shade of covered sidewalks as best he could.

Charles caught up quickly. "Thank you, dear fellow. I had no idea of what to expect when I got here. I have to admit I was a little afraid. So thank you kindly for your hospitality."

"Happy to do it," Logan said. "Helping someone out always makes one feel good."

Charles gazed off momentarily. "You know, I believe you are right on that point, dear fellow." He scanned the buildings, the street, the people, his head constantly moving while his mouth gaped open. "This is quite amazing. I've never experienced anything like this. Rugged, rustic, yet quaint and charming all at the same time."

"I guess you could describe Craig that way." Logan found this Charles fellow anything but rugged, but he did hold a certain charm that whetted Logan's curiosity.

As they approached Sunny's Place, the aroma of fresh bread and slow-roasted beef wafted Logan's way. "Whoa, smells extra good today," he said, licking his lips.

"Have you had your lunch yet?"

"No, no I haven't."

"Then why don't you join me?" Charles held his palm out toward the door.

"I'd like nothing more, but . . ." Logan thrust his hands into his pockets. One dime and five pennies. He doubted it would be enough. And then how would he buy those crackers he was hoping would last him until payday?

"This is on me. I've recently come into some money. And as you put it, 'helping someone out always makes one feel good.'"

"Well, if you put it like that, how can I refuse?"

"I can tell already I'm going like the people here in this town." Charles nodded approval. He pushed the door open, and they stepped inside.

Sunny's new girl seated them immediately and handed them each a menu.

"What do you recommend?" Charles asked.

"I can't rightly say." Logan's mouth was watering over the description of the chicken and dumplings. "I don't eat in here all that much."

"What, is the food no good?"

"No, the food's plenty good." Logan tightly clutched his napkin with his free hand. It reminded him of that supper out at Celeste's. And then he thought of how he'd never be able to court her properly and take her out to Sunny's if and when she came to town. "I just gotta watch where I spend my money, that's all." He wished that was all.

"Believe me, I've been there, my dear fellow. And I didn't care for it at all. It nearly cost me the woman I loved. But I'm doing something about that as we speak. I've got this investment plan in place. It's going to make me a wealthy man. I'll tell you about it after I get some good food in my belly and a good night's sleep. Speaking of which, is there a decent hotel in this town?"

"Yeah, the Craig Hotel is right nice." Logan pointed through the wall. "It's across the street and down a block. You can't miss it: the tall red-brick building with the fancy curtains in the windows."

"Thanks, Logan." Charles sent him a sideways glance. "Is it all right if I call you Logan?"

"Of course."

"What's your surname, Logan?"

"You mean last name?"

"Yes, your last name."

"Jones, Logan Jones."

"I like it," Charles's mouth curled up slightly on one side. "It has a friendly ring to it."

"Thanks." Logan could see this fellow and him becoming fast friends. "What's your last name?"

"Mine?" Charles bobbed his head. "It's not quite so friendly sounding. Some folks have told me it sounds rather snobbish, but I hope you'll not judge me by my name." He ran his hand through his curly hair, pulling away a wayward lock that had fallen into his eyes. "Weathersby. My name is Charles Weathersby."

"Naw, I don't think it sounds snobbish at all," Logan said.

Chapter 15

CELESTE TRIED TO STRAIGHTEN THE wrinkles in her skirt as best she could as the wagon reached the outside of town. Maybe she should have worn her brown one. It didn't show wrinkles as much. But the blue one she had on was nicer. Oh, bother! Why was she fretting over such a simple decision? Weren't the big decisions enough? It had taken her the past two days to decide on even coming with Pa today, even after she told him she wanted to. She removed her bonnet and smoothed all the loose strands of her hair somewhat back into place.

"You're as pretty as they come," Pa spoke up for the first time in miles. This particular trip into town she'd found him less talkative than usual. "I'm guessing you could be dressed in a gunny sack and your hair cut to the quick and Logan wouldn't care a whit."

"Oh, Pa." Celeste brought her hands down from smoothing her hair and folded her arms tightly across her waist. She hoped her pa wasn't correct, that Logan wouldn't care. It'd taken her all afternoon yesterday to iron her dress and wash her hair, and then this morning, she got up at the crack of dawn to get ready. Would her efforts even catch his eye? The things that caught men's attention back in New York apparently didn't work on Logan. Neither did he seem interested in kissing her when the moment was perfect. She thought back to the Fourth of July and exhaled her frustration. Yet he had held her hand and even held her close at times that night. He must be at least partially interested in her.

"I'll stop at Ma's office first and let you off so you can fix your hair in her mirror if you want." Pa pulled the wagon onto Yampa Avenue. "Then I'll head on over to the mercantile."

"Thanks. That would be grand," Celeste said, having barely listened to her pa. Her mind scrabbled for ideas of how to win the heart of a man who was so unlike all the others she'd met. She glanced under the seat to check on the apple pie she'd baked yesterday. Hopefully, that would help. And hopefully that wouldn't be the only avenue that would work on Logan, because Ma was almost out of bottled apples.

"After that, I'll be over at the bank in case you're unable to locate Logan and you want to ride back home with me. But today's Friday. I believe he's working the livery stable today." Pa looked over at her. The up-and-down jostle of the wagon made it look like he was nodding. "'Tis something he knows, is it not? That you're paying him a visit?"

"Not really." Celeste chewed on her lip. "This is hardly New York, where there are telephones or where couriers of one's messages are plentiful to be found."

"Yep, one of the joys of the West," Pa said. This time, it was obvious he nodded his head. "Makes things more interesting, though. When you pop in on Logan unannounced, it'll be more exciting for the both of you."

"You really think so, Pa?" Celeste feared maybe this wasn't such a good idea after all.

"I know it would be for me." Pa scratched his chin. "And I don't suspect Logan is any different than any other man."

"That would be nice," she muttered under her breath, "if he wasn't that different." Then she'd have more of a clue as to how to get him interested in her.

"What's that?"

"Nothing, Pa." She cleared her throat. "Say, Pa, how long are you planning on being over at the bank?" She certainly hoped Logan was at the livery stable. What if for some reason he went out to the Circle J Ranch or his sister's place?

"I can't answer that. I don't exactly know. I'm mostly looking for information on how best to invest some money."

"You have extra money lying around, enough to invest?" Celeste had talked to enough young men about such matters in their attempts to swoon her. It had only served to bore her.

"Your grandma sent Ma a small sum, wanting her to invest most of it for our retirement. It was very thoughtful, 'cause I hadn't thought much about it. I just figured I'd work my sheep ranch till the day I died, never once taking into account that there might come a time that my body was too old to do what I used to and all my children choose to move away from this high-desert wilderness."

"That was kind of Grandma." Celeste sighed. "She *can* be thoughtful at times."

Pa pulled the wagon in front of the saddle shop. "Here you are. The key is hid under the—"

"I know where it is, Pa. Unless Ma's moved it." Celeste climbed down from the wagon.

"Nope, same place as before you went off to school."

She reached under the seat for her pie. "Maybe it's time we convince Ma to find another hiding spot."

"Naw, this is Craig. It'll be fine." Pa eyed the pie in her hands. "Good-looking pie. I don't know a man alive that wouldn't enjoy such a gift. Especially when it was made and served up by such a beautiful young lady."

"Aw, Pa." She batted her hand at him. "Stop it."

Pa picked up the reins. "I guess you know you have my full approval."

"Of the pie?" Celeste thought it *was* her best-looking one yet. She offered a coy smile, figuring Pa meant something else and wanting him to elaborate.

"Logan. You have my approval for him to court you."

Celeste kept her demeanor calm, although she was thrilled. After that lecture he'd given her on thinking her ideas were always the best, she worried Pa would frown on her plans to pursue Logan. What was that little talk all about, then? She shrugged it off and nodded her approval of Pa's declaration.

"Or convince him to court you—however you decide to tackle this," Pa continued, his crooked grin lighting up his face. "I like the boy, always have." He cleared his throat. "Under the circumstances, I guess I better quit calling him a boy, now, hadn't I?" He flicked the reins, and the wagon pulled away.

Celeste smiled at her pa as she ascended the steps to Ma's office at the side of the saddle shop. She could never fool Pa. He'd obviously seen right through her when she'd tried to keep her intentions toward Logan to herself. Ma probably figured it out too. As for her brothers? When it got right down to it, she no longer cared if they knew or if anyone else knew. It might even be a good thing if other people knew. Then maybe they could help her convince Logan that it was time for him to find a wife and settle down, and everyone knew just the girl to help him do it. Her!

With her bag looped over her elbow, it pulled her arms to one side and made the pie difficult to carry. Perhaps she should have left it down in the saddle shop. After she freshened up in Ma's office, she'd need to carry it right back down. Mr. Hoy would have kept it safe for a few minutes. It's not like he would slather it up with saddle grease or anything. She smiled at the ridiculous thought, and the smile lingered as she realized Mr. Hoy was easy enough for her talk to. So was his wife, Ethyl. It was like Logan had said; she just needed to get to know people. *Logan.* She definitely needed him by her side. He was good for her.

At the top of the stairs, she set the pie on the landing and opened the box Ma had put there years ago for people to leave her notes. Sure enough, there was the key, under the pad of paper. She took it, opened the door, and brought the pie inside.

Ma's office hadn't changed much from the way it was five years ago, before Celeste had moved away. She did have two chairs now in the waiting area, painted yellow instead of blue like the one before. But the exam table still stood in the middle of the room, and her two cabinets with cut glass in their doors so as to reveal her medicines and tools still lined the inside wall. It seemed such a nice office for a doctor who opened it once or twice a week and then saw mainly maternity patients, now that there was another doctor in town. But Ma chose to do it that way so as to not take all her time away from her family. She did, however, leave at a moment's notice, to anywhere in the county, when the word came in that a woman was ready to give birth. She stayed for days at a time, in some cases, to deliver a child and take care of the mother. Celeste's heart warmed with appreciation for her stepmother. She hoped she could become more helpful and loving to others like Ma. But Ma didn't have problems talking to people or have bouts of melancholy. Yes, Celeste definitely needed Logan's help to overcome her anxieties.

After brushing her hair and stacking it again atop her head and pinning it securely in place, she grabbed her pie and descended the stairs. She glanced up and down Yampa Avenue just in case Logan was out and about like he often was, talking to people as he ran errands for Gus. There was no sign of Logan.

She did, however, catch sight of a man in an expensive suit that seemed out of place in Craig. His face was turned away from her, but his slight build and the way he walked reminded her of Charles Weathersby. For a moment her heart sped, which made her catch her breath. She cast the ridiculous notion aside and strolled down the street in the opposite direction of the man, toward the livery stable.

It was a lovely day to take a morning stroll. The sun had not risen to where it shone mercilessly upon her, and a slight breeze blew in from the west, making the temperature perfect for her and her pie. Birds chirped in the distance, and the laughter of children running down the opposite sidewalk cheered her spirits. The smell of freshly cut hay wafted in from a farm to the south, bringing a smile to her lips. This town felt a world away from Millbrook, New York, and Miss Bennett's school.

"Howdy, miss." An older man in cowboy boots and dirty trousers lifted his hat as she passed him.

Celeste nodded to him. A minute later, two middle-aged women walked toward her, each seemingly involved in their conversation. When they reached Celeste, both smiled.

"Good morning, Miss McCurdy," one of them said.

"Glad to have you back," the other said.

"Thank you. It's good to be home," Celeste said, noticing her knees weren't trembling at all.

They did, however, wobble a bit as she approached the livery stable. She paused for a moment outside the small door and breathed deeply before walking in.

The door jingled as she stepped inside.

"Be with you in a minute." Logan's voice came from the direction of the stalls.

It held that familiar cheerful tone and calmed Celeste. "Don't hurry on my account. I'm just stopping by to visit."

"Celeste?" His voice rose in pitch such that she dared hope he might be a tad bit excited. "You're here?"

"I rode in with Pa this morning. He had a few matters he needed to take care of in town."

Logan emerged from the farthest stall, wiping his hands on his trousers. "How long will you be staying?"

"It depends." Celeste stared at the manure caked to the bottom of his trousers, sweat stains on his shirt, and some sort of filth smeared across the palms of his hands.

"Depends on what?" Logan hobbled toward her, wiping his hands on his shirt now.

"I was kind of hoping you would have some time for me today, you know, that we could take a stroll down by the river or sit in the park and reminisce about the Fourth of July." She paused when the smell of perspiration and manure overwhelmed her as he came closer. "But . . . it appears you are quite busy at the moment."

"Yeah, I kinda am. Got two horses that just came in, and I've got to rub them down right away. And the manure in this place is getting out of hand. It needs shoveling and new straw put down." Logan's forehead wrinkled. "If Gus were here, I know he'd let me off for a while, but he's over in Hayden until later this afternoon." He stopped a foot or so away from her, hunched his shoulders, and spread his hands out toward her. "Sorry. If I'd known you were coming, I could have arranged better."

"I understand. It's not like we've got one of those new telephone machines at our house." Celeste offered a soft laugh.

"Wouldn't that be the day?" Logan laugh sounded more nervous than amused.

"What time do you figure Gus will be back?" She'd really hoped Logan would be taking this line of thinking, not her. "Could we take a walk then . . . uh . . . after you clean up, of course?"

"I don't know exactly." Logan scratched his stubble-covered chin. "And I more than reckon he'd let me go once he got here. But I imagine your Pa will be long since done with his business by then and be wanting to head back." He let out a sigh. "Sorry. I'd have liked to visit with you today. Liked it a heap, but . . ." He swept a hand toward a pile of manure. "This here's not the place." A horse whinnied. "And the horses are waiting for me."

Celeste held back her frustration and firmed her jaw. "Say, I have an idea. If you are amenable, how about I wait at Ma's office until Gus gets back from Hayden. She's got a book or two there. Then you clean up, and we take a stroll until suppertime. We could dine at Sunny's Place, and we'd still have time to make it back to my place before it gets dark. You could spend the night in the barn like before and then ride out in the morning first thing. Just let Gus know you might be a little late coming in tomorrow morning."

"Uh, uh . . . I don't know," Logan stammered.

"What's wrong?" She had thought it was a perfect idea. "Would Gus not allow you to come in late?"

"Naw, that'd be no problem. Besides, I'm delivering mail tomorrow, so I could just take it with me. But . . ."

"But what?"

"I'd have to take one of Gus's buggies with you not wearing trousers today." Logan motioned to her dress with his hand while his eyes lingered on her face. "And looking so pretty." He moved his gaze to the floor. "I'd have to leave it at your place while I made my deliveries, but I guess I could pick it up by backtracking on my way back to town."

"Ma's got a spare set of trousers at her office."

"Oh, well then . . ." Logan swallowed hard.

"Gracious be, Logan Jones. If you don't want to take me back home tonight, just say it!" Celeste brought the pie out from behind her back, where she'd been hiding it all this time, waiting for the right moment to give it to him. "Here! I made you a pie. I'll give it to you right now and be on my way. If I hurry, I can catch Pa." She shoved the pie toward Logan, but he held up his filthy hands and stepped back while his mouth gaped open. "I don't know what I was thinking telling Pa to leave without checking with me first." She kept hold of the pie and turned to leave.

"Celeste, please, no, don't go." Logan's begging tone tore at her heart.

She turned back around.

"More than anything I want to spend the day with you, whether down by the river or at the park don't matter, so long as I'm with you. And I'd be more than willing to take you home in Gus's buggy. But . . ." He stared at the floor again before gazing into her eyes. "I've got ten cents to my name right now. I can no more buy you a supper at Sunny's than take you to New York and treat you to those fine restaurants you're deserving of."

"That's it?" *Money.* Celeste's shoulders relaxed. "That's the only reason you've been dragging your fee—being so hesitant?"

Logan nodded.

"Logan, Logan, money, or rather the lack thereof, should never overshadow the desires of one's heart." Celeste wondered if she should encourage him to take the postmaster job. She gazed at him, his dirty face expressing desire and helplessness together in a most endearing quiver of his lip. It would be cruel to force him to dwell on his lack of income now. "How about I cook us a meal at Ma's office instead? She's still got that tiny kitchen in the back room. With your dime, the handful of change I've got, and this pie for desert, we'll have a fine supper." She held up the pie.

"Oh, Celeste, that sounds wonderful." Logan reached out to her but quickly stopped himself, pulling his soiled hands behind his back.

She cleared her throat. "I'm going to insist you clean up first before, um, we meet up this afternoon."

Logan glanced down at his shirt and laughed. "Yeah, that might be a good idea." He tipped a hat that wasn't there upon his matted, sweaty hair. "See you as soon as I possibly can." Then he looked into her eyes, as if reaching down to her soul and thanking her heart. "Thank you, Celeste. You are a jewel."

Celeste felt a blush of heat rise to her cheeks. This was exactly why she was here. "You are most welcome." She reached out and touched her hand to his check and let it linger a brief moment. *Should I kiss his cheek? No, it'd be too forward.* An impulse from somewhere inside made the decision for her, and she found herself brushing her lips quickly across a clean spot on his face.

"I shall be waiting for you," she said softly, then turned and walked out the door.

Chapter 16

LOGAN HAULED OUT THE LAST bit of manure from the stables and dumped it onto the pile out back, his heart still tingling from that kiss Celeste gave him an hour ago. He hurried back inside and washed down the stalls as best he could with a bucket of water and a rag. The floor could really use a good cleaning. If only it was made of concrete like he'd learned some of the livery stables in those big cities had. As he laid down fresh straw on the damp parts of the floor, he doubted Gus would ever put out that kind of money, especially with the fate of the livery stable in the hands of those automobiles.

The front door bumped its bell as it opened. Logan stepped out of the stall and looked toward it. "Gus!" He dropped his handful of straw and hobbled toward him. "I got a big, big favor to ask."

"Shoot."

"I need to leave early, right now, preferably." Logan shifted his weight from one leg to the other, trying to contain his feelings.

"What's so all-fired important that it's got you dancing like a schoolboy?"

"Well, there's this gal I'm—"

"Well, I'll be, our Logan's finally got his eye on someone." Gus slapped Logan on the back. "Who is this lucky girl?"

"Well . . . in case she changes her mind, I'd rather not—"

"Say no more. Get out of here." He shooed Logan toward the door. "And for goodness' sake, take a bath before you go calling on her."

"For sure." Logan ran out the door.

He hurried to his place and rifled through his clothes, trying to find something that was clean and not too full of holes. It was due time he bought himself some new duds. *This payday for sure.* Before now, he'd rarely spent money on clothes—hadn't needed to. And his paychecks had been sufficient to take care of his needs. But they could never take care of two people's needs. But should he wait to ask Lucas for permission to court Celeste until he officially got the postmaster job or take the gamble and ask Lucas the first chance he got? Either way, he wanted to court her. Wanted it more than anything. She made him feel like she cared for him, perhaps even loved him. The hope of being cherished by someone felt real now after that kiss, not just a dream.

Logan went back and forth with what to do. Deciding what to wear proved infinitely easier than deciding on when to approach Lucas. He picked his white Sunday shirt, the only shirt that hadn't been worn since he'd done laundry, his black pants, which could be made presentable with a damp rag, and his favorite belt with the silver buckle with a horse engraved on it. He slipped off his work boots and pulled on his good ones. Bringing a fresh change of underwear and socks and his razor with him, he ran out the door. Porter's Bathhouse lay two blocks away.

A block away from the bathhouse, he heard footsteps approach him from behind. He tried to walk faster, but as he did, the footsteps became faster. Now was not the time for someone to stop him for a neighborly chat.

"Hold on there, my dear fellow. You're making it awfully hard to catch up with you."

Logan slowed his pace and let this new friend fall in step with him. "Afternoon, Charles. I can't really stop to talk now; I've got somewhere to be. First, I've got to go to Porter's Bathhouse."

"Ah, so that's where you fellows clean up. I was wondering about that when I discovered the hotel rooms don't come with their own bathrooms."

"A lot of things are different out here," Logan said, huffing a bit.

"Yes, I am finding that to be quite the case. One difference I've found that I quite like is the people. Fellows like you, the Browns, the Tuckers, the Hoys, and Miss Sunny—you're all friendly people, much more so than my old friends back East."

"You've met all those people already?" Logan asked.

"Yes, I've been busy the last three days."

"I'm downright impressed," Logan said. "Say, I forgot to ask you last Tuesday—and thanks for the chicken and dumplin's by the way—what exactly brought you out West? It don't sound like it's the kind of place a fellow like you would gravitate to." He stepped on the wooden sidewalk in front of Porter's.

"I'm afraid I'd keep you from your appointment if I were to go into that right now." Charles motioned to the bathhouse door. "Don't fear. I'll meet up with you later. For now, let me say opportunity drew me to this place." He lifted his fancy hat. "Good afternoon, my dear fellow."

"Afternoon." Logan removed his hat and walked inside, glad he'd squeezed in that quick chat with Charles without having to stop. He had to wonder, though, what kind of opportunity could have possibly brought a man like Charles Weathersby to an out-of-the-way small town without a railroad?

On the wooden sidewalk outside the bathhouse, a man sat in a chair with his legs crossed, waiting and wagging his foot in time to the tune he whistled. Logan didn't know him. *Yeah, Craig is changing, growing.* Logan walked up to Owen Porter at the stove in the middle of the room. He appeared to be heating up water for the other fellow's bath.

"Owen, how fast can you fill me a tub? I don't need you to heat it up."

"Fifteen minutes or so."

Logan grimaced. "I'm kind of in a hurry."

"Okay, ten minutes."

"That'll be fine." Logan walked to a set of sinks, both with mirrors hanging above them. "Do you mind if I borrow a sink and give myself a shave while I wait?"

"Help yerself." Owen motioned to the sinks while he poured a bucket of steaming water into one of his five tubs that lined the wall opposite the sinks.

Logan lathered his face with the soap and brush Owen provided his customers for a penny extra. He hoped Owen would be willing to give him the soap and bath on credit.

"Getting gussied up for a gal?" the man in the tub hollered across the room to Logan.

"Yep." Logan moved his mouth to one side to give his razor an easier time with his face.

"I wondered why you was in here so soon," Owen said as he poured a bucket of water into the tub closest to Logan. "Usually it's a couple of weeks before I see you again."

"That'll be changing." Logan ran the blade up the other side of his face.

"Anybody I know?" Owen asked.

"Maybe. Maybe not. Craig is changing. Folks don't know everyone who lives here like they used to."

"So tell me her name, and I'll tell you if I know her or not." Owen dipped his hand into the water. "Kinda cold. You sure you don't want at least one pail of hot in there? I've got one ready."

"Sure, heat it up all you can 'til I'm done shaving."

"So are you going to tell us her name or not?" said the stranger at the far end of the room. "Who knows, I might even know her."

"I'd rather not say," Logan admitted, "just in case things don't work out between the two of us."

"Why, that doesn't sound like the Logan Jones I know. Usually you're the optimistic one."

"Like I said, Owen, things are changing around here. Oh and by the way, could I put today's visit on credit?"

"I suppose." Owen didn't sound all too thrilled.

"I promise I'm good for it, Owen." Logan ran his hand over his face and neck. "Smooth as a baby's bottom. You dumped that hot water into my tub yet?"

"Nope." Owen sloshed a bucket's worth of water into the tub. "Now I have."

"Great." Logan peeled off his clothes, realizing now how filthy they really were, and held them at arm's length. He let them drop to a pile on the floor and stepped into the tub. Tepid water engulfed him. It felt good; the room had been way too warm.

As soon as Logan could get himself scrubbed, dried, and dressed, and splashed a dash of Owen's special tonic onto his neck, he darted for the door.

"That'll be a penny extra for the aftershave," Owen spoke up.

"Put it on my tab." Logan hurried out the door. "Yep," he muttered, "things around Craig are changing."

Though he wanted to walk as fast as his legs would allow, he took his time going to Kate's office. The late-afternoon heat beat down on his back, and he didn't want to work up any more of a sweat than he had to.

When he reached the bottom of the wobbly steps, he stopped and took a breath. He never did like taking that many steps all at once. He started up the steps wearing a smile. Celeste was more than worth it.

At the top of the stairs, he took off his hat, raked his fingers through his damp hair, and knocked. There was another thing he needed to do come payday—get a haircut.

"Coming." Celeste's voice came through the door, and Logan's heart beat a little faster. Moments later, it opened. "Logan! You made it." She took a step back and looked at the whole of him. "You have cleaned up very nicely."

"Thank you." He fumbled the words out, so glad he'd taken a little extra time at Porter's.

"And what perfect timing," Celeste said. "Supper is almost ready."

"But—" How would he put this so as to not sound pathetic? He couldn't; it did sound pathetic. "I never got a chance to pitch in my money."

Celeste flicked her hand in the air as she led Logan through the office. "Don't worry about it. I caught Pa before he left, and he paid for what I needed at the mercantile."

"Oh." Logan gulped. Now Lucas knew he was dirt poor. What if Lucas wouldn't give him permission to court Celeste? He'd better rein in his feelings for her until he got a solid go-ahead from her pa.

"We're having steak, new potatoes, and peas. And apple pie for dessert, of course." She motioned for him to sit at a small table set just outside the back room. "Oh dear, Miss Bennett would probably faint if she knew I was entertaining a young man alone and unchaperoned in my ma's office." She breathed out what sounded like a sigh of relief. "But nobody here cares about her rules, do they?"

"No, I can't say that they do." Logan lowered himself slowly onto one of the two chairs. He, for one, didn't care. But what about Celeste's parents? He knew Celeste enough to know she did her own thinking. He'd better make sure his behavior was impeccable, for Lucas's and Kate's sake. He didn't want to do anything that would jeopardize obtaining their permission to court Celeste. "Wow, I'm not accustomed to eating like this," he said to change the subject.

"Well, that should change." She stepped into the kitchen area.

Logan wondered if by that she meant to do something about that and cook him more lovely meals or that he should take it upon himself to change his financial situation so he could feed himself better. He really couldn't tell from her voice.

"Smells real good," he said. Then he thought of another possibility. It was more likely she thought that should change so he could afford to feed a family. And she'd be right. Hopefully Lucas would be okay with the knowledge that Logan was working on that. The government should be making a decision on that postmaster position any day now.

"Thank you," came Celeste's voice from the kitchen. A moment later, she emerged carrying two plates heaped with food. "I hope it will taste good too." She placed a plate in front of Logan and one in front of her chair and then sat down. "Would you offer a prayer of thanks?"

"Me?" Logan panicked. He hadn't blessed his food in front of someone for nigh onto thirteen years, since he'd basically lived on his own. His prayers had always been in his heart. But he'd clung to them because Susannah had taught him to pray, like their ma had taught her. And in some small way, it connected him to his ma. "I'm afraid I'm a little rusty with praying out loud. But that don't mean I'm not thankful," he added quickly. "God knows that. He hears them fine coming from my heart."

"I appreciate that, Logan. How about I say the prayer?" She placed her hand on Logan's as it rested on the table.

Logan heard very little of her prayer. The caress of her fingers against his consumed his thoughts all the way through to the *amen*.

She removed her hand from his, picked up her knife and fork, and began cutting up her steak. The smallest of a bite Logan could imagine went into her mouth, and she chewed with such dainty motions of her jaw. She swallowed and looked across the table at Logan. He had yet to take a bite, as enthralled as he'd been in watching her.

"Are you not hungry?" She pointed her fork at his untouched food.

"No, I'm famished. I'm just enjoying my view," he said, his eyes still on her.

"Oh, Logan, that is so sweet." She waved her fork at his plate. "But you need to eat so we can get going before it gets too late. And save room for pie. I made the same one as you liked so much on the Fourth of July. "

"Oh, I'll not need to save any room. I could eat that even if I was plum full." He spoke the simple truth. "You made that for me 'cause I liked it, didn't you?"

She blushed. "Yes."

Logan blinked away his disbelief and dug into his food. Could this really be happening? Things were working out better than if he'd daydreamed this Friday up.

Except for the money part.

Chapter 17

After Celeste and Logan cleaned up the dishes in Ma's back room, Logan went outside and down the stairs while she changed into a pair of Ma's trousers. With her skirt and petticoat stuffed into her bag, she hurried down after him.

Logan was walking his horse toward her, with reins in hand. He watched her every step with nary a blink. "I think it was good we decided against our stroll."

"I agree. Getting on the road right away will allow us to take our time and stop along the road if we choose. It'll be just like our stroll, only your horse will be walking for us."

"Good ole Bootstrap." Logan patted his horse on the neck. "He's used to doing a lot of my walking for me."

Celeste handed Logan her bag. "Here, hold on to this while I mount your horse." In one fluid motion, she mounted his horse and nestled onto the blanket he'd placed behind the saddle."

"Whoa, where'd you learn that?" Logan handed her back the bag and mounted.

"One of my best classes at school was my equine course."

"Eck wine?"

"That's the upper crust's way of saying 'horseback riding.'"

"Oh." Logan chuckled and prompted his horse onto the street. "Does this mean if I round you up your own horse, we can go riding together—real riding, like in a friendly race or two?"

"That would be lovely."

"Aw, come on now, Celeste. We're talking horses right now, here in the West, not back East. *Lovely* sounds . . . I don't know, just too fancy for what we're doing."

"You are absolutely correct." She wrapped her arms around Logan's waist as Bootstrap picked up speed. "It'd be to my liking," she corrected herself, "just like this is." She squeezed him tighter.

As they rode through the last block in town, Celeste caught a glimpse again of that man in the fancy suit who reminded her of Charles. He was walking into the telegraph office, so she didn't get a look at his face this time either. Old memories stirred, and the pain felt raw. She shuddered.

"What's wrong?" Logan asked.

"Oh, nothing. I just saw someone who reminded me of a person I knew back at school. That's all."

"Those days are behind you. There's no need to fret about them anymore. You hear me?"

"Yes, Miss Bennett." Celeste giggled. "She used to always ask, 'Do you hear me?' Only not as nice as you."

"What? I thought I was being stern. Even a little downright mean."

"You, Logan? I don't think there is a mean bone in your body."

Logan turned his horse to the east and headed out of town on the road to Hayden.

"I'm glad we didn't end up taking a buggy," she said. "It would have slowed us down considerably. So thanks, Bootstrap," she patted Logan's horse, "for letting me share your back with Logan."

"He don't mind at all," Logan said over his shoulder.

"So you can speak for your horse, can you?"

"All the time. We know what each other's thinking too."

"Interesting." Celeste loved the breeze moving past her face, and this conversation too. "What's he thinking now?"

"That he has the most beautiful gal in the world riding on his back."

"Tell him that is very kind of him to say." Celeste's heart swelled. "And tell him that he has the sweetest, kindest man in the world riding on his back with her."

She felt Logan's hand rest atop hers. Tingles of excitement danced up her arms. No other man's simple touch had ever made her feel like this.

Craig soon slipped out of sight behind the poplars of the river bottom, and Bootstrap settled into an even pace. Silence fell between them. Celeste loved how she didn't feel pressured to make trite conversation. Logan's presence, like always, felt like a soft blanket of comfort. She turned her head to one side and laid it against Logan's back. It felt firm, a reminder of the hard worker that he was. Contentment filled her, and she found herself dozing in and out, enjoying the pleasant scent of sage and cedar with each breath she took.

The sun had set by the time they reached the ranch. Pa sent the boys to bed, and he and Ma played cards with Celeste and Logan until Ma declared she was "done-in."

Celeste walked Logan out to the barn, stopping before going in. Enough of Miss Bennett's etiquette rose to the surface this time to disallow herself to go any further. She loved how Logan respected her, and that heightened her respect for him. Dining alone with him and giving him that quick kiss on the cheek next to his lips was as far as she would push the boundaries of decorum. She cringed inside as she remembered wanting to sit on his bed in the barn to tell him her "bedtime story" that first night he'd come over. What had possessed her to want to do so? Desperation to convince Logan to court her, she supposed. Thank heavens he'd saved her from her foolish decision. And thank heavens she no longer had to try to convince him. True, their courtship wasn't official yet, but she sensed it was only a matter of time. A short time.

She latched on to Logan's arm, moving her hand down and entwining it with his when they stopped just outside the barn. "I had a lovely evening. Thank you." She kept her hand in his.

"Me too." He took hold of her other hand and pulled her slightly closer. "Thanks so much."

She felt another tug to her hands and anticipated a strong pull that would bring her into his arms, ultimately culminating with their lips meeting and a most tender kiss.

He just stood there, unmoving, except for his eyes, which stared at the ground. Finally, his gaze moved up to meet hers. "It's getting late. I should probably hit the hay. I need to get up early."

"Yes, yes, that would probably be best." She let go of his hands and couldn't help but let her shoulders slump. "Good night."

"Good night, Celeste." He turned away from her and limped into the barn.

She walked back to the house, folding her arms tightly to her body. What had just happened back there? She'd thought things were moving along so well.

U

The next morning, when Celeste came into the kitchen for breakfast, she saw only Ma there, cleaning up the dishes. "What? Everyone's already eaten?"

"Yes, dear."

"What time is it?"

"Nearly seven."

"You should have woken me."

"I tried," Ma said, wincing a bit. "Somewhat. But you wouldn't stir. I figured you needed the sleep. I heard you tossing all night. Is everything all right?"

"Yes, perfectly fine. Except now I'm a bit angry. Is Logan still here?"

"No, he ate his breakfast with your pa and rode out even before the boys were up."

"Mother! I didn't even get to say goodbye. *Why* did you not wake me?"

"So we're back to 'Mother' now, are we?" Ma placed her hand on Celeste's shoulder as if to calm her, but it didn't work. "Logan insisted we not wake you. I really believe he was merely thinking of you."

"That's a pretty lousy way to think of me, by not saying goodbye." Celeste dropped into a kitchen chair.

"Would you like a fried egg?" Ma asked in a gentle voice. "I can cook you one up in a minute or two."

"No, thank you." Celeste sagged in her chair and splayed her legs out in front of her. "I'm not hungry."

"It's a long time until dinner." Ma waved a wooden spoon at her.

"Fine, but I can make my own egg. You get back to your chores." Celeste pulled herself up from the chair. "I'll get to mine when I get to them. Maybe tomorrow. Maybe I'll walk into town. Why do we have to live so far away from Craig?"

"You sounded exactly like you did five years ago, your voice, your words, everything."

"Yes, well maybe you should send me away again."

"Celeste, you make it sound like we did that to punish you."

"Well, didn't you?"

"No, not at all." Ma lowered herself into the chair and urged Celeste back down into hers. She took Celeste's hands in hers. "Living so far away from town like we do was one of the major reasons we sent you back to your grandparents to go to school. There was no place in Craig for you to stay the night, and we couldn't very well drive you to school every day in the wagon. Especially with the winters we have around here."

"What about the boys? You teach them at home. Why couldn't you have done that for me?"

"Oh, Celeste." Ma squeezed Celeste's hands. Ma's eyes appeared wet with threatening tears. "We did what we thought was best at the time. Every child is different."

"Ma, I'm sorry. I didn't mean to upset you." She leaned over, hugged her ma, and stood. "I'm just a little frustrated. I guess from not being able to say a proper goodbye to Logan." *Or from him not saying goodbye to me.*

Was she fooling herself about their relationship? Did Logan really care for her, or was he just being his kind, friendly self? Or, even worse, accepting her advances toward him because he didn't want to be unkind to the daughter of his good friends?

Celeste fried herself an egg, then dragged herself outside to pull weeds out of the potatoes in the garden and thin the carrots. Back at school, she'd found very quickly that moping never actually made her feel better, so she'd just as well get to work and get her chores out of the way.

By mid-morning, she'd made it to the carrots. As she pulled out the little carrots every inch or so to thin them, and carefully saved the tender roots for supper, Pa walked by the garden on his way to the barn.

"Ah, Celeste, take a break from the garden for a minute and join me in the shade of the barn. 'Tis something I wish to tell you."

Celeste found her father's tone peculiar. It weighed her down. Had Logan said something disturbing to him this morning? Is that why he had left without saying goodbye?

"What is it, Pa?" She sat atop the wood pile next to him.

"I met a young man while I was in town yesterday, a stranger to Craig. I talked to several folks after he left the mercantile—'tis where I first met him. No one at Decker's store had ever met him before this week, yet they all carried on with him like he was their brother."

"So you met this man more than once, I take it?"

"Aye." Pa stroked each side of his chin with his thumb and fingers. "I'm thinking he must have overheard me talking to Lavender. I'd told her about the money your ma's ma sent us and how I was heading over to the bank shortly to deposit it." He sat on the chopping stump and folded his arms like he was settling in for a while. "'Cause he stopped me right before I walked into the bank. He seemed to appear out of nowhere, hurrying toward me, calling out my given name like I was a longtime friend."

"Why are you telling me this?" Celeste's puzzlement hushed her voice.

Pa kept going like he'd not heard her. "Funny thing was I could have sworn he was an old friend. Leastwise, that's what the fellow made me feel like. He had this infectious smile. Put with his gentle voice and friendly manner, it made me like the fellow right off. He wasn't much to look at, kind of a scrawny young man with a big nose and lots of laugh lines etched in his face. But I have to admit, after I first met him, I never noticed those things."

"Why are you telling me this, Pa?" Celeste enunciated her words better this time.

"Because . . ." Pa hesitated. "It appears you know him. Or at least, he knows you."

Celeste stood. "Charles Weathersby," she muttered.

"So you do know him, then?" Pa rose beside her.

Celeste nodded as old memories filled with delight and pain flooded her mind. "Did he say why he came?"

"He told me it was because he saw Craig as a land of opportunity, a perfect place for him to share his investment opportunity. Said he was looking for open-minded folks who could use a few extra bucks in their pockets." One side of Pa's mouth lifted in a sorry version of his usual smile. "That was pretty close to his exact words."

"Was that his only reason?" Celeste heard the disappointment in her own voice. She'd not intended for that to happen. She hurried and added, "I meant to say, did he come out West in search of an adventure, like so many young men do?"

"He spoke of nothing else." Pa's voice lowered into a serious tone. "But I sensed he came out here in search of something he never mentioned. I saw it in his eyes when he said your name. And now that I've spoken with you, I'm afraid it might be true."

"Just tell me and tell me straight." Celeste's voice wobbled.

"I believe Mr. Weathersby came out here searching for you." Pa turned his head away and stared at his flocks in the nearby field. "Logan Jones is a good man. There's none finer, just saying."

"Yes, Logan is a good man." Celeste dusted off her knees. She gazed at Pa, whose eyes were still focused on his sheep. "But he has yet to ask me to court him officially. And I have made it as plain as I possibly can that I wish for him to court me—without coming right out and saying so." She contemplated the ache Logan's diffidence had created in her heart. "So if Charles happens to show interest in me again and requests your permission to court me, then I might very well accept."

Pa's head snapped around, and his eyes met Celeste's. "But what about Logan?"

"Has he asked your permission to court me?" Celeste said with a note of defiance, figuring Pa would have told her so if it were the case.

Pa's eyes veered off to the side. "As a matter of fact, he did this very morning."

"Oh." Celeste's insides warmed without warning. "What did you say to him?" She awaited her pa's confirmation. Her head and her heart felt in a muddle.

"Being the responsible father that I am, I asked as to his plans to take care of you. I asked if he'd decided to accept the Circle J from his sister, since rumor said it was his now."

"And?" Celeste couldn't believe it. Was that really a possibility?

"He said taking on the Circle J was not an option. But he had other possibilities in the wings, and he'd ask me for my permission again when he knew for sure he had the means to take care of a family. Then he hurried out of here like he didn't want to be here no more. He barely took the time to wish me good day."

"Really? That doesn't sound like Logan."

"Aye."

Celeste wondered if Logan was going to apply to the postmaster job after all. If he didn't get the position and the rumor about the Circle J was just that—a rumor—what then? She grew weary of her feelings for Logan rising and falling like the paddle of a butter churn, and she swore his feelings for her rose and fell the same way.

"Now, tell me, Pa, what is it that Charles said to you to make you believe his intentions were to search me out, even though he mentioned not a word of it?" Celeste felt that familiar flutter she used to feel when Charles came to call on her. He had this way of making her laugh. She loved and missed it. If he was indeed here to see her, there must be a logical explanation as to why he had disappeared from her life those six months ago. The fluttering in her stomach told her it would only be fair to give him the opportunity to explain.

"He did say that he knew you and that he had escorted you to a number of dances while you were back at school. He also said he considered you a good friend and he hoped you considered him the same and thus would love to see you again. He seemed to know I was your pa, and I think he was reaching out for some sort of permission from me to come out to our place to call on you."

"So did you give it to him?" A small niggle of excitement grew in her chest. If Charles's explanation was viable, perhaps she could forgive him for disappearing without a word. "Your permission? Did you tell him where we live?"

"I didn't have to tell him about our ranch. He appeared to know all about it." Pa pursed his lips.

"Did you give him permission to call on me?" She persisted.

"No, no I didn't." Pa's brow wrinkled. "My mind was still on matters of investing your ma's money with him. That's what we were talking about when he brought up that he knew you."

"Charles? Invest with him?" Celeste was certain her face had twisted in a most unbecoming fashion. "He's as poor as a church mouse." Maybe that was why she and Charles had gotten along so well. She thought she'd made that clear to Logan too, that money, or rather the lack thereof, should not affect the leanings of one's heart.

"Apparently, Mr. Weathersby is not poor anymore. He's teamed up with some fellow who's found a way to turn one's investment around and make you a thirty-percent profit in as little as three months." Pa shook his head. "How he makes such a hefty commission on mine, or anyone else's for that matter, is beyond me. That's why I'm still thinking on this."

"So Charles has money now?"

"'Tis what he says."

She was glad for him but also became sad for him as Reverend Francis's voice spoke in her head. "We are molded by the things we love. Those who covet money pierce themselves through with many sorrows. They are never satisfied with what God has given them, and they become unhappy." She hoped Charles hadn't fallen in love with money like so many people she knew back East. He'd always been such a happy soul.

She tried to shake thoughts of Charles from her head, wanting to get back to thinning carrots. That task had left her feeling much more at ease. Her rubbed-raw fingers were preferable to the dilemma that now faced her. "Why did you see the need to tell me about Charles Weathersby, Pa? Especially if you did not give him permission to call on me."

Pa lowered himself back down onto a stump and looked up at Celeste. "Because I don't want you to hurt Logan's feelings. 'Tis in his eyes and every word he says about you, dear Celeste. He cares deeply for you. Just give him time for his tongue to untangle."

"Still, you might have said nothing of Charles. Why bring him up if you've basically told him to stay away?" She vented her frustration with a long exhale. "It would have been easier on all of us."

"Because," Pa heaved a sigh, "I believe he will not give up his desire to see you so easily. And I fear the fellow's so dang likeable that I won't have the presence of mind to stop him. So I had to tell you about him. 'Tis going to be your decision what you do about Mr. Weathersby."

"Oh, Pa." She shook her head, not finding this situation fair at all. Pa knew how she struggled with making decisions.

Chapter 18

THE SUN DIPPED LOW IN the western sky. Logan patted Bootstrap's neck as they approached town, still thinking about the opportunity he'd had last night to kiss Celeste but didn't dare take. It had occupied his mind all day while he'd delivered the mail—after he'd let go of the stupid idea of giving up on Celeste because of what Lucas had said. "It's been a long day." He'd had enough of his heart and his head battling it out with each other. She didn't seem too bothered by his shortcomings. So why should he be?

Wrong. She talked about me applying for the postmaster job. His measly income must bother her. It obviously bothered her pa. Maybe he *should* take on the ranch.

No! He'd vowed to heaven and hell he'd never do that.

Enough of this! At the moment, he wanted only to curl up with a book on his cot in that lonely back room and eat the rest of the apple pie Celeste had left with him.

Gus was still at the livery stable when Logan got there. Gus sat outside with Ned from the telegraph office and that new fellow, Charles. Being close to sunset, the front of the stable was in the shade. It looked rather inviting to sit and play checkers at that makeshift table Gus had made out of a big stump and a board. He'd have to round himself up a stool from the back of the stable if he wanted to sit down; the three stools Gus kept outside by his table were taken.

"Enjoying a game of checkers, I see," Logan said as he approached.

"Yep," Gus said.

"Em-huh," Ned mumbled and jumped his red checker over two black ones.

Logan dismounted and led Bootstrap past the three of them, toward the half-opened double doors of the stable. "Mind if I join you after I take care of my horse?"

Gus jumped his black checker over a red one. "Not at all. You can watch like this new fellow here." Gus glanced up at Logan. "His name's Charles. You two should get on like two peas in a pod."

Charles patted Gus on the back. "I've already met your fine friend." He looked to Logan. "And I have to admit, I do get along with him just dandy. I hope he feels the same, because if I were to share a pea pod with anyone, I'd just as soon it be you, good fellow." He smiled at Logan.

"Well, thank you kindly," Logan responded, feeling a smile stretch his lips. It felt good. He'd not had the whim to do so all day. He was still feeling the urge to kick himself around the block for not asking Celeste directly to court him. His twisted notion that Lucas would do the hard part and ask Celeste for him had backfired. He'd not expected Lucas to bring up his finances. He thought the man would trust he'd be able to take care of his daughter by the time they tied the knot.

Tomorrow was Sunday, his day off from both part-time jobs. Perhaps he should ride out to the McCurdy place and spurt out the question the moment he saw Celeste so he wouldn't have a chance to let his shortcomings stare him back down. First, he'd better find Rosie and see if she'd heard any word back about him getting the postmaster job. If only he could bring himself to tell Ron he would accept the Circle J. But he couldn't. He'd thought about it plenty, more than plenty. The pain was too deep. He could never enjoy taking care of his pa's ranch, not enough to do it well, when he knew Pa never wanted him to have it in the first place. It would always eat at him with each improvement he might try to make. It also wouldn't work to do as Ron suggested and keep out enough money to survive on and just sell the dang ranch. The postmaster job might not be so enjoyable either, but at least it wouldn't remind him of Pa's disdain toward him.

"How would you like to play me as soon as these gentlemen have finished their game?" Charles looked at Logan.

"Love to. Let me go rub Bootstrap down, and I'll be right out."

After Logan got Bootstrap all taken care of and settled for the evening, he hobbled toward the checker game with a stool in hand, dodging a sizeable pile of manure. He couldn't see his three friends, but a light breeze blew in the half-opened big set of doors as their voices carried into the stable as clearly as if he was out sitting with them.

"So do you think you might like to invest that three-hundred dollars you've got sitting there under your bed like you'd mentioned, collecting dust instead of interest?" Charles's voice held that same easy-to-listen-to tone it had each time he'd spoken with Logan.

"I don't know," Ned Clark said. "Let me talk it over with my Constance, and I'll let you know in a day or two."

"What's for yer wife to decide?" Gus's voice rose in pitch like the times he'd tell Logan to quit being so bull-headed. "It's a guaranteed return on your money, Ned."

Logan stepped outside of the stable, and all eyes turned to him.

"Ah, Logan." Gus motioned him over to the table with a sweep of his hand. "You don't need that old thing. Come take my chair. I gotta get some work done inside before I head home for the night. Gladys is gonna be furious enough with me as it is." He pointed his thumb at Charles. "But lands, when this boy gets you talkin', you just can't stop."

Charles held his hands out and up like he'd been caught. "Hey, I just happened by. These gentlemen coerced me into sitting down and watching them beat each other up with endless games of checkers."

Gus eased out of his chair and nudged Logan into it. "Unless you've got something better to do," he said to Logan.

"Not really," Logan said, "except go make myself some supper."

Ned rose from his stool. "I'd best get going too. Constance has probably been keeping my supper warm for so long now it'll be tough as an old shoe." He laughed and slapped Logan on the back. "Oh to be young and carefree, like you two fellows. Enjoy the fine evening now."

While Gus and Ned lumbered away from the checker table, Charles lifted a brown paper bag from the ground and set it to the side of the checkerboard as best he could. "I had Sunny's Place make me up a cold supper. I was just on the way to my hotel room when Ned and Gus invited me to sit and chat. Would you care to join me?" He pulled out something wrapped in a piece of butcher paper and unwrapped a huge roast beef sandwich with a slice right down the middle. "Don't worry. There's plenty. I had a big lunch."

Logan reached for a half but hesitated. "You already paid for my supper once. I should return the favor before taking advantage of your hospitality again." His stomach growled, and he rushed his hand to his belly to make it stop.

"Who's keeping track?" Charles picked up half the sandwich and pushed the other half and the paper it sat on toward Logan. "Besides, I've already paid for this. You're doing me a favor so it won't go to waste."

"Are you sure?" Logan eyed the sandwich, and his mouth watered.

"Positive." Charles took a bite of his half of the sandwich and laid the checkers out on the board. "Do you want to be red or black?"

"Don't matter to me. You choose."

"I'll take black," Charles said.

"All right. I'm red. I like red anyway. You go first," Logan said and took a bite of the sandwich. He chewed it a long time before he swallowed. The savory beef and the tangy sweet sauce tasted like heaven. When it made it down into his stomach, it was even more delightful. "Thanks again for the food. I haven't eaten since this morning, and I guess I was hungrier than I thought."

Charles moved the first checker out. "You really need to eat more often, my good fellow." He motioned for Logan to move a checker and then pointed at Logan's middle. "Your belly's as lean as a stray dog's. Where is it you said you were employed?"

"I never told you." Logan moved his front, far-right checker, the one he always led out with when he played—which wasn't often, as of late. Not only was Craig changing and there weren't as many checker games to be found on the street sides, but he also didn't seem to have the spare time he used to.

"You are right, Mr. Logan Jones." Charles moved another checker. "So tell me, where do you work? Whomever your employer is, I daresay it's time you ask him for a raise." He pointed to the tear in Logan's shirtsleeve that had been there going on three months now.

"One of them is Gus," Logan said.

Charles cringed. "No, don't do that to poor Gus. I know he can't afford to give you one. With the advent of the automobile, he's rather concerned he won't be able to make a go of things long enough for him to retire in ten years."

"My other job is delivering mail two times a week. I already knew the job didn't pay much when I took it. I didn't care at the time because I'd been delivering folks' mail since I was thirteen, and I figured I may as well get some extra pocket change for doing it. Plus, I enjoy it."

Charles moved one of his checkers that was already way out front. He then leaned slightly over the board and looked Logan in the eye. "You know what you need? To supplement your income."

"I ain't got enough time to hardly work the jobs I've got." Logan felt exhausted just thinking of adding one more thing to his routine—except for spending more time with Celeste, which would be nigh onto impossible if he took on another job.

"I'm not talking about working for another employer. Heavens, two is plenty. You could whittle that down to one, perhaps none, if I let you in on my little investment secret." He jumped one of Logan's red checkers, picked it off the board, and stuffed it into Logan's hand. "Let's pretend this is your investment. You give it to me." He motioned for Logan to hand him the checker. "I'll invest it for you in my boss's company, and in three months, I'll be able to give you not only your initial investment back," he stuffed the red checker back into Logan's hand, "but this much more." He snatched up two of his back-row black checkers and stuffed those into Logan's hand as well. "That's what they call a hundred-percent return on your money. What do you think about that?"

"I'd be thinking that'd be too good to be true." Logan shook his head, not feeling comfortable at all with Charles's proposal. "I haven't much, if any, experience in such matters, but I do pride myself in being levelheaded."

"Of course you're levelheaded. I could tell the first time I met you. That's why this is perfect for you. It makes so much sense." He placed his black checkers back on the board and moved one without giving it but a quick glance. "Would you like to hear how it works?"

Logan studied the board for a second or two, moved a checker, and then said, "All right, if you want, go ahead and tell me." He studied out his next move, which would be easy if Charles continued to be as absentminded as he appeared.

"Being a mailman like you are, I think you'll understand this better than anybody else here in town who is interested in investing in the Securities Exchange Company." Charles quickly moved a checker to the next square. "Mr. Charles Ponzi who founded the company, whom I work for and share his first name," he sported a proud grin, "has found a loophole in the international postal coupons issued by the US Postal Service. Are you familiar with postal reply coupons?"

"Somewhat," Logan said as he jumped his checker over three of Charles's. "Someone living here in the US who's got more money than, say, their granny back in the ole country across the ocean, and wants them to write them back when they send granny a letter, buys a postal coupon here and sends it in with their letter. Then when their granny gets the coupon, she uses it like money to buy stamps."

"That's better than I could describe it," Charles said.

"We haven't had a large call for them here in Craig. Will that affect any of the folks who have given you money to invest?"

"No, not at all." Charles moved a checker. "See, how it works is that Mr. Ponzi has someone in Europe purchase postal coupons over there at a cheaper price than what they sell for in the US. Then they send the coupons over here, and Mr. Ponzi cashes them in for stamps, which he sells and makes a profit on. All he needs is investors to help fund the purchase of the coupons, and in return, he is able to pay himself and people like me who he hires to help him out, and there is still plenty of profit to pass on to investors like your friend Gus. Or you, if you care to invest. My boss promises to double your money in ninety days." Charles held up his hands. "Hey, I wouldn't be telling you this or be trying to persuade you if I hadn't seen my own return with my own eyes. I gave Mr. Ponzi one hundred dollars I borrowed from my uncle, and sure enough, ninety days later, I had two hundred dollars in my pocket."

"That's all fine an' dandy," Logan said. "But I ain't got no money to invest."

"You said payday was on Monday. How about then?"

Logan thought of all the things he needed to buy now, not ninety days from now. He also couldn't explain it, but something didn't quite feel right about this, even though he could see how money could be made by taking advantage of that oversight in the international postal coupon program. "No, my mind won't change before then."

"Seriously, my good fellow?" Charles moved the whole checkerboard off to one side of the table and reached his hands out toward Logan with his palms up. "There is a limited number of investors Mr. Ponzi and I are taking into our confidence. You being one of them."

"Thank you kindly for considering me," Logan said. "But as I told you, I got nothing to invest."

"You could always borrow a hundred dollars like I did. In ninety days, you pay it back to whomever you borrowed it from, and you have a hundred dollars in your pocket. It's that easy. Don't tell me there's not something, or someone, you'd like to spend that money on."

"Well . . ." Logan's mind immediately went to that image of Celeste's beautiful face.

"Let me guess." Charles's smile lines really showed up this time. "It's some pretty young lady you've got your eye on, isn't it? And you don't quite have enough money to treat her like she deserves to be treated. Am I right?"

"Well . . ." Logan still didn't feel like he should do this. But he did nod his head.

"You know why I know this?" Charles's smile lines relaxed, and his face grew serious. "Because that's exactly what happened to me. There was this beautiful girl who stole my heart, and I believe I even captured a bit of hers. But I was poor as dirt. I had nothing to offer her. How could I ever ask her father for her hand in marriage if I couldn't even feed myself?" Charles rubbed his forehead as if it hurt. "Then I did something stupid. I let her go."

"I'm sorry." Logan ached for his new friend. He knew exactly how Charles must feel. Being tempted to let Celeste go the moment he left the McCurdy place this morning had left him feeling like he'd eaten bad meat. Thankfully, he'd wised up by the time he started delivering the mail.

"But I'm rich now, and I'm going to win her back." Charles slapped his hand on the table, causing checkers to fly this way and that. "You, my good fellow, should save yourself the pain I am going through. Make your money now, and treat your girl right before you lose her."

"Maybe you're right," Logan said, ignoring the uncomfortable feeling in his gut.

"That's the spirit. Shall we forgo the checker game?" He pointed to the scattered pieces and laughed. "I'll come find you on Monday, and we'll discuss this more. It's getting late, and tomorrow is Sunday."

"Yes, yes, I'd like to wait until then, at least. Give me time to sleep on it."

"But don't sleep on it too long, or you might lose your girl like I almost lost my dear Celeste."

It felt as though a saber had stabbed Logan's heart. He must have heard Charles wrong. He had to have. "Celeste, you say? That's the name of your girl you're wanting to win back?"

"Yes, Celeste McCurdy." Charles's face took on a dreamy look, similar to how Logan always felt when he thought of Celeste. "It's one of the main reasons I came to Craig. Do you know her? More importantly, if you do, could you take me to her house?"

Logan shook his head, more out of disbelief than as an answer. All along he'd imagined some faceless man named Dudley as the enemy. He didn't want to have "despised Dudley" feelings toward his friend Charles.

Chapter 19

SUNLIGHT PEEKED OVER THE EASTERN hills, sweeping away the gray light of dawn. Celeste moved the old hen to one side and gathered one last egg into her basket. "It's unfortunate for all of us that I began my task so early, girls," she spoke aloud to the half-dozen hens in the coop. Ever since she'd come home, these little chats with Ma's hens had been some of her favorite conversations. "Sorry, but I need to save the sunlight for the garden. It's not my fault your eggs are white and easier to see than weeds." As she stepped from the coop, she said over her shoulder, "And thank you kindly for breakfast. Ma will be tickled with all your hard work."

She took her time, surveying the landscape as she strolled toward the kitchen. The mid-July heat had taken its toll. The fields and hillsides had lost the vibrant green they showed off when she'd first arrived home a month ago. But the expansive blue sky, with its billowy white clouds, practically took her breath away with its grandeur. And the dull green fields dotted with the dirty-white woolen creatures that kept her family's ranch running held a beauty of its own. Or so she told herself.

The past few days, she'd gotten better at dwelling on the important things in her life like Reverend Francis and Logan had taught her. They both had been correct; such an outlook helped to lift her from her bouts of melancholy. Ironically, the reason for this latest bit of melancholy was Logan.

She carried the basket of eggs toward the house, knowing Ma was waiting for them to make breakfast. By the time she reached the big cottonwood tree, she noticed a bit of dust following in the wake of what appeared to be a buggy headed down their lane. She walked toward the house, curious as to who came this way so early in the morning. Could it possibly be Logan? If so, was he coming to ask her, personally, to court him? Her heart danced at the thought.

Then she quickly dismissed the idea. Logan would be on Bootstrap, not in a buggy. Whoever it was, she'd let Ma or Pa greet them. She'd prefer to scramble the eggs.

"Someone's coming," she said to Ma the moment she stepped into the house. "In a buggy. At least, it appears so. Would you like me to cook these eggs so you can meet our guest properly?"

Ma wiped her hands on her apron. "Yes, dear, I would appreciate that." She glanced out the window. "Whoever could it be? Oh my, the place is a mess. Where is your pa?"

"I believe he is out in the barn with the boys."

"Please, leave the eggs be and go get him for me." Ma continued to gaze out the window as she straightened the dishes in the sink. "It appears we have a gentleman calling on us, and he doesn't look the least bit familiar to me."

Celeste ran out the back door and toward the barn.

"Pa!" she hollered the moment she stepped inside.

"Yes?" Pa's voice drifted down from the loft, where he and the boys were pitching hay to store for the winter. "Is breakfast ready?"

"No, Ma needs you. A strange man is driving a buggy down the lane, and she doesn't care to greet him all alone."

"Coming." Pa climbed down the ladder, meeting Celeste at the bottom. He glanced over his shoulder at the loft as he walked briskly alongside Celeste. "You boys keep working 'til Ma calls you to breakfast."

"Yes, Pa."

Celeste darted outside with Pa.

The buggy pulling into the front yard carried a man dressed in a dark suit. He also wore a white skimmer hat with a blue band around its crown. It reminded her of the fashion back in New York and stirred up a plethora of painful memories. Pa didn't bother stepping into the house first but walked around the side. Celeste figured he wanted to meet up with their guest before he made it to the front door.

"Good morning." Pa's voice carried around the side of the house. He'd offered the greeting like he would to someone he knew. Celeste appreciated her pa for giving Ma a few extra minutes to tidy up the house before their guest would come inside, if Pa saw fit to invite him in. Celeste slipped behind the lilac bush at the front corner of the house, curious as to who this man was. She peeked through the branches of the bush and gasped. *Charles Weathersby.*

She turned around and darted to the back door, smoothing down her hair as she ran, unsure if she was excited, nervous, or upset at the idea that Charles was actually here.

"He is most likely here to chat with Pa some more about investing his money," she muttered to herself before opening the back door. *Yes, that is it. He would have come when he'd first arrived in town if he'd intended to visit me.*

Inside the kitchen, Celeste returned to her task of cooking the eggs, wanting to be busy if, by chance, Pa brought Charles into the house. A flutter of sorts unsettled her stomach. Just hunger. He didn't deserve for it to be anything else. The hurt had healed, and she cared not to reopen that wound. He'd slipped out of her life without a word. She certainly wasn't keen on the idea of him slipping back into her life as silently as he had left.

She cracked ten eggs into a mixing bowl, added a bit of cream, then some salt and a dash of pepper. Ready to start whisking them into a froth, she wondered if she should add two more eggs. For Charles. She picked up an egg in each hand, ready to crack them into the bowl. A wave of heartache swept through her chest. Then anger. The urge to throw the eggs at him instead burned strong. She restrained herself and cracked the shells with her hands, letting the contents drop into the bowl. She would be neighborly. Just because he had sent her into a three-month melancholy when he'd vanished didn't mean she should treat him poorly. He'd never treated her poorly, even when she'd been in one of her "moods." Unless she wanted to count his vanishing without a word as poor treatment. *I don't want to count that.* Logan would never hold such a grudge, and she was trying to follow his example. She hoped this would help her find the secret to his continually cheery temperament. She whisked the two eggs in with the others, figuring if perchance Charles didn't stay for a bite of breakfast, Rob would gladly gobble up the extra portion.

"Ma, where's the bacon fat so I can get started on these eggs? It's not where it's supposed to be." Celeste moved the box of salt on the shelf by the stove to see if it was hiding.

"Sorry, dear, I used it all in the potatoes last night. You'll have to cook up some more."

"That could take some time," she said, wanting these eggs to be done as quickly as possible. "Might I use butter instead?"

"Yes, I guess that would be fine." Ma motioned for Celeste to step to the side while she opened the oven and pulled out the pan of biscuits she'd made earlier.

Celeste placed the largest cast-iron skillet onto the hot stovetop and dropped in a spoonful of butter. As she stood there, waiting for the butter to sizzle, she wondered why she was so anxious to get these eggs done. Was she not wanting Charles to have his biscuits grow cold while he waited on her eggs to be done? Or head out before he had a chance to eat? Both notions were ridiculous. She poured the eggs into the hot skillet, spilling a good portion on her hand, and stirred them into the best batch of scrambled eggs her brothers could care to have. Then she wiped her hand on Ma's faded old work skirt she had on, not caring one whit what she looked like if and when Charles walked in that door, because she didn't care about Charles any longer. "I don't," she whispered, convincing herself.

The eggs cooked up nicely. She stepped over to the window and hollered toward the barn. "Rob, Patrick, breakfast is ready." After giving the eggs one last stir, she grabbed an extra potholder to place under the skillet, removed the skillet from the stove, and placed it on the table next to the plate of biscuits. No sooner had she done this than the back door flew open and the boys ran in.

Then the front door opened as the boys and Celeste settled in around the table.

Pa walked in. "Kate, I hope 'tis not a bother, but I've invited a friend to breakfast." He stepped to one side and motioned for Charles to enter. "This is Charles Weathersby."

A friend? Celeste fumed. It appeared Charles hadn't lost his uncanny knack to make friends with everyone. She wasn't so sure she was comfortable with him making friends with Pa. At least not so quickly.

Charles removed his hat and held it to his chest. "Good morning, ma'am." He nodded at Ma. "Boys." He nodded to them. "And good morning, Celeste." He nodded at her, but his eyes remained fixed on her face while that charming smile of his did crazy things to her heart. "It is so nice to see you again. You'll never know how often I have dreamed of this moment. It is even more delightful than I'd imagined."

Ma jerked her head toward Celeste. "You two know each other?"

"We were acquaintances from my time at the Bennett School."

"Oh, I daresay I had hoped you would remember me as more than a mere acquaintance," Charles said to Celeste. He turned to Ma and Pa, who now stood together at the head of the table. "You see, we had courted for a brief time while Celeste was at school. Personal matters took me away from New York, and I took my leave without a word to your daughter." He turned to Celeste. "For that, I apologize profusely and beg your forgiveness." He returned his attention to Ma and Pa. "I wish to start up where I left off and thereby seek your permission to officially pursue your daughter's attention once again, if I may."

Ma shrugged her shoulders. "Celeste is her own person. Even if I grant you my permission, ultimately it is she who must make that decision."

Charles looked at Pa with that smile of his. "And you, Lucas, what do you say?"

Pa breathed deep and glanced at Ma. "I share my wife's sentiments."

"I thank you both for your graciousness." He turned to Celeste. "And now to the person whose answer I esteem yet distress over most of all. May I have your permission to resume courting you?"

"Uh . . ." Celeste wanted to chastise him for trying to ignore all that had happened with such a simple apology. Why wouldn't the words come? Her mouth felt as if it was full of cotton. For months, she'd consigned herself to the idea that she would never see Charles again, and *if* for some reason she did, the only thing she'd feel toward him was animosity. Yet here he stood a few feet from her, smartly dressed in a nice suit and wearing that infectious smile, evoking a flurry of excitement inside her.

She quickly squashed the excitement like she would a snail that had invaded her garden. He'd been in town for at least two days—that she knew of. Why had he waited until now to call on her?

"I realize this must be a bit of a surprise, dropping in unannounced," Charles said while crimping the brim of his hat with both hands. His fingers' tight grip appeared to be releasing some inner angst. "I would have written first, but I didn't have your address. All I knew was that you came from Colorado and your parents lived outside a town named Craig."

"That's all the address you would have needed," Celeste said, wishing he would have written first. That would have prepared her better for the confused feelings churning inside her. "Celeste McCurdy, Craig, Colorado. It would have made it to me. Our mail carrier knows everyone and where they live." Logan's face took form in her thoughts and served to stir her jumbled feelings further.

"Again, I apologize," Charles said. "I had no idea such a vaguely addressed letter would have made it here. That is why I came in person." His eyebrows raised slightly, and he peered directly into her eyes. "Dear Celeste."

"Oh." Celeste fought off the feelings unsteadying her heart at hearing that special tone again. Like before, she delighted in the musical sound of his voice as he declared her as his "Dear Celeste." She chided herself. She should be angry at him, not endeared by him.

"I did not want to take the chance that my letter would not be delivered. You see, I am a changed man. I have made something of my life. I am financially secure. I will never again have the need to run off and leave you without a word." He walked to her, lowered himself down onto one knee, and took her hand in his. "Give me another chance, dear Celeste. Please allow me to resume courting you."

"Uh . . . if only it were that simple," Celeste responded, scrambling to sort out her feelings for Charles—and Logan.

Charles's eyebrows drooped. "Has someone else asked permission to court you?"

Celeste heaved a sigh. "That is none of your business."

"Well, I say, if a fellow does not have the gumption to speak up and voice his intentions when the most beautiful, wonderful woman in the world is within his grasp," Charles smiled and winked, "then he doesn't deserve you, and you deserve better."

"Oh," Celeste uttered quietly, her feelings for Logan and Charles entangled and muddled. Unfortunately, his words made more sense than she wanted them to.

"But of course, that is for you to say, not me." Charles rose to his feet. He placed his palms together in front of his chest, almost like he was praying. "For today, how would you feel if I simply escorted you to church? I know how much you enjoy going." He motioned out the window with a sweep of his hand to the buggy he had arrived in. "That was my original intention when I came out here so bright and early on this fine Sunday morning. I guess I kind of got a little carried away with my words when I saw you, dear Celeste. Please, give me another chance."

"Church?" Celeste had to admit church could be a safe setting to spend some time with him. "It has been some time since I last attended, and I do miss it so." Though she did often sit on the back row and rush out the moment the service was over. She always had been the odd one, her roommates had said, going to church to worship, not to socialize. "But is there time?"

"If we leave in the next half an hour, we shall be fine," Charles said, pulling out his pocket watch. "I checked with the reverend. Worship service begins at eleven. It took me an hour and fifteen minutes to come here. It is half past eight as we speak."

Ma grabbed a plate and fork from the cupboard and placed them on the table across from the boys, who were starting to fidget. "Come then, everyone, let's eat breakfast so we have time to clean up before we leave." She glanced at Charles. "Do join us. There is plenty."

"Don't mind if I do." Charles walked around the table and sat down next to Celeste.

Pa looked across the table to Ma. "Dear, will you offer the blessing?"

Ma nodded and prayed.

After the murmur of amens, Celeste turned to Ma, touching her lightly on the arm. "What did you mean by 'We have time to clean up before we leave?'"

"I am coming with you," Ma said.

Celeste straightened her back, not liking the idea of Ma butting into her private affairs.

Ma glanced at Charles. "If that is amenable?"

"But of course," Charles responded in his usual cheerful manner.

Celeste wondered if he really meant it. Was he merely trying to win over her parents? She had never been in this kind of situation with him, so she couldn't rightly say. Maybe it wasn't such a bad idea after all if her ma came. Celeste seemed to be acclimating to the coarser ways of the West quicker than she'd expected. Perhaps it would be good to dust off some of Miss Bennett's lessons, utilize some proper etiquette at this moment, and be grateful Ma, rather than her old teacher, was her chaperone.

"Is there enough room in your buggy?" she asked.

"There's room for three." Charles smiled and looked across the table as he accepted the plate of biscuits when Celeste passed it to him. "But sorry, boys, there's no back seat. I guess that means you won't be able to come this week."

Rob and Patrick poked each other and laughed.

"It's fine," Rob said, still laughing. "I'll manage to get over my grief."

Pa stared at Rob. "T'would only need be for a week. I think next Sunday we'll get our chores done early and take the wagon into town. And all of us McCurdys will be attending church." He turned to Charles. "That way, you won't be needing to come all the way out here to fetch Celeste if she wants to go to church. And once she gets there, she don't have to sit by us. She can decide whom she sits by: her family, you, or whomever else tickles her fancy." He glanced at Celeste with a concerned look.

She guessed Pa was referring to Logan. But Pa didn't know that Logan was just as busy as Pa was, and he, too, rarely made it to church. She'd hoped to find a churchgoing man for a husband. Faith in God was one of many qualities she hoped for. Charles had many qualities she liked. The most important of all was that she felt at ease with him; she could be herself with him. Of course, Logan had that same quality.

But Logan hadn't asked her to court him. True, he had asked Pa but then hightailed it away from their ranch without a word to her—like he'd changed his mind. That happened all too often. It seemed every time they took a step forward and shared a tender moment, and she swore he desired her company in the same fashion she desired his, he took two steps backward the next day. As much as it pained her to realize it, she couldn't afford to put all her eggs in a basket that might be full of holes.

If Charles was sincere and Logan was hesitant, it wouldn't hurt to entertain the idea of courting Charles again. If for no other reason than to help her figure out where her heart lay.

Chapter 20

Logan stepped out of Porter's Bathhouse rubbing his clean-shaven chin and thinking how three baths in one week must beat some sort of record set by straggly bachelor cowboys of the area. At least it was a record for him. Same with shaving. Once a week was his norm. But that was all going to change. *Treat your girl right before you lose her.* Charles's words sliced through Logan's thoughts like a sharp scythe. Excellent advice. The most painful edge of the blade came from the fact that he might very well lose Celeste to Charles.

"But not if I can help it!" He patted Bootstrap in the way of greeting and untied him from the hitching post outside the bathhouse. "Sorry to make you wait outside in the sun," he continued as he mounted up, "but I needed to be going the second I finished cleaning up. And I didn't want to take the chance of getting smelly by fetching you from the livery stable. So there."

Bootstrap whinnied his understanding.

Logan settled into his saddle and headed south on Yampa Avenue, figuring he could make it to the McCurdy place by noon if he hurried. He stopped by Sunny's Place and picked up a picnic lunch he'd asked Sunny to put together. Thankfully she agreed that he could pay her tomorrow after he got paid. Boy, he sure had a passel of things that paycheck from Gus needed to take care of. But he'd calculated things out, and there'd be enough of it to go around. Barely.

With the picnic lunch of a couple of Sunny's famous roast beef sandwiches and four pickles wrapped in butcher paper and stuffed into his saddlebags, Logan took off. He pulled out his pocket watch, the only thing he owned that had come from his pa. Quarter to eleven. Yep, he had plenty of time to make it to the McCurdys' without having to work Bootstrap, or himself, into a sweat. Once there, he would boldly assure Lucas he would be able to take care of his daughter, obtain his and Kate's blessing, and then invite Celeste on a picnic down by the river bottoms on her pa's land. It was pretty, just like she was. He smiled with anticipation. Then he would talk to her all nice and enjoy her friendly chatter. She would then tell him how much she needed him because he made her feel at ease. Then he would feel confident at that point to finally spit out the words he'd meant to ask her long before now: "Celeste, may I officially court you?"

Then her eyes would brighten and give off that beautiful shade of green like they did when she got excited, and she would say, "Of course you have my permission, Logan Jones. I have just been anxiously awaiting for you to ask me because, after all, you are the perfect man for me, and I wish to marry you someday soon."

His thoughts flowed from his brain and settled in his heart with such a contentment that he wondered why on earth he'd not done this sooner. He found himself tipping his hat at every man, woman, child, and dog he passed on his way to the edge of town.

Just before he reached the intersection of Yampa Avenue and the road to Hayden—Victory Road as it had been officially named a few years ago—he noticed a buggy carrying three passengers approach from the east. As it neared, their faces took form, and his heart felt ripped from his chest. He rode closer. His heart felt ready to fall to the ground with a thud, and he scrambled for ideas as to what to do next. He hardly dared to pass by them, for it would be obvious he was all dressed up and headed out of town. Certainly they would see him and ask where he was headed. If he were to say, "Visiting someone in Hayden," Celeste would think he had another girl tucked away over there, and she would never give him a fighting chance to court her. But if he were to tell her the truth, then Charles and even Celeste might say, "Why didn't you come out to the McCurdy place sooner?"

He glanced down to the end of Yampa Avenue to the little white church and then at his cleaned-up self. "Well, Bootstrap, now's about as good a time as any to become a churchgoing man. Lord knows He's been waiting long enough to see me there again. I may as well make someone happy today." He kept going straight, expecting to see Charles's buggy turn right, head into town, and remove the painful image of Celeste sitting hip to hip with Charles in that buggy. He made a quick glance at them to make sure that's where they were headed. For the first time, he noticed Kate. Why was she there with them? A chaperone? Was that something he should have thought of those times he'd spent alone with Celeste? Had he been doing things all wrong? It was not like he was experienced in the matters of courting. He'd had neither a ma nor a pa from which to learn.

His heart about flew from his chest again when he realized that Charles steered the buggy into a left turn. They were heading for the church too. Logan frantically looked for a logical, legitimate place he could ride to at this point other than the church, other than the same place Charles and Celeste were headed, where they'd obviously share a pew and the next hour together, and who knew what other plans Charles had for the remainder of the day. The only possible place Logan could ride to at this point, other than the church, was down the lane that led to old Matthew Cromwell's pig farm, a rather disagreeable spot to visit for Logan, even in his worn-out trousers and sweat-stained shirt he usually wore to deliver mail—the only reason he ever visited the bad-tempered old man.

He kept Bootstrap pointed toward the church and then tried to act surprised when Charles pulled the buggy alongside him.

"Ah, Logan, my good fellow," Charles spoke up, his side of the buggy being closest to Logan and Bootstrap. "On your way to church too, I presume?"

"It would appear that way," Logan said dryly. Never before had he had such difficulty in engaging in conversation.

"Do you two know each other?" Celeste's voice rose slightly above its usual pitch.

Logan couldn't bring himself to look at her face, so he wasn't exactly sure what her higher voice was meant to communicate. Was it possible he had just been a distraction for Celeste until she could be with Charles again? The thought felt like a knife to his heart. "We've met a couple times," Logan stated.

"Logan, so good to see you out and about this fine Sunday morning," Kate spoke up. "Would you like to sit with us? The pews seem to be built for four."

Logan braved a look at Kate. "Good to see you too." He avoided the other question and sneaked a peek at Celeste. That was a mistake. She looked beautiful as ever. Her eyes even held a spark or two.

"Good morning, Logan," she said in the sweet voice he was used to.

Logan's throat felt extra dry. He managed a "Good morning, Celeste."

"Wait a minute here," Charles said and slowed the buggy to a near crawl. "I was just about to tell my new friend, Logan here, my good news." He spread his arm wide, indicating Logan. "That this was the girl," he motioned to Celeste, "I had been telling you about, the one I let slip through my fingers and was determined to find and make things right. But now it appears that you two know each other." Charles's brow furrowed, and he studied Logan for a moment. "Why did you keep quiet when I asked if you knew of her and where she lived?

Logan gathered his courage and pushed down the feelings of awkwardness that threatened to smother him. "Because," he took a deep breath, "Celeste was the girl I had hinted about, the one I also cared to not let slip from my fingers."

Charles straightened his back. "Well, this is quite the awkward predicament now, isn't it, my good fellow? Whatever should we do?"

Celeste cleared her throat. "Ah-hem. You two seem to forget that there is someone else to be considered in what you, Charles, have deemed as a predicament. Have you not thought about how it tears at my emotions to have two men I care about, who are friends with each other no less, look at each other with disdain in their eyes?"

"Oh, yes, dear Celeste, I am so sorry. But of course, you are the most affected of all here."

"Quite agreed," Logan said, finding a slight bit of solace from her mention that she still cared for him and had not automatically declared Charles her choice. Even though she sat very close to him. "I'm sorry, Celeste. The truth is that I was on my way out to your place to ask you if I could court you proper-like." Logan stared at Bootstrap's neck. He then looked at Kate. "If you and Lucas'd allow me, I'd like to call on Celeste next Sunday." He focused on Celeste, determined not to back down. "If they are okay with me courting you too, I would love a chance to take you to church next week. You too, Kate." He shot her a glance. "I can be out to your place as early as you'd like." He gazed at Celeste, awaiting her answer.

Kate answered first. "I'm answering for Lucas here too, and I know he wouldn't object. Yes, Logan, you have our permission to court Celeste. But as I told Mr. Weathersby, it is ultimately Celeste's decision whom she wishes to court."

All eyes turned to Celeste, and she squirmed in her limited space on the buggy's seat.

"I suppose that would only be fair." She looked at Charles. "I'll go to church with you today." Then she looked at Logan. "And with you next week." She folded her hands neatly in her lap and stared at the chapel, which now stood before them. She seemed to be the only one who'd realized they had arrived at their destination.

Logan had barely noticed, but only because Bootstrap had stopped on his own, as did Charles's horse, Brownie. Logan should have known Charles would have rented his horse and buggy from Gus. He would have noticed sooner if he'd been working this morning. But even if he had, what would he have done? Put burrs under Brownie's harness? He'd never do that to a horse. Nor to a friend. He'd thought of Charles as a friend—before he'd found out they liked the same gal.

Why should that change their friendship? It really was the best thing for everyone if Celeste was the one to do the deciding.

Logan dismounted and handed Bootstrap's reins to the church hostler. "You still okay with me sitting in the same pew with you folks?"

"I certainly am," Kate said.

Celeste's face held a look of uncertainty.

"I'm okay with it," Charles said, "as long as you sit on the other side of Mrs. McCurdy and she's between you and Celeste."

Celeste's expression relaxed. "I suppose that would be fine. And then next week, that is where you will sit, Charles. And Logan will be sitting next to me." She motioned for the four of them to walk toward the open church doors. "Yes, I do believe the best way to deal with this dilemma is for me to take turns courting each of you."

"All right, if that's what you want." Charles pointed to Logan. "But I'm sorry, as much as I like this fellow, I don't care to have him accompany us on every outing I take you on." He smirked. "I don't like him that much."

"Well said," Logan agreed and smirked back.

"No, it won't be like that at all," Celeste said. "I would find that very uncomfortable and ineffective as well." She now reached for Charles's hand, which he eagerly gave, and she patted it. "Starting today, I will spend the next . . . ah, two weeks with Charles. Yes, I believe spending two weeks in a row would be more conducive than one in getting to know each of you. During that time, Charles will be free to court me in a manner he sees fit." She motioned to Logan. "The following two weeks, starting with you bringing me to church, I will spend with you, Logan, allowing you to court me as you see fit." She motioned for everyone to resume walking.

Kate clamped a hand to her hip and let out a sigh. "I hope you can make your decision quickly, for I fear I shall become dizzy at trying to remember whose week is whose, and who is coming for supper and who is not on any given day."

"I agree, Mother. Hopefully, one month's time should be sufficient to make my decision." Celeste gazed sweetly into Logan's eyes and then Charles's. "For I would hate to drag either of you fine gentlemen down a disappointing road for too long. It wouldn't be fair. But if I need more time than one month, the pattern shall continue. So if either of you want to back out of this . . ." she cleared her throat, ". . . unconventional idea of mine, I would certainly understand."

At the bottom of the steps, Charles crooked his elbow for Celeste to take hold of. "I am not backing out. And since it is my week, Celeste, allow me to escort you to church."

"I'm not backing out either." Logan hobbled up the steps behind Celeste and Charles, unsure if the annoyance he felt bubbling inside him was because of Charles or Celeste.

Kate was by Logan's side and leaned in close so only he could hear. "Good for you, and you've got my vote."

Kate's encouragement gave him the boost he needed to keep climbing the stairs—and the challenges that obviously lay ahead, especially as he made out bits and pieces of Charles and Celeste's conversation.

"Don't forget, right after church I've got reservations for dinner at Sunny's Place. Best seat in the house, and the sky's the limit on what we order."

"Oh, Charles, you shouldn't have," Celeste said as he escorted her inside.

Logan stopped just outside the chapel doors. He couldn't go on. He couldn't bear sitting in the same pew as them, even if he had been invited. It would be too painful, and he didn't care to listen in on any more of Charles's extravagances.

"Kate," he said to her over the chatter of the gathering congregation.

She appeared to be following Celeste, but she took a step back and moved to his side. "What's wrong, Logan?"

What's wrong? This whole day—month—is wrong! "Ain't it kind of obvious?"

"Yes, it is." Kate placed her hand on his arm. "I'm so sorry about Celeste. That girl has a mind of her own—a mind, unfortunately, that struggles so with finding her place in this grand scheme called life. Please be patient with her. She just has to work things out her way; then she'll see where her heart lies and who is really the right man for her. I'm sure of it."

"Still, I think I'm going to sit in the back by myself, if you don't mind." Logan wondered if Kate's omission of his name connected with the "right man" was unintentional or not.

"I understand entirely." Kate gave his arm a squeeze. "Don't worry, Logan. When she's with you, she'll realize what she was missing with Mr. Weathersby and see for herself you are the best choice. And I promise I won't be a bothersome chaperone. I might not even feel the need to go to church that week." She winked at Logan and made her way to Celeste and Charles, pulling her daughter aside and speaking into her ear.

Logan slipped into an empty spot on the back row by the door and tried to get comfortable. His leg ached from trying so hard not to limp around Charles. His head ached too. He didn't feel like joining in with the opening hymn. And when Reverend Brown began his sermon, he chewed on Kate's words instead of the reverend's. Logan was sure Kate had only meant to be encouraging. But the thought of Charles spending the entire next two weeks with Celeste, with all that spare time and money of his and fancy, eastern manners and knowledge about courting a woman properly, Logan felt as though he'd fallen into the deepest, darkest well ever dug. There was little chance of him climbing out of this hole smelling like a field of clover.

One thing was sure: he was glad he'd applied for that postmaster job when he did. Rosie had said he'd know by Tuesday if he got the job. That would certainly help his chances with Celeste. At least that was one thing to look forward to this week. For now, he was going to eat himself two sandwiches as soon as church was over and not think about the money they cost and how it could have been used better elsewhere.

Chapter 21

"I REALIZE THIS IS A rather unconventional way for me to court a man," Celeste whispered when Ma grabbed her by the elbow and pulled her away from Charles on their way down the chapel's aisle. "But I have to admit it might be what I need."

"You are a 'wee bit unconventional,' as your father always says," Kate said with a roll of her eyes.

"Mother, listen to me," Celeste continued to whisper. "I realize now that I care for both Charles and Logan. But there are also things about each of them that I'm not so fond of."

"Too bad you couldn't combine the best of both men and make one." Kate smiled ever so slightly. "Then you'd have someone like your pa."

"Ah, Mother." Celeste batted her hand at her ma. "Things are not that simple. Especially for me. But perhaps this mix-up is my good fortune. To court two men at once is a chance most girls would never have."

"Or want." Kate shook her head

"No, Mother, I do want this. And I think it is a grand idea, so I'm going through with it. You know how I struggle with decisions. It will be simple, just like Miss Bennett taught me in that household organizational skills class. When an important decision needs to be made and you're having fits trying to decide between two good choices, you simply line them up side by side and compare them tit for tat."

"For everyone's sake, I hope you aren't making a mistake."

"Me too," Celeste said under her breath. Then, moments later, she and Charles filed into the pew after her ma.

A few minutes into the sermon, Celeste fidgeted in her seat. Of all the subjects the reverend had to choose from, of all days, why did he have to give a sermon on kindness? What she was putting both Logan and Charles through was not very kind at all. Obviously, one of them would have to walk away from this ill-thought-out idea of hers hurt and rejected. A little while ago, it had sounded like a great way to navigate through her indecision. But now it sounded rather cruel. Frankly, she hadn't really expected both Logan and Charles to go along with it, and maybe that's why she'd suggested it. Surely one or both of them would have told her the idea was absurd or showed they weren't as serious as the other. Now she was stuck. She'd told Charles she was his to court this week and next, and she'd stick to her word.

She wanted to look over her shoulder and sneak a peek at Logan to see if his whole face still drooped in a frown. He'd looked so handsome all freshly shaven, cleaned up, and his clean hair curling at the nape of his neck when she and Charles met up with him on the way here. Frowns didn't become him. She'd rarely seen them on his face before. Pushing good manners aside, she gave in and glanced back, hoping Logan's frown had faded.

Her unperceivable gasp paled to the sinking of her heart. He was gone, that spot on the pew empty. Her eyes pulled back to the pulpit, skimming past the windows on their way. Sunshine and glimpses of the green grass from outside caught her attention first. Then she caught sight of Logan preparing to mount his horse. He pulled something out of his saddlebag. It appeared to be some kind of food. She recognized the butcher paper Sunny wrapped sandwiches in. There were two bundles. He crammed them both back into the saddlebag with force.

Celeste's throat tightened. *Those were meant for a picnic. He was heading out to take me on one.* And now she was sitting in church next to Charles, who kept moving his hand closer and closer to her on the pew. She knew he wanted her to hold it.

Not yet, Charles. Not today.

She could tell by the way Logan mounted his horse, like he was an old man carrying a heavy burden, that he was not feeling like his usual self. *What have I done?*

Nothing. You have done nothing wrong. You need to find out where your heart lies.

She did. She really did need to know if Logan was truly the right man for her. She needed to know that he wasn't just her over-active imagination conjuring up her perfect mate, and then convincing herself that Logan was that person. If she hadn't been doubting her decision to pursue Logan, fearing his feelings didn't match hers, then maybe she wouldn't have been in such a vulnerable spot when Charles showed up this morning. But she had been. And even though she'd been flustered during breakfast, Charles had been as friendly as ever. He reminded her of their delightful times together.

Maybe it was best to sit back and let these two men convince her, by their own merits, who would make the best husband for her.

"Amen," she verbalized her own support of her latest idea.

Both Charles and Ma turned and stared at her. She felt her face flush with warmth, realizing she'd uttered louder than she should have and at a time when it was not called for at all. She quickly shrugged and set her sights on the reverend, figuring she'd better listen.

U

It was almost three o'clock in the afternoon by the time Celeste and her ma left Sunny's restaurant and walked to the livery stable where the horse and buggy Charles had rented awaited them.

"I hope you ladies have had enough to eat." Charles helped Celeste climb aboard so they could head back to the ranch.

"If I ate any more, I'm afraid I would burst," Ma said as Charles assisted her into the buggy. "And you needn't have paid for my meal. It is Celeste you are courting, not me."

Charles laughed. "Ah, Mrs. McCurdy, you have quite the wit."

"I must agree with Mother." Celeste held her stomach. Her tongue also. Ma's statement had not expressed wit; it merely stated truth. She felt like Charles had been trying to get on Ma's good side back there at Sunny's Place as much as he'd tried to put his best foot forward for her. All in all, he was trying *too* hard, if anyone were to ask her. "You have fed me too well," she added.

She wanted neither her remaining family, nor the townspeople of Craig, to know about her fickle-sounding plan to choose a husband. People would certainly deem her years of finishing school a total failure. If she, Ma, and Charles were to remain closed-mouthed about this, then chances were no one would pay notice that she happened to be riding with one fellow this week and a different one the next. The people of Craig hardly knew her anyway.

But Logan knew everybody. Would he keep quiet?

Her full stomach churned uncomfortably.

"Are you sure I can't convince you two women to remain in town a tad longer? What kinds of entertainment does this town have to offer?"

It was Ma's turn to laugh. "Having lived on the East Coast my whole life, until fifteen years ago, I can confidently tell you that Craig offers nothing in the way of entertainment on Sunday, except for the two activities we have just completed."

"Unless you want to consider a game of poker at the Buckthorn Saloon," Celeste said dryly.

Ma glared at her. "I hardly think so!"

"Ma, I was teasing."

Ma raised an eyebrow. "Since when have you been the teasing type?"

"Are you serious, Mrs. McCurdy?" Charles said. "The Celeste I know is quite the ingenious tease."

"Only because you tease me first. It's merely a reaction to your inimitable sense of humor." Celeste had to admit that she did like how Charles always seemed to bring out the lighter side of her personality. Logan didn't do that, but he did bring out a calmness in her that she valued immensely. She glanced at Charles, practically feeling his smile warm the side of her face. "And you need not smile at me such. You know how it makes me laugh so unladylike. And with my mother here, well . . ."

"I am sure she loves a good, hearty belly laugh now and again." Charles glanced at Ma as he climbed into the buggy and grabbed the reins.

"Though I do like to laugh, I do not care to engage in laughter with all this food in my stomach." Ma motioned to the reins in his hands. "It is time to take us home. I know I am ready."

"Is that what you wish?" He looked at Celeste.

"Yes, I am ready for you to take me home as well." Celeste gave his hand the slightest squeeze. Despite her moments of misgiving, she had enjoyed her time with Charles. She definitely needed this full two weeks to sort out her feelings toward him. "Thank you for bringing me to church and for the lovely meal."

Charles flicked the reins, and the buggy shot forward. "You are most welcome."

It proved to be a delightful afternoon for a covered-buggy ride. A breeze blew in from the west, along with a few clouds, cooling the July air to where it felt comfortable. Celeste didn't bother donning her bonnet, as she loved the feeling of air blowing across her neck that the confining nature of a hat didn't allow for.

Charles talked of his job and how many investors he'd signed up already in Craig. Ma told of the last baby she delivered. And Celeste just listened, enjoying the company of two people she felt at ease with. She would wait to talk with Charles about personal matters, like why he'd not sought her out when he'd first arrived in Craig. Or, more importantly, his goals and desire for a family, matters that needed to be brought into the light so she could make an intelligent decision on who was the best man for her to marry. Ma being there made that too uncomfortable.

A drop or two of rain now and again tapped against the roof of the buggy by the time they reached the turnoff to the ranch. It developed into a healthy pitter-patter when they pulled into the front yard.

"Such wonderful timing, Mr. Weathersby." Ma didn't wait for Charles to come around to help her down but hopped out by herself. She looked at the rainclouds and headed for the house. "I daresay you'd better hurry back into town before the roads get too muddy," she said over her shoulder.

Charles was around the buggy and helping Celeste down as Ma ran into the house. "Thank you again, Celeste." He lingered there next to her like he didn't want to leave or move to give her passage to the front door.

"You are welcome, Charles. I enjoyed my day with you." Celeste leaned to one side and gazed at the front door Ma had left open. "I'd invite you in," she offered a teasing smile, "but Ma is right. If this sprinkle works into a summer rainstorm, you'd best be on your way as soon as possible. It was a good thing we left for home when we did."

Charles gazed into the sky. "It doesn't look all that bad."

"Charles, these roads aren't kept up like the ones back in Millbrook. And there're no neighbors for miles if by chance you got stuck. It would be especially bad if you stayed for a while and got stuck in the rain in the dark. Trust me. Go home. Now."

"When will I see you again?" he asked.

"That is up to you," she said, managing a wincing smile. "You are courting *me* this week and next, remember. You are in charge of any itinerary. I will simply say yes or no to what you have planned."

"May I pay you a visit tomorrow morning?" he asked.

"For how long?" she responded.

"All day?" He smiled that charming smile.

"As much as that smile of yours tempts me to take you up on that idea, I have chores I need to tend to. And to spend the remainder of the day together . . ." For some reason that sounded exhausting to Celeste. "Well, let's work into that. Perhaps by the end of the week, we could spend an entire day together. For now, let's keep our outings brief."

Charles mouth flattened into a straight line. "If that is what you wish."

Celeste thought his expression looked a bit like that of a spoiled child. "Haven't you heard the saying 'absence makes the heart grow fonder'?"

"No, I haven't." His smile returned to one side of his face. "And I know why; I don't care much for that saying, so I probably never listened." He tipped his hat and moved out of her way. "Nonetheless, I shall be going."

"Goodbye, Charles." She stepped around him.

He leaned into her way. "May I call here around nine? Do not fret; I will take my leave by early afternoon."

"Yes, that would be fine." She did look forward to seeing him, and that length of time sounded perfect.

He moved out of her way but not without first grabbing hold of her hand. He raised it to his mouth and kissed it. "Until tomorrow, dear Celeste."

"Yes. Until tomorrow." She pulled her hand away, clasped it together with her other one, and glanced at the sky. "I can see myself to the door. In fact, I shall run. Goodbye," she said as she hurried to the door to avoid the increasing number of raindrops.

Later that evening, while Celeste helped her ma with the supper dishes, she noticed they were alone in the house. Pa and the boys were outside seeing to the animals before night set in. "Ma, may I ask a favor?" she spoke over the clank of the pots in the dish water, wanting to take advantage this private moment.

"Certainly, dear."

"Charles is coming by in the morning for another visit. I would prefer it if I could spend our brief time tomorrow without a chaperone. Could that be possible?"

"That depends."

"Please, Ma. I feel bad that I'm stringing these two good men along like I'm doing, but I have to know I'm not making a mistake. I can't choose solely on what I know about Charles or Logan right now. Weighing out my words because someone is listening in won't help me at all."

"I understand."

"You do?"

"Of course." Ma wrapped her wet hand around Celeste's shoulder. "I only weaseled my way into your outing today because I wasn't sure if you *wanted* to be with Charles or not. I thought maybe you were just being gracious."

"At first maybe I was," Celeste admitted. "But being with him reminded me of the reasons I do like him. He's funny and charming and makes my heart lighter. And he could provide well for us. Those are different from the reasons I like Logan." What *was it* about Logan she liked besides his kindness? It was hard to put her finger on. "The world just feels right with Logan. Like I said, I only hope in a month's time I can decide whom I want to court seriously. Because regardless of the outcome, I do care for each of them and desire not to hurt either one."

U

The following morning, Celeste watched as Charles drove his rented buggy down their lane, the same buggy he'd driven to church. It wasn't a big concern, but still, it was one. Charles did not know how to ride a horse. Horseback riding was something Celeste loved. Besides that, how would he survive out West?

"Good morning." Charles waved at her as he pulled into the yard.

Celeste strolled over and met him. He hopped out, ran around the buggy, and helped her in. Then he turned and looked at the cabin. "Are we to be alone today? No chaperone?"

"That is correct. I convinced Ma it would only prolong my decision-making process. I hope you don't mind."

"Not at all." His voice sounded exceptionally cheerful.

"I trust your behavior will be stellar, as always." She hoped not having a chaperone wouldn't be a mistake. Reminding herself she wanted to make her decision quickly, she brushed aside the concern, knowing Charles was nothing like Dudley. "'Tis a lovely day." She scanned the pasture and hillside of her pa's land while settling into the seat.

"Picking up a bit of your pa's accent, it sounds like." Charles's smile held a different twist to it than she'd not seen before.

"Does that bother you?"

"Uh, no, not really." Charles commanded the horse to turn the buggy around. "Your diction was one of the things that attracted me to you when I first met you. Among myriad other attributes, of course," he quickly added. "I just find it interesting that you have picked up on the local drawl so soon. But it doesn't bother me. No, not at all," he added just as quickly and headed down the lane.

"Have you considered that perhaps I didn't pick up on this way of speaking but rather returned to it?"

Charles raised both eyebrows. "Oh."

"And that all those years at Miss Bennett's school I was suppressing the way I really wished to speak?" Celeste said, digging her voice into him a little louder than perhaps was called for. She loved the way her pa talked.

"Oh?" His eyebrows remained raised.

"Speaking of adjusting to the unfamiliar," Celeste said, careful to speak with such diction that Miss Bennett would be proud, "do you have plans to learn how to ride, or is that a skill you deem unnecessary?"

"Funny that you should mention this, for it is a matter that has been on my mind ever since I came west." He smiled now like he usually did, both ends of his mouth curling up dramatically while all the smile lines on his face sprung to life. "I have the perfect solution to my fear of horses." Taking his eyes off the road, he looked at her in earnest. "Sorry I haven't told you before that I am mortified by the creatures, but I'm telling you now. Should we not be revealing our warts and moles as we get to know each other better?"

"Yes, I agree." Celeste couldn't help but smile. He'd always had a knack at getting her to do that. "But I do not care for the terms *warts* and *moles*." She kept smiling but inside now. This was exactly what she wanted. Hopefully, Logan would be willing to reveal his "warts and moles" too. "Couldn't we just say we are getting to know each other thoroughly?"

Charles laughed. "That description *is* rather coarse. My apologies."

"No need to apologize, except maybe for getting off subject," Celeste said. "I am rather curious at your solution for a lack of riding skills."

"Ah yes, a wonderful solution, if I say so myself. I'm sure you will love it. You would be the talk of the town riding down Yampa Avenue in a new Oldsmobile."

Celeste's mind flashed back to the parade. "You don't mean one of those horseless carriages, one of those automobiles, do you?"

"That's exactly what I'm talking about!" Charles beamed.

"Oh, Charles, I'm sure those contraptions are very costly."

"Who cares? I can afford it." He patted her hand. "And I insist on only the best for my lovely Celeste. In fact, that is what our little outing is all about today. I've arranged with Lavender Decker at the R.H. Hughes Mercantile to meet with us at eleven. She will go through all of her catalogs and help you order two new dresses and every accessory imaginable to go with them: new shoes, handbags, parasols—the works."

"Oh, Charles, I cannot allow you to do that. We are not officially courting, merely kind of pre-courting to determine if we shall officially court." *Oh, that sounds awful.* "What if I decide not to continue on with you?"

"Doesn't matter. I'd still love to shower you with gifts. What good is money if I can't spend it on a lovely lady like you?"

"No, I wouldn't feel comfortable with you spending such money on me. And if you insist on it, I shall refuse to go any farther in this buggy with you. Now promise me you won't spend any money on me today, other than a spot of dinner."

His face clearly showed his disappointment. "May I at least buy you a new handkerchief or a lacy shawl?"

"Oh, I presume a handkerchief—something small—would be acceptable. I hate to see you so sad."

His eyes lit up. "Wonderful."

Celeste refused to speak any more about his purchasing gifts. This trial period was supposed to be about getting to know each other, not him trying to sway her with niceties.

"Charles, there are some things I need to know. First of all, why did you wait several days to call on me once you arrived in Craig?" She turned toward him and stared, expecting at least a glance her way, but he kept his eyes focused straight ahead. His silence prompted her to continue. "Second of all, you've never really told me why you left so suddenly in New York. Can you tell me the reason?"

"Uh . . ." Charles raked a hand through his hair. "Your first question is easy. I was gathering my courage. The second question . . . well . . . that matter was really out of my control. But be assured, I was merely trying to find a way to make a good living, with the sole intent of coming back and being able to court you properly."

"Oh really." Celeste cleared her throat. "Why couldn't you have told me that before you left?"

"I, um . . . just couldn't bring myself to do so at the time. I do apologize for that." Charles flicked the reins, and the buggy picked up speed.

They rode in silence for about a mile. Charles spoke first, describing his new job and then his ability to take care of her. So she talked about the weather, trying to figure out if he was one who could endure the winters of northwest Colorado or if he would want to run back to New York with the first Rocky Mountain blizzard.

By the time they'd made it to town, Celeste hadn't learned much more, if anything, about Charles. She told herself that she was, however, impressed by how he waved at practically everyone they passed. He genuinely acted as though he knew them as he said hello, which very well might be possible. Charles was so much like Logan in that way. His having no problem talking to people would take that burden off her shoulders. As of yet, he had not tried to get her to step out of her shell to talk to these folks like Logan had done. That was a plus on Charles's behalf. Yet Logan had thought it good to make her stretch, and she *had* become better friends with Mrs. Hoy.

As much as she struggled talking to people, she was happy to be here today. Being on the ranch day in and day out, doing the same activities over and over, wore on her. Though she didn't miss most things about the Bennett school, it had spoiled her. She'd constantly been barraged by dances to dress up for, teas to attend, and new classes to learn from—or the classes she repeated every year. Her equestrian course had her attending contests every few months and thus practicing every day after school. That was one of the few things she did miss.

"What else do you have planned for us today?" Celeste asked as Charles pulled the buggy to a stop in front of the mercantile. "I fear purchasing a handkerchief will hardly fill fifteen minutes' worth of time."

He smiled. "Ah, do not fear, my dear Celeste. We'll think of something. Or maybe nothing. Just being together is sufficient for me. I would hope it would be so for you."

Was he asking her? Or telling her? In either case, her tongue felt tied. Why? Today would be a good time to ask each other hard questions, to learn more about each other's "warts and moles." Unfortunately, at the moment, that sounded as appealing of a task as mucking out the stalls in Pa's barn. She offered him a demure smile as he helped her down, telling herself she would enjoy this partial day with him, face each situation as she came to it, and adjust accordingly. For now, she needed a new handkerchief and appreciated Charles's generosity.

As they headed to the door of the mercantile, Celeste noticed Logan walking down the sidewalk toward them, his distinctive gait very familiar. Her heart skipped a few beats ahead.

"Logan! Good morning." She held back saying more to him for Charles's sake, though she would have liked to ask what he was doing, obviously heading for the mercantile himself in the middle of the morning. It was Monday, his day to be tending to the livery stable.

"Celeste!" Logan's eyes brightened as they rested on her. "Morning to you too." He glanced at Charles, and his face blanched. "Oh, and don't worry, Charles. I'm not here to horn in on your time, just picking up my mail."

Charles's flat expression was hard to read. "I am not worried, my good fellow. But it does seem rather curious that you see the need to pick up your mail at this exact moment, when, as I recall, you are a mail carrier. It would make more sense to me that you would collect your own mail the days you come in to deliver the mail. It's not like you are some high-class business executive who needs to check his mail every day."

Celeste glared at Charles, feeling that statement was uncalled for.

"I'm expecting an important letter *today*," Logan said with emphasis. He turned to Celeste and appeared to be holding back a smile. "I applied for the postmaster job and was told they would let me know yea or nay by letter today."

"Oh, Logan, that's wonderful!" Celeste enjoyed her grin and the feelings inside that put it there. "I'm sure their answer will be a yes. There's no one more qualified than you." This was great news, especially given how her heart was finding it more difficult to give Charles a fair chance than she'd expected.

"Ah-hem." Charles cleared his throat, opened the door to the mercantile, and held the door for Celeste to enter.

"Thank you," she muttered to Charles. With a nod to Logan, she said, "My best wishes," and entered the store.

Lavender uttered a wobbly greeting the moment they stepped inside. "Good mornin', Celeste. Good mornin', Charles. Oh, and mornin' to you too, Logan." She stood behind the counter, straightening a display of soaps. She wore a smile, but it lacked the spirit it used to when her husband, Sam, was still alive.

"I'm just here to pick up my mail," Logan said and beelined it to the back room. "Is Rosie here?"

"Yep," Lavender said without a shred of emotion.

Celeste mourned for Lavender. Her life surely had been turned upside down because of Stanley Jones.

"Good morning, Lavender." Celeste walked toward her, not bothering to take hold of the elbow Charles extended. This sweet old woman was one she'd always felt comfortable around. "You look lovely today," she added.

Lavender batted a hand at Celeste. "Oh, gracious be. Lovely and Lavender don't go together—except when it comes to that little purple flower my ma done named me after." She let a tiny laugh escape.

That prompted a healthy smile from Celeste. "We're here to look at handkerchiefs." She motioned for Charles to take his place by her side at the counter. "Charles will be paying for it, so show me your most economical ones."

"Quite the contrary!" Charles placed his palm atop the counter, almost slapping it. "My dear Mrs. Decker, I insist that you show us the nicest, most expensive handkerchiefs this establishment has to offer."

Lavender's smile transformed into a smirk. It was good to see a little of the old woman's spunk rise to the surface. "How about I just show 'em all to you." She pulled out a box from beneath the counter. "You've got all of five to choose from. Unless, of course, you want me to pull out the men's handkerchiefs. They ain't as pretty, but they sure as heck are a lot more practical."

"I'm sure I'll be able to find one among the women's handkerchiefs that will suit me fine, thank you." Celeste considered selecting a man's handkerchief just to see how Charles would react. She held back a chuckle, but her grin refused to be dampened. Logan having applied for the postmaster position partially fueled her urge.

Lavender pulled five different handkerchiefs from the box and laid them out on the counter. "Here you go, Celeste. Pick which one is to your likin'."

Three were trimmed with lace. One of those did catch Celeste's eye. She touched its half-inch border of lace. It felt soft. She touched the lace on the other two. They both looked lovely, with fancy tatted lace each bearing a different design, but their wide borders were much too scratchy and impractical for her taste. The other two had simple, turned edges. The smallest did hold an embroidered pink flower in one corner, which was nice.

"These are all very lovely," Celeste said, "but I think I'll choose *this* one." This decision was easy. She pointed to the large, plain one, knowing she already had a fancy one her grandmother had given to her for special occasions. She needed a practical one to stuff in her pocket while she tended to her chores.

"Surely not that one!" Charles's voice rose in pitch. "My dearest Celeste, you are with me. Please, remember, money is no object. I was wanting to buy you a new dress—two new dresses. At least let me buy you this one." He pointed to the fanciest, most impractical of them all.

Celeste was about to protest when she noticed Logan slink from the back room. His head hung low, and she could only see his profile. It was sufficient to read the disappointment. *He didn't get the position.* Pain shot through her heart. For him. If she were to choose him over Charles, life wouldn't be easy, but with Logan's good work ethic and God's help, they would find a way to manage without that job. She pulled her gaze away from Logan and let him weave his way quietly through the displays of merchandise on the far side of the store without the pain of her eyes on him.

She looked instead at Charles. It was obvious he had the means to provide for a family. Everything he did for her was a reminder of that fact.

"I know what I want, and you'll not influence me otherwise," she stated in a firm voice, feeling on edge. "This plain, simple one suits me best." She snatched it from the counter and handed it to Lavender. "Ring this one up for me. Thank you."

The cash register drawer opened with a ding as the front door slammed closed.

Celeste whipped around. Through the large front window, she saw Logan trudge past with his hands fisted. His face looked dark—and not because of the tilted brim of his cowboy hat.

Chapter 22

LOGAN HADN'T MEANT TO SLAM the door that hard, but darn it all, he had to do something! As if reading that letter of rejection from the postal service wasn't enough, Charles's voice reached into the back room and rubbed salt into his gaping wound. "Money is no object," he mimicked Charles's words with disdain.

He dragged both feet toward the livery stable, in no hurry at all to get back to his part-time job he used to love. He used to love his mail-delivery job too, but now they felt like a pair of boulders tied around his neck, taking all his time while not paying him enough money to court Celeste like she deserved. He certainly wouldn't be taking her to Sunny's Place every day or to Decker's store to buy a handkerchief—not with the money he had left in his pockets after paying all he owed yesterday. What kinds of activities would he take Celeste on once it was his time to court her? They could go horseback riding. Gus might even let him borrow a horse for Celeste without charging him. His heart sagged further. That's all he ever did with her, take her horseback riding. But what else could he do?

Maybe she would enjoy a walk with him, where they named wildflowers and picked up interesting rocks. He could tell stories to her, or they could sing—more like he'd let her do the singing and he'd listen. She liked dancing with him. If his leg wasn't too tired, they could do that. They could have fun cooking together or . . . He couldn't think of anything else. He certainly couldn't do like Charles and take her shopping.

He shoved his hands into his pockets and fingered a dollar bill and a couple of dimes—all he had left of his paycheck from Gus. It had to hold him until he got paid by the postal service next week. What if he didn't eat and didn't rack up his bill at Porter's Bathhouse? "Naw," he muttered to the breeze. A dollar and twenty cents would hardly come close to putting him on equal ground with Charles anyway.

He stopped in his tracks just outside the livery stable, reality hitting him like an anvil to the head. He didn't have a chance in Hades with Celeste, not against a rich, well-mannered, well-dressed, likeable fellow like Charles Weathersby. A few weeks ago, he wouldn't have cared. He would have graciously backed down from this competition recognizing that he was obviously the loser. That was before he realized he loved Celeste. Now . . . the thought of going through life without her sounded worse than Stanley rising from the grave and having to go through another twenty-six years of life with him as a brother.

Stanley! The money and time Charles spent on Celeste was nothing compared to what Stanley had once had at his fingertips. A ranch and its money could be Logan's. All it would take was his signature.

He reached for the handle to the livery stable door and hesitated. Why should he go back inside that smelly stable and work his back into a fit for ten cents an hour? If he took the ranch—that was rightfully his—he could sit in the saddle all day and wine and dine Celeste all night and still have enough money to take her to Europe for a honeymoon or travel the world after they got married. And then dress her in the prettiest darn clothes ever to be laid eyes on in Craig, Colorado.

He'd sworn he'd never take that money. The pain of Pa's abandonment rose to his throat, and he let it fester there for a moment, reminding him of his decision to abandon that money.

Anger and frustration boiled inside him. He grabbed the door handle with force, pulling it partially loose from the wood, and stormed inside. A strong whiff of ammonia nearly knocked him over. A large pile of manure awaited the shovel and his strong back. Apparently, it'd been ignored by Gus this morning. And why not? Why should Gus do such dirty work? He was the boss. He owned the place. That's why he hired Logan.

If Logan owned the Circle J, he could hire a new foreman; he didn't have to keep Tom, Stanley's mean-as-a-badger foreman.

No. What was he thinking? First of all, Gus didn't deserve such sour thoughts. Second of all, he was *not* going to take the ranch! Or *any* of Pa's money!

But I wouldn't be doing it for myself.

It was for Celeste. Maybe she could be happy with the plain and simple man he was, but she deserved more.

"That still would be takin' it," he grumbled through gritted teeth. His feet felt rooted to the ground there in the doorway of the livery stable, not wanting to step inside and get back to work at the job he now saw as a dead end. Neither could he back out. Where else would he go? A man with a bum leg was not in high demand.

"So sorry to hear about your bad news, my good fellow."

Logan let go of the broken door handle and whipped around. Charles had brought his rented buggy to a stop in front of the stables. Celeste sat in the buggy's seat next to Charles. Her eyes held concern, whereas Charles's held mirth.

"Did no one ever teach you it ain't nice to sneak up on a fellow like that?" Logan clenched his jaw, wondering how Charles knew.

"I certainly didn't think we were sneaking up on you. We saw you standing in the doorway there, neither coming nor going, and wondered if you were all right." The smile on Charles's face didn't fit his words.

"Are you all right?" Celeste's wrinkled brow and pursed lips *did* match the concern in her voice. He swore she really cared, and it made Logan want her all the more.

"You must have been so preoccupied with your thoughts that you didn't hear me drive up. I can't say that I blame you. To not get awarded the job you so sorely needed is a blow, to say the least."

"Who told you I didn't get the job?" Logan struggled to keep his voice calm.

"That woman named Rosie." Charles held up his hands as if Logan had pointed a gun at him. "She came out of the back room just as you left. She was concerned about you too."

"Too?" Logan's insides felt on the verge of exploding. "You didn't really stop because you're worried about me like Rosie. You stopped because you wanted to gloat, right?" That was it. Logan knew it was so with every fiber of his gut. He didn't have to take this. Between the ranch and Pa's holdings, there would be so much money at Logan's fingertips he could make Charles Weathersby look like a beggar living on the street.

"Oh no, it was not like that at all," Charles backpedaled—the hesitancy in his voice condemned him.

"It was I who made him stop," Celeste spoke up. "Don't lose heart, Logan. You'll find something else that suits you even better."

"I'm sure of it," Logan responded. "And thank you, Celeste. Good day." He lifted his hat.

Charles cleared his throat and appeared ready to say something.

"Goodbye, Charles." Logan grabbed hold of the loose handle, for the door had swung closed during this bothersome conversation. "I have work to do," he said and stepped inside the livery stable.

Gus looked away from the horse he was rubbing down. "Ah, Logan, finally. I've been waiting for you to quit yakkin' out there and come get to work. There's two more horses that need tending to, plus that pile of manure is getting out of hand."

"Sorry, Gus, but I'm quitting. I just came in to tell you before I headed over to Ron Smith's office."

"Quittin'?" Gus's sad expression nearly tore Logan's heart down the middle. "But . . . I need ya." He rubbed his forehead. "How come? Have I treated you poorly, boy?"

Logan regretted the mean thoughts he'd had for Gus earlier. His heart tore further. "No, you've done nothing but treat me like the closest thing to a real pa I ever had." He took in a deep breath—big mistake with all the ammonia seeping out of that pile. Admitting this out loud would mean he couldn't back out. "I've come into a little money. I don't need this job no more. What I do need is more time to court this gal I've got my eye on. So given all that, I gotta let go of this place."

Gus slapped a hand on Logan's back. "I understand, boy. It'll be hard to carry on without you, but I understand. Especially the part about the gal." Gus's smile spread across his face. "It's about time you found yourself one and settled down. Sorry, but I can nary afford to pay a fellow enough to support a family. That's why I usually just hire on boys." His smile faded, and he chewed his lip.

Logan wasn't a boy anymore, and his reasons for taking the ranch felt better and better to him. Gus had been like a pa, and his agreeing with Logan's decision helped him feel like it was justified.

"Thanks for sticking with me all these years. I always knew you'd have to move on. Just never wanted to admit it." Gus pulled Logan close.

Logan gave Gus a hug. When he released his boss, he eyed the knee-high pile of manure. "I'll finish out my shift today. But come tomorrow . . ." He winced. "Sorry, but I've got other work I need to attend to pronto-like." *Before it's my time with Celeste.* "If you're ever in a pinch, though, don't hesitate to give me a holler."

Chapter 23

CELESTE WALKED AHEAD OF CHARLES, following Sunny to their table. He placed his hand on the small of her back, and she bristled. She didn't need to be guided, nor did she enjoy that simple touch of his like she had two weeks ago. Tomorrow would be Logan's turn to court her, starting with church. The very thought prompted a sigh of relief. Charles had grown more intense with every passing day in his efforts to sway her. This whirlwind two-week courtship had worn her out.

At least it had fulfilled its purpose and had helped her to see that Charles was not right for her. He had changed from the Charles she'd met a year ago. She couldn't put her finger on it exactly—more self-serving? Her guess was that his newfound wealth was to blame. His manner and their conversations had felt more genuine when he was poor.

Charles pulled Celeste's chair out for her to sit down. "I've tried to make tonight special, my dear, seeing how this will be our last evening together until the next two weeks have passed." He squeezed her shoulder as he scooted her and the chair to the table.

Celeste stiffened, knowing she should tell him this night was it. But to be fair, she would spend as much time with Logan in the upcoming two weeks and not say anything to either man about her decision until two weeks from tomorrow. She made an effort to relax her back and shoulders and looked up at Charles, dressed in the fanciest of his three new suits.

"Yes, 'tis our last night together," Celeste said in the cheeriest voice she could muster. "But I can't imagine what you could ever do to make this night more special than the others. You really have outdone yourself with the activities you've planned." She would have never imagined finding so many things to do in Craig.

This past week they'd watched a horseshoe-tossing contest behind the black-smith shop, complete with some of old Mrs. Hoy's infamous barbequed pork, gone on a moonlight picnic in the park serenaded by the same musicians who played for the Fourth of July dance—which caused her to think about Logan that night much more than Charles—and, among other things, spent an afternoon reading at the new library, which was more like listening to Charles carry on to the librarian about all the books he'd purchased and were on their way as his donation to their collection. It was nice that he was doing well, but it made her feel awkward when he kept flaunting his wealth.

"Ah, nonsense," said Charles. "I have just done what any man worthy of your attention would do. Anything less would be an insult to you, my dear Celeste."

"Oh, really now." Celeste pinched her lips together. She sensed this was meant as a dig at Logan, who could afford nothing even close to what Charles had shelled out to court her thus far.

"As for tonight," Charles continued, "I have hired this establishment's head chef to create a new menu item in honor of you." He took the printed menus awaiting them on the table and handed them to Sunny. "We won't be needing them, as you know. Your chef already knows what we're having tonight."

Sunny sheepishly took the menus. "Oops. Forgot about that. I'll go tell George you're ready for what he's whipping up for you." She raised an eyebrow and looked at Charles. "What was it again he's making you all?"

"Tender braised lamb *à l'orange* over a bed of celestial au gratin baby potatoes and steamed greens reminiscent of the green pastures of Ireland—all in tribute to my dear Celeste."

"Yeah, right." Sunny pointed her pencil at Charles. "I'll see how George is coming on those fancy lamb chops and get them right out to you."

"Uh . . . thank you," Charles mumbled.

"Oh, Charles, you needn't have done this. It's too much. In fact, you've spent way too much money and effort on me. The whole idea of these two weeks was merely for us to get to know each other better." Celeste stared down at her hands clasped and lying in her lap. "At least that had been my intention, not to make either of you spend your hard-earned cash on me."

"First of all, it wasn't all that hard to earn." He stuck out his chest. "Please, keep in mind that you shall never want for anything if you were to choose me over . . ." He paused, as if weighing his words. ". . . over someone who has to struggle daily and spend all his time eking out a living and have no time to spend with you or your children."

He'd brought up the ease of earning his money before. She'd always felt uncomfortable with it but hadn't dared ask. Whether she decided on Charles or not, it was something she wanted to know, especially since this morning Pa mentioned he'd invested five hundred dollars with Charles's company. "How is it that you don't have to work very hard? Your job and the investment returns you promise sound like something out of a storybook. It sounds rather too good to be true."

"My dear Celeste, don't worry your darling sweet head over such matters. Trust me when I say I know it works. I've seen it all laid out, and there truly is a loophole in the foreign postal coupon system. There is profit to be made there." Charles shook out his napkin and tucked it into his collar beneath his chin. "I have nothing more to say on the matter. Now, when is our food coming?"

"I have just one more question. Answer me this, and I promise I'll bother you no more. I agree. I've seen how there is money to be made buying these coupons across the Atlantic, then redeeming them for stamps in the US, and then selling those at a profit." Celeste exhaled loudly. "But is there not a limit to how many of those coupons are sold over in Europe? With all the investors you've bragged—told me you've brought in, not to mention untold numbers your boss is recruiting, it seems to me that there wouldn't be enough of those postal coupons to generate the income needed to pay back your investors, especially since each coupon brings only a few pennies of profit with each exchange."

Charles patted Celeste's hand. "My dear, Miss Bennett's financial wellness class has filled your head with worries that belong not to your gender. Trust me here. I've seen it with my own eyes. I invested a hundred dollars with my boss, and not more than two months later, I was returned not only my hundred dollars, but an additional hundred dollars. The money's there. I promise you, it works." He went from patting her hand to pulling it into his and giving it a squeeze.

She didn't return the squeeze but pulled her hand free and picked up her napkin. She took her time flattening it on her lap and then took hold of her fork—anything to keep her hands busy and her concern off Charles's chosen vocation. "I, too, wonder where our meals are," she said, feeling more comfortable with mindless conversation at the moment. It might very well be so for the remainder of the evening, for she was in no mood to speak of serious matters with Charles. No, she really didn't need even a week with Logan to decide. She could imagine happily discussing any matter with Logan.

Sunny scurried by, stopping by their table barely long enough to say, "Your lamb chops are almost ready," and she went off to seat a new customer who had just walked in.

Celeste couldn't see the customer's face, as he was turned away from her, but his shoulders looked broader than most men's, filling out his expensive-looking suit rather nicely. His hair was dark, the same color as Logan's but cut short—no adorable locks to curl up beneath his white hat at the scruff of his neck. *What is it with those skimmer hats in Craig lately?* Her guess was the man was going to meet a gal here. Why else would a single man in Craig dress up to eat at Sunny's

Place? Something about this man intrigued her, and she found herself following him with her eyes as Sunny led him to a table. His shoes looked brand new, with their well-polished black leather. She found it interesting that he wasn't wearing cowboy boots. Charles was the only other man in this town who wore round-toed shoes. She caught her breath. This man's shoes had a much thicker sole on the left than on the right. *It couldn't be!*

Celeste's eyes moved up from the man's feet past his legs, which were barely limping. Her suspicion was confirmed when he turned slightly to slip into his chair ten feet away, an empty table sitting between them.

"Logan?" She couldn't hold back the surprise in her voice.

Charles turned and stared, his eyes surveying Logan from head to foot. "Ah, what brings you here this evening?" he said loud enough to be heard by Logan over the chatter filling the restaurant. "Your turn doesn't start until tomorrow. Might I suggest you save what you got left of your paycheck, after buying that new suit, and use it another night when you'll need to pay for her meal too?"

"Do not worry, my good fellow," Logan said in poor imitation of Charles's voice. "I have plenty more money where this came from." He tugged at the lapels of his suit jacket. "As for being here tonight, I have as much right as the next guy to be seated at Sunny's Place for a bit of supper. Ain't that right, Sunny?" He leaned back on his chair and tapped Sunny on the arm as she pulled her notebook out, ready to take an order at an adjacent table.

"Well, lands be, Logan Jones. I didn't recognize you when I seated you— or I would have given you a bit more personalized attention." Sunny scratched her head and stared at him. "Where on earth did you get the money to buy that suit? My dear Pete had one just like it, God rest his soul, and I can tell you, it cost him a pretty penny. You don't have money like that."

"I do now." Logan sat up straighter than Celeste had ever seen him sit in a chair. "You're looking at the new owner of the Circle J Ranch."

"What?" Celeste could hardly believe her ears.

Sunny took a step closer. "But I thought it went to your sister after Stanley was han—uh, passed away."

"Susannah gave it all to me—the ranch, Pa's money," Logan explained. "Said she and Joseph didn't need it like I did, which I finally realized was true," he mumbled under his breath. "I signed the papers almost two weeks ago. It's official now. I'm rich."

"About time you got what was rightfully yours." Sunny clapped her hands to her chest, notebook and all. "That's absolutely wonderful, Logan. I'm happy for you."

"I'm happy for you too," Celeste said in a daze, still trying to take it all in.

"Yes, wonderful for you." Charles's smile did not reach his eyes. "Now, if you would excuse Sunny so she could get back to her job, I'm sure her other customers would appreciate that."

Sunny turned her attention to another table, took their orders, and scurried off to the kitchen. A minute later, she returned with two delicious-looking plates of braised lamb, creamy au gratin potatoes, and a helping of steamed chard.

Celeste breathed in the savory aroma that made her mouth water. "Smells wonderful," she said as Sunny placed it before her. She looked at Charles. "Thank you. This is my favorite meal that Ma makes. This must have taken some clever tactics to figure out, seeing that you and Ma have rarely talked without me around. This is very thoughtful, Charles."

"You are very welcome," Charles responded, his voice quiet. He obviously no longer wanted to be heard by Logan. "But it appears this will be too little too late."

"Whatever do you mean?" Celeste took a bite of the lamb. It tasted heavenly—much better than her ma's.

"I never told you this, but it's about time I did." Charles set his fork down and looked intently at Celeste. "Last year, when I slipped out of your life without a word?"

"Yes, I remember." Celeste wondered what he was getting at, bringing up this painful subject.

"It was not actually out of my control, like I had said."

"No?" Celeste bristled.

"That was when I discovered the Securities Exchange Company, and Mr. Ponzi said if I dropped everything and joined him immediately in Boston, he would train me to earn the kind of money he did. I was forced to make a very difficult decision. I could either stay in New York and continue trying to court you as a pauper, competing for a beautiful princess along with those filthy-rich fellows Miss Bennett brought in for her practice 'society' dances, or I could take a chance and leave you for a moment so as to make my fortune. And then return on an equal footing with all the other men vying for your attention. I thought I finally had a chance when I came to Craig. Not only were all of your other suitors left behind back East, but now I had the means to take care of you like you deserved. I was a little disconcerted when I discovered that in the few short weeks since you returned home, you already had another man here in Craig with his eyes set on you."

"Logan," Celeste murmured.

"Yes, Mr. Jones, the first friend I made here in town." He hung his head. "I wished it hadn't been so." He looked back up. "But it was. I immediately realized the only thing I had going for me, that he didn't have, was two good legs—and money."

Celeste reached out to him, wanting to soothe the pain she detected in his voice. He was still her friend, and she cared for him as such. "No, Charles, that's not true."

"It is." He squeezed her offered hand momentarily, then returned his hands to his lap. "I knew you, knew Logan's legs would not be an issue with you. So it was only my money that gave me an edge over my competition. Now even that is gone." He rubbed the sides of his head by his eyes. "The saddest part is I left you hanging without a word for nothing. I hurt you for nothing. It was all for *nothing*. I fear that after I wish you good night, I shall never be privileged to enjoy your company, one on one, again. I will have lost to the likes of Dudley *again*."

"No, that is not true," Celeste said without thinking. She just couldn't bear to see Charles so disheartened. It was so unlike him. But neither did she like feeling as though she was a prize to be won. At the moment, however, Charles needed cheering up more than her gripe needed to be heard. "You didn't lose to Dudley. Dudley was never in the running. Why people continually think he was is beyond me." She'd been amazed that this heartless man's fame had even made its way into Logan's concerns. "The only thing that Dudley had to offer me *was* money." She placed her hand on his. "Charles, I assure you, money is not what I am looking for in a man. True, one needs to make an honest living, sufficient to raise a family, but beyond that, what I want in my future husband is a good heart and the inherent qualities that come with it. So don't worry that Logan has suddenly come into money. That will not sway my decision either way."

"So you're saying after you court Logan for two weeks, I shall have the privilege to court you again the following two weeks?" His eyebrows raised in obvious anticipation.

"I'm saying that none of us, you, me, or Logan, should jump to any conclusion at this point. I shall court Logan for his allotted time, with my eyes open just as when I courted you, looking at your inner qualities. Hopefully, I will be able to make a decision by this time two weeks from today as to whom I shall continue to court seriously. For I believe it is safe to assume than none of us desire to continue this unconventional triangle of courtship. It's not fair to you or to Logan." *And I don't care for it.*

"Are you certain, my dear Celeste, that money shall not play a factor in your decision?" Charles sounded more than hopeful.

"Absolutely." Celeste turned her attention to her plate and took another bite of lamb, wanting to enjoy it before it got cold and thinking it was rather sweet of Charles to arrange this meal as he had. He did have a good heart.

Chapter 24

Logan offered Celeste the crook of his elbow and escorted her out of the church as soon as the worship services were over, anxious to be shed of Charles's presence. Of all the gall that man had, coming into the chapel during the opening hymn, slipping past him and Celeste while they stood to sing, and then sitting down on the other side of Celeste when the hymn was through . . . Sure, two weeks ago, Charles had invited him to sit with him and Celeste, but Kate had been with them. And Logan had the decency to sit elsewhere and give them their privacy.

"Beautiful day," Charles said, looking up at the sky as the three of them stepped outside. He glanced at Logan. "What a lucky fellow you are, being able to spend the whole of it with such a lovely lady."

"No more lucky than you were the last two weeks." Logan would have liked to hurry down the steps and into his new buggy and be shed of Charles, but even with his new "orthopedic shoes," as the catalog called them, he'd never be able to take steps as fast as Charles.

He'd paid a pretty penny for those shoes, having to spend a tremendous amount for them and his two new suits to be delivered in time for him to start this week with Celeste. He had the money now. And with money, it seemed, came power to accomplish almost anything. He looked at Charles as he walked down the steps on the other side of Celeste, wondering if there was some way he could pay to have Charles go away. Gazing at the sky without noticing it, only wanting to make a point, Logan said, "Yes, it is a beautiful day to spend with Celeste. Sorry for leaving you behind, but we've got a day full of plans ahead of us, and my buggy only fits two."

"Goodbye." Celeste offered Charles a parting wave of her hand.

Logan simply gave him a nod and led Celeste to where his buggy awaited, the church's hostler busily hitching it to his new horse, Prince.

"Where's Bootstrap?" Celeste asked as Logan helped her climb into the buggy. "I'd meant to ask that when you first picked me up this morning, but I forgot, what with all the rambling on you did about your busy week taking on the responsibility of the Circle J."

"Oh, he's out in the pasture at the ranch. Frolicking, I daresay, at the prospect of not having to haul me or anyone else around no more." He pointed to the purebred sorrel-brown stallion before them as he settled into his seat. "Prince here is a more fitting choice to be pulling this new buggy. You deserve better than to be hauled around by a motley old horse like Bootstrap." He flicked the reins, and Prince pulled the buggy forward with a smooth transition befitting a horse of his breed. Oh, it was nice to have money. He had only ever dreamed of owning a horse like this.

"But I like Bootstrap," Celeste said. "And I thought you did too."

"Oh, I do. I still like Bootstrap—a whole lot. Just like I do my favorite pair of boots. But sometimes you've got to get a new pair so you don't look like something the cat drug in."

"I admit, Bootstrap wasn't the handsomest horse, but he had his own kind of beauty." Celeste stared forward at Prince, though it appeared that horse was not where her focus lay.

Her words jabbed his conscience and his heart. He had to admit he did miss Bootstrap. Sure, Prince was a fine specimen of a horse, one worthy of showing off, and he loved all those stares and compliments that came his way as he rode or drove Prince through town. But he couldn't talk to Prince like he did to Bootstrap. Prince was in his own world. Logan was merely his master, not his friend. "Tell you what, we can pay Bootstrap a visit as soon as we get to the ranch."

"I'd like that," Celeste said, her eyes sparkling the way they did when she was content.

Logan wanted to keep her eyes sparkling like that continuously. Fortunately, he now had the means to do so. "And while we're there visitin' him—" He cleared his throat and spoke with more care. "I mean, *visiting* him, I can show you that surprise I told you about when I first got to your place this morning."

"Oh, I thought that was Prince and your new buggy." Celeste wrinkled her brow. "There's more?"

"Yes," Logan said proudly, and he could hardly wait to show her. "But I'm not saying any more. You've just got to wait and see."

"Oh." Celeste looked at the trees at the side of the road. "All right."

He'd expected more excitement from her. Her reaction of getting to see Bootstrap had bested everything so far today. Even when he'd shown her his new shoes and told her how they got rid of his limp. This next surprise, though, would best everything. Celeste would surely wrap her arms around him, kiss him again—at least on the cheek next to his mouth like she had that one time—and tell him it was the best gift anyone had ever given to her. When he'd seen these two magnificent twin horses over at that breeder in Hayden this past week, he knew immediately he'd wanted them both. One for himself and one for Celeste. He was so excited to show Celeste her horse, he could barely endure the mild pace at which they rolled out of town.

"It was a nice sermon Reverend Brown gave this morning," Celeste said after several minutes of silence between them.

"Yeah, it was," Logan said, realizing he'd basically spoken a lie. He hadn't heard a thing the reverend had said. His mind had either been on Celeste or Charles, sitting way too close to Celeste, or on Princess—Celeste's new mare waiting back at the Circle J Ranch.

"I especially liked the part where the reverend talked about loving one's neighbor with an open heart." She turned her head and gazed at him, apparently looking for his response.

"Yeah, I liked that part too," Logan responded, feeling the uncomfortable lie dig deeper into his gut.

"I knew you would." She placed her hand atop his as he pulled the reins to guide the buggy around a bend in the road.

The sensation of her fingers against his made him smile clean through his body. "How'd you know that?"

"Because that is who you are, Logan Jones. I think that is what has always attracted me to you."

"What? Not my dirty, worn-out clothes, long hair, and my gosh-awful limp?" Logan tried to smile at his pathetic attempt at humor, but those things were too close to the truth. They were things he never really smiled about when alone.

"Oh, Logan, you say that like you are ashamed. You have nothing to be ashamed about. Life had dealt you a poor hand. You were playing the game as best you could with what you had." She squeezed his hand. "And I think you've done more than anyone could have expected."

He turned and glanced at her, noticing her eyes were still on him. "You'll be glad to know those days are behind me, Celeste. So you needn't worry, about anything. I promise."

Her focus shifted to the horse that gracefully pulled them along the bumpy road. "I was never *really* worried," she stated and then paused. "Before now." She spoke the last two words softly, almost as a whisper.

"What on earth are you talking about?" He couldn't make sense of her words.

"Nothing. Nothing of importance. Forget I said anything." She glanced at him, offering a tight-lipped smile.

Logan was glad to forget about it. He wanted nothing to taint the moment he presented Celeste with her new purebred mare.

They arrived at the Circle J Ranch mid-afternoon. As Logan climbed out from beneath the shade of the buggy's roof, he felt the full forces of the merciless sun. He removed his hat and fanned at the sweat gathering beneath its brim, wishing at that moment for his old summer cowboy hat that let in more air than this fancy new one he'd bought. He placed it back on his head as he rounded the back of the buggy, wanting to look his best as he helped her down. His eyes caught hold of her sitting there, looking the vision of loveliness as she waited for him, and his heart beat erratically. It was definitely worth wearing this blasted new hat. He would never be as handsome as she was beautiful, but his new clothes and commitment to a regular shave and haircuts would help. She deserved it. And he was glad he could now afford to give that to her.

"You've never been out here to the Circle J before, have you?" Logan asked as they headed toward the front door, having left his new horse and buggy in the care of one of his ranch hands. Mercy be, it was nice not having to tend to such details anymore and being totally free to spend all his time with the gal he was falling deeper and deeper in love with. Surely she would see how nice that convenience was too.

"No, I have not." Celeste turned to one side and then to the other, obviously taking in the scope of the land and ranch house that belonged to Logan now. "It certainly is big."

"Yes, it is." Logan offered her his elbow. "Do you like it?"

"I-I guess I do." Celeste seemed taken back by his question. "There is a certain beauty to it, with all that land and all those cattle dotting the gray-green with their black hides."

"It's the ranch house isn't it?" Logan said quickly. "It doesn't have a woman's touch to it at all. That's because Stanley had it built for him. I could build you a new house, one just like the old ranch house my ma designed. It had two stories with fancy carved gables painted a different shade of blue from the rest of the place. It was right pretty—before it burned down."

"Logan, stop." Celeste squeezed his arm at the elbow. Not gently, not affectionately, but almost like she was chastising him. He couldn't help but stop in his tracks. "That would be a ridiculous waste of money," she continued. "Besides, your ranch house is more than sufficient for you or anyone else's needs."

She motioned to the door and for them to continue walking. "Come. Show me inside before I faint from this sun."

"Of course." Logan opened the front door and motioned for her to enter. He took her hat, placed it next to his on a rack of hooks on the entryway wall, and then proceeded to give her a tour of the ranch house. He started with the large living room directly off the entry toward the back of the house. Her eyes gravitated to the elk, moose, and bear heads hanging on the walls above eye level, and she didn't look pleased.

"The hunting trophies are Stanley's. I haven't had time to make the place my own yet." Logan would have liked to add he was wanting to wait until the place could have a woman's touch, specifically Celeste's touch, but he didn't dare. Yet.

"I see," she said and turned toward the huge dining table tucked into a nook off the living room. "Is the kitchen beyond that door?" She pointed to a swinging door in the dining room wall.

"Yes. Would you like to see it?"

"Yes, that would be lovely." She shuddered as she passed under the bear head on her way to the dining room, glancing down the right hallway as she walked. "What's down there?" she asked and pointed to the darkened hall.

"Bedrooms. I never go down there," Logan admitted. "Don't need to. My room's down the left leg of the house, along with a den and a room Stanley kept his poker table in."

Celeste glanced to the left, to the east end of the house toward his room, then back to the west. "This is a big place to live in all by yourself," Celeste said with a curious edge to her voice. "Why would Stanley build a house with so many bedrooms when it was well known he was a confirmed bachelor?"

"Because he could." Logan didn't care to think about his brother. "At least, that's what my sister said. Money was no object, and he liked spending it, so he did. He built a bigger house than he needed simply to have a bigger and better house than all the other ranches in these parts."

Celeste responded with a sigh followed by an expression that looked close to one of pain. "You don't do all the cooking and housekeeping for this place by yourself, do you? You'd get nothing else done, I'm afraid."

"Oh, no, I have a housekeeper. She has a cottage for her and her husband down by the ranch hands' dormitory. I just told her to take the afternoon off, that I didn't need her to come back until supper time. You know, for our meal. You can stay for supper, I'm hoping."

"I could stay if we eat early enough. The sun doesn't set until eight." She breathed in the aroma of pot roast as they stepped inside the massive kitchen.

The kitchen held two stoves, one at each end of the long, narrow room. A large butcher-block covered table stood in the center of the floor. In the middle of the long outside wall, directly in front of a large sink, was a sizeable window overlooking the open pastures full of cattle. Logan pointed to a small kitchen table with two chairs tucked away in an alcove next to the far stove. "That's where I usually eat. And half the time I tell Mrs. Crandall—that's my housekeeper— that I can whip up something myself. In fact, I tell her not to bother to come in to cook until supper time and then only clean the house when she thinks it needs it. She was afraid I was going to cut her pay at first, cutting back on all her work like I had. But I assured her it wouldn't be that way."

Celeste slipped her hand into his, surprising him and nearly sending him through the roof with the thrill. "I'm so glad to hear you haven't really changed," she said softly, right next to his ear, sending a tingle down his neck. "I was afraid . . ." She brought her hand to her chin and rubbed. "Never mind. Say, what time was Mrs. Crandall coming back? Do you think she would like some help with supper? I mean, this kitchen would be a delight to be able to cook in. I would deem it a pleasure more than a chore."

Logan smiled inside. The thought of Celeste cooking for him every day in this kitchen sounded exactly like what he'd been looking for when he'd decided to bring her out to see the ranch. The happy feeling faded as quickly as it had flared up. Celeste need never set foot in this kitchen if they were to marry. He kept forgetting he could afford servants now.

"I have no idea when my cook will be back. 'In time to finish supper' was all she said. Besides, you are my guest. What kind of suitor am I to expect you to help my housekeeper cook for me?" He took her by the hand and pulled her toward the back kitchen door. "Come on. I got more to show you outside."

"I cooked for you before, and I didn't mind," Celeste said in that same quiet voice she'd used a moment or two ago. Reluctantly, she let Logan lead her to the door. "The sun is rather merciless today. Couldn't we look at the rest of the house first, at least until closer to evening when the inside becomes warmer than outside?'

"But I've been waiting all day to show you this." Logan was nigh onto bursting at the seams with excitement. "This is the surprise I've been talking about. I'll show it to you fast, and then we can sit in the shade."

"All right then." Celeste walked out the door Logan held open.

He stepped out into the backyard after her. The sun beat down on his head, but he didn't want to bother going back in for their hats. "This won't take long," he said as much for himself as for Celeste.

"Where are we going?" Celeste shielded her eyes from the sun and glanced toward the bunkhouse and the Crandalls' cottage. "Over there?"

"No," Logan responded as they left the edge of what was supposed to be the backyard. "I apologize for the weeds back here. I promise, I'll have this spot cleaned up into a right proper yard, with a garden space and maybe even a swing tied on to that old cottonwood." He pointed to the lone tree that lay between the ranch house and the barnyard.

"Logan, you don't have to apologize for anything. This is not a competition between you and Charles for who can best show me how wonderful each of you can make my life. Today, and the next two weeks, I want merely to get to know *you*, not what you can do for *me*." She swiped a wayward lock of hair from her forehead. It must have been bothering her, because she appeared frustrated. Or perhaps it was a bead of sweat. "Charles, too, fell into that rut."

"Rut? What rut?"

"Of thinking he had to impress me. I hope that is not what you are doing."

"Uh . . . no," Logan muttered, feeling like the wind had been knocked out of his lungs. He took a deep breath to steady himself. "This way." He motioned toward the corral. "I just wanted to show you a horse. That's all. You know how much I like horses, and now that I've got a few extra dollars, I guess I kind of went crazy and bought me more than I rightly needed."

His gut wrenched from all the lies he was spewing out. When they reached the corral, he gripped the top rail of the corral's fence and squeezed hard to vent his frustration. He knew darn well he'd bought Prince and Princess to impress Celeste and make himself look better than Charles. The only truth he'd told had been about buying more horses than he rightly needed.

"I understand." She placed her hand atop his, and he relaxed.

"You do?"

"Of course. I know how much you love horses. And you own a ranch now, so buying a couple of extra horses to help run the place makes sense." She let go of his hand and climbed up onto the first rung of fence rail. She leaned into the sizeable corral, surveying the horses it held. "Is that your surprise? You wanted to show me yet another one of your new horses, besides Prince?"

That was true. Partially. "Ye-eah," Logan drew out the word, hoping she wouldn't think he'd bought this new mare to impress her—even though it had been his original intent—and to give to her. He climbed over the top rail and hopped into the corral. "Let me go fetch her." He grabbed the rope coiled and resting over a fence post and headed toward Princess.

The mare shied away from him as he approached. He called out to her, and she moved further away. "Stupid horse. Don't she know I'm her master now?" he muttered. Then he felt a nudge to his shoulder. He turned. Bootstrap stood next to him and nudged him again. "Sorry, boy, I don't have no time for you again today. But if you could do me a favor, I'd appreciate it." He pointed to Princess. "Fetch that new mare over my way so I can lasso her without having to run halfway across this here corral in the heat. Okay?"

Bootstrap reared his head and neighed. He trotted off toward Princess. Mere moments later, he'd herded Princess to Logan's side, where he was able to slip the rope around her neck with no problem. He led the mare to Celeste.

"This here is Princess," Logan said, bringing the horse close so Celeste could see her properly. "She wanted to come meet you."

"Is that so? It looked more like she wanted to run away from me. And you." Celeste chuckled and patted the mare's nose. "If it wasn't for Bootstrap," she said to Princess, "I believe you'd still be out there. Good ole Bootstrap. Is he your friend too?"

Princess raised her nose as if nodding.

"She's a smart horse. So is her brother, Prince." Logan couldn't hold back all of his pride. Though he figured now was not a good time to spill everything about this expensive set of horses, that he'd wanted a matching set of horses for him and Celeste.

"Oh, so Prince and Princess are brother and sister?" Celeste said, like things were making sense. "I thought they looked a bit alike."

A bit? "They are actually twins," Logan blurted out.

"Oh, that's nice," she stated, like it was the most common thing in the world. She fanned her face and turned her back against the sun. "How come you didn't bring Bootstrap to see me? I quite adore that horse. I would have liked to have said hello to *him*." Her eyes twinkled with teasing.

"Bootstrap?" Logan's gut tightened. "He's not what I'd call a surprise. And I told you I was going to bring you a surprise."

"So . . . your surprise is to show me Prince's twin sister. Am I correct?"

"Uh, em, yeah," Logan stammered.

"Good." Celeste rubbed her forehead and then flicked the perspiration from her hand. "Because for a moment there, I thought maybe you were going to tell me that you were going to put Bootstrap out to pasture and Prince and Princess were going to take his place."

"No, Bootstrap's not going anywhere." Logan couldn't tell if she was serious or if she had figured out his plan and was teasing him. In either case, he got the sense that Celeste didn't care much for his new horses. She just needed a little more time with them. That was all.

Celeste brought her hand to her forehead to shield her face from the sun. "I think I've had my fill of greeting horses." She swayed to one side and then back upright. "I think I need to get out of this sun, Logan. Help me dow—"

Logan barely made it to her in time. She fell off the bottom fence rail into his arms. He rushed her to the house, all the while yelling silently to himself for taking her outside in this heat to show her a horse she didn't care about one whit and not only forgetting her hat, but not offering her a drink of water first. The whole trip out here from church they'd had nothing to drink. He should have known better. What was wrong with him?

Chapter 25

CELESTE GLANCED AT THE CLOCK set on Pa's hand-carved fireplace mantle as she finished cleaning up the kitchen from breakfast. It read a quarter past nine. Logan could be here in as little as fifteen minutes. She should have been thrilled at the prospect. Last month, she would have been. Today she would have liked to crawl back into bed if she'd had the choice. Perhaps her body clung to the effects of the heat exhaustion she'd suffered yesterday. That must be it. After all, she'd fainted—not something she'd given in to like so many of her fellow classmates at school. She'd felt bad for having Logan take her home before supper. But she'd felt nauseated and wouldn't have been able to eat anyway. And she'd been exhausted. That's why she'd agreed to have Logan come out to their ranch this morning and take her on a horseback ride: to be fair. Otherwise, she would have rather waited until Tuesday morning

She breathed out a sigh. Logan was acting no different from Charles. It was like they were trying to see who could buy the biggest and best gifts for her.

She sighed again, deeper than before, feeling like a trapped animal caught in a snare of expensive gifts she didn't want. It was all her fault. She'd caused every bit of this mess with her un-thought-out idea of courting two men at once. Her pa's words came to mind. *It's great to be a free thinker, but to think your ideas are always right will lead you to be anything but free.*

"But I'm not courting them at the same time," she said aloud, convincing herself rather poorly. "I was merely trying to decide which one of them I should *actually* court." She gave the table a good wipe with her dishrag, taking the last remnants of biscuit crumbs with it. "It sounded like a good idea at the time."

She rinsed out the dishrag and hung it over the lip of the sink, then pumped herself a big glass of water and drank it. She was going on a horseback ride with Logan, and she'd better make sure she had enough to drink this time. Thankfully, Logan promised they'd be back long before noon, when the sun began its merciless heat.

She hurried off to her bedroom and changed into her riding clothes. They were a little worn, having been a secondhand set of breeches she'd purchased from a girl at school. The girl decided she hated the equestrian courses and sold them to Celeste at a price she was able to afford from the allowance Grandma had given her. She hadn't dared write home and ask Ma and Pa for the money, but it had been a necessary item to own to be able to sign up for the classes. It had been her best purchase ever, for those equestrian courses had been her haven while at school.

She pulled the breeches from the drawer and ran her fingers down the gently worn fabric and leather with affection before she pulled them on. They fit perfectly, and for a moment, she relived that excitement she felt every time she'd headed off for class wearing them. Maybe today's ride with Logan wasn't such a bad idea after all. She was just grateful she could be confident he wouldn't be showing up at her door in one of those newfangled automobiles. She feared Charles would be doing that come next month if she didn't stick to her guns and end this "competition" after her two weeks with Logan was done.

As she donned her riding clothes, a smile formed on her face. It felt good. "Logan would never be so foolish as to buy one of those cars. He knows the roads out here would rip those silly tires to shreds, and he'd always be stuck." She liked Logan's love of horses. At least horses were practical.

The front door flew open, and Patrick ran in. "Celeste!"

"Yes?" She walked out of her room.

"Logan's here, and you just gotta see the two horses he's got with him. Pa's out there drooling over them right now—says they had to have cost Logan an arm and a leg. Especially after he found out Logan bought them from that fancy horse breeder over in Hayden." He took Celeste's hand and pulled her toward the door. "Come on."

Celeste let her little brother drag her outside, not wanting to dampen *his* excitement. "I've already seen Logan's new horses. They're named Prince and Princess," she stated and then realized her dull voice could very well have dampened the day for anyone who heard her. "Unless he's purchased even more horses," she said to rectify things. That idea sat with her about as well as drinking soured milk, especially when she realized that could very well be true, what with the way Logan was spending his new fortune.

"Ah, you're not fun." Patrick let go of Celeste and ran over to join Pa in stroking the new mare's neck.

Logan sat atop Prince, holding the reins to Princess. "Good morning, Celeste." He greeted her with a smile. "Are you ready to do some riding?"

"I suppose," she responded, noticing Princess wore a brand-new saddle. Celeste recognized the intricately tooled leather as Stewart Hoy's work, having seen enough of his quality-made saddles, with Ma's office being above his shop. Surely the Circle J would have had plenty of saddles from which Logan could choose. Why did he need to buy another? As she walked closer, she was able to see the leather tooling in more detail. There within the floral design was etched the name Celeste. She stopped, stared, and felt her stomach sink with the realization that he'd bought that saddle for her. That sinking feeling worsened. What if he'd purchased Princess for her as well? Then she noticed Logan's saddle looked just like the one on Princess. If Logan were to dismount would she see his name stamped in the leather in similar fashion? She chewed on her lip, nearly biting right through it.

"When you invited me to go riding with you yesterday I had supposed it would be like before," she said, hearing a hint of her sadness come through in her voice. "The two of us together on top of Bootstrap."

His smile vanished. "Uh . . ." He looked as though she'd punched him in the stomach.

At that moment, she knew that's exactly what Princess and the personalized saddle were: gifts to sway her.

"Well, you young folks enjoy your ride." Pa put his hand on Patrick's shoulder and quickly led her brother away.

". . . Uh, I'm afraid Bootstrap ain't feeling too good today," Logan said when Pa and Patrick were out of sight. His eyes lost their spark, and Celeste knew he was lying. "So I decided to bring my new horses. They needed the exercise, and I thought it would be quite the treat for the two of us to ride matching horses."

Celeste reached out for him to hand her the reins to Princess. "Yes, I suppose sitting in my own saddle would be preferable." She hadn't meant it as a dig, but Logan's pained expression spoke volumes.

"You liked sharing the saddle with me?"

"Yes, and I liked Bootstrap," Celeste stated. "He's such a gentle horse. This mare," she patted Princess's nose, only to have the horse jerk it away, "seems a bit high-spirited for my taste."

"But I thought you could handle any horse after them fancy horse classes at school."

"Every horse in the school's stables was as tame as the school days were long. Miss Bennett couldn't afford to have them throw one of her students and have those rich parents up in arms."

"Oh." Logan gave Princess a nervous glance. "She's a tiny bit spirited but just when you first mount. I'll hold the reins while you do that, and you'll be just fine. She's a real good horse. Promise." He dismounted. And as if having a second thought, he reached into his saddlebag. "Oh, I forgot. I've got something for you." He pulled out a brown paper-wrapped package and handed it to Celeste. "This is for you."

Celeste reluctantly took it, wondering what little trinket he'd brought her this time and wishing again he wouldn't feel the need for such gift giving. She pulled away the paper to reveal a new pair of riding breeches. Having shared a dormitory with girls, most of whom were from extremely wealthy families, she recognized these breeches as being identical to the ones Silvia Dreyer had. It was well known that Sylvia's parents bought her only the best money could buy.

Celeste held out the breeches, still partially wrapped in the brown paper, and shoved them toward Logan. "This is very kind of you, but I have a set of riding breeches that are all broken in and that I love. Plus, this is not a contest between you and Charles to see who can buy me the best presents. I finally got to where I refused anymore gifts from Charles. I'm going to do the same with you, starting now."

"That's hardly fair." Logan frowned. "Couldn't you at least have waited a little longer 'til you quit taking my gifts? Charles got to give you a whole passel of them."

Celeste shook her head. "You just don't get it, do you?"

"Get what?"

"Obviously not." She shook her head again. "My whole reasoning behind courting you for two weeks, and Charles the same, was to help me decide which one of you could give me what I need in here." She patted her chest. "Not who could give me the most in here." She pulled open the pocket of her breeches and pointed inside. She exaggerated her movements, and Logan appeared hurt. His expression tore at her heart, but she knew it had to be.

"I'm sorry," he said. "I can hardly help myself. For the longest time I've wanted to buy you something nice, and I couldn't. You know how embarrassing it is to have a gal pay for your supper?" He didn't wait for an answer. "I guess I just kind of got carried away, that's all. It's so gosh darn fun buying things for a gal you care for when you've finally got some money to do so."

Celeste ducked her head. "I'd not thought of it that way." She looked back into Logan's eyes. "So . . . you care for me, do you?"

Logan nodded emphatically and opened his mouth to say something.

Celeste placed her finger on his lips to silence him. "Don't tell me," she said softly, mere inches from his ear. Being so close to him made her heart thump faster. She would have liked to kiss his cheek but refrained. "Show me . . . in ways that have nothing to do with money."

Logan gulped. He took hold of the hand she had to his mouth, spread out her fingers, and kissed them one by one before releasing them "If you say so."

She felt his other hand pressed against her lower back, sending tingles up her spine. He pulled her close, his mouth meeting hers with such tenderness she gasped her delight. For so long she had awaited this moment that anticipation transformed to passion, and she returned his kiss with rawness.

When at last their kiss ended, she laid her head against his chest and snuggled up under his chin, enjoying his arms still wrapped around her. "There. This cost nothing, but it has been my favorite moment of this day." She easily smiled. "So far."

"This is my favorite so far too." He sighed.

"I'm so glad we agree on something." They remained in each other's arms a minute longer, until Celeste broke the silence. "I do love horseback riding. How about we just forget we're riding on matching, purebred horses and merely concentrate on being together. What do you say?"

"I say yeah."

As Logan pulled Princess into position for Celeste to mount, she blurted out her thoughts. "Though it would have been more fun in the saddle with my arms around you."

Logan appeared to steady himself and then steadied Princess instead. "Next time I'll make sure to only bring one horse," he said and then whispered under his breath, "Go ahead, Charles, buy your automobile. A gal can't cozy up to the driver of a car like she can to a rider on a horse."

Smiling to herself, Celeste stuck her foot in the stirrup and mounted flawlessly. She noticed Logan watching her. His eyes held a gleam of pride. "Let's ride down to the river bottoms," Celeste suggested once they were both mounted.

"Sounds like a good idea. Let's cut through that field over yonder." He pointed to a freshly cut field of alfalfa bordering her pa's land. "Already in the week and a half since I've owned the Circle J, all the ranch hands have commented on how much smoother things are running. The hay getting cut on time being one of those improvements."

It didn't take long for them to make it to edge of Logan's land. Celeste thought having Logan live so close could be a silver lining to him acquiring the Circle J. As they neared the heart of the ranch, Celeste's attention gravitated to the bunkhouse. "This will take us by the bunkhouse, won't it?"

"Yes. It's still one of the best ways to get to the prettiest part of the river bottoms," Logan said.

"I'd rather go a different way." Celeste's insides tensed. "I don't want to take a chance of running into that ranch manager of yours, Tom."

"I let Tom go the first day I was here," Logan said. "He was Stanley's manager, not mine."

"Good decision." Celeste was glad Logan was still able to make good ones. So many decisions he'd made of late certainly did not fall into that category. "Were you able to find a replacement that quickly?"

"Naw. I still don't have one. You might say I'm doing it all."

"Who oversees things when you're gone? The next two weeks are ours together. You might be gone a fair amount of time."

"Don't worry. I'm paying Mr. Crandall extra to keep an eye on things. He's the housekeeper's husband, remember?"

"Yes, I remember." Celeste chewed on her fingernail and slowed her horse down. "Does he have any experience managing a ranch?"

"Not really. He's the onsite blacksmith. But he's a big man, so I'm sure things will be fine. Besides, the hands all like me."

"And you're positive Tom is gone?" Celeste turned in her saddle so as to look at Logan straight on.

Princess reared up on her hind legs. Celeste's movement must have spooked Princess. The next few seconds played out as if part of a slow-moving bad dream. The horse hurled her into the air. The next moment, she lay on the ground with Princess's front hooves coming straight down toward her head.

"Roll!" Logan screamed.

Miraculously, Celeste managed to move from her back to her side; Princess's hooves landed mere inches away.

Logan dismounted and rushed to Celeste's side, shooing both Princess and Prince away. He gazed into her face, worry lines standing out in his forehead. "Are you able to sit?"

She nodded. "I think so." She sat up slowly with Logan's help. "Luckily, I landed on my backside. But other than getting the wind knocked out of me, I think I'll be fine."

He scooped her into his arms. "I'm taking you back to the ranch house. Darn temperamental horses!"

"Thank you." She wrapped her arms around his neck to help him support her weight. Being cradled in Logan's arms at any other time would have quickened her heartbeat, but now its thumping came from being scared out of her wits. "I think we're done with horseback riding for today." She ran her fingers along the base of his neck. Normally, she would have felt those soft curls. The action had brought her comfort the last time she'd done that. A little comfort would be nice. "I miss your long hair. I liked how it reached down to your shoulders."

"Are you pulling my leg?" Logan's face twisted. "What a strange thing to say at a time like this. At least you're talking. That must mean you're not hurt too awful bad. That's what I'm hoping."

"I'm fine." Celeste's hip ached, and it would probably have a large bruise by tomorrow, but she *was* okay. And now was as good a time as any to share some more of her feelings. They had yet to discuss such matters. "I'm serious about your hair. I liked the way it curled up on the back of your neck." She brushed his cheek with the back of her hand. "And I liked your short beard too, when you trimmed it."

Logan laughed and seemed to enjoy carrying her back to the house in his arms. "And all this time I feared I'd turned your stomach, making you look at a man who couldn't afford to keep his hair cut or buy a new razor."

"Oh, I do like it when you're clean-shaven too." She caressed his chin, finding it enjoyable as she made this important point. This was good. Communication was vital in a courtship.

"So a clean-shaven—or trimmed—face is more important than being presented with a new horse, saddle, and riding breeches?" He shifted her weight in his arms, continuing to carry her like it took no effort.

"Absolutely," she responded. "But even more so is respect for my requests." This day was finally going as she'd originally hoped it could.

By the time they made it to the house, Celeste was touching her hip gingerly. Apparently she'd bruised it more than she'd thought. Her playful mood became hard to maintain.

He laid her carefully on the sofa in the great room and then turned toward the kitchen. "Can I get you something? A drink? A sandwich to hold you 'til supper?"

"A drink of water would be good." She situated herself on the sofa and couldn't keep back a moan when she put pressure on her hip. A wave a nausea hit her. "I don't think I'll be staying for supper." She looked up at him before he left the room. "I'm afraid I'm not feeling as well as I'd thought. It would be best if you took me home, and I think it might be best if you didn't call on me tomorrow." She offered him a weak smile. It was hard to muster much more.

"Are you sure?" Logan's voice sounded strained.

"Just because this is your time to court me, don't feel like you've got to see me every day. I've heard it said that absence makes the heart grow fonder."

Logan's hand made a fist. "Let me guess, Charles said that," he said, clenching his jaw. "He most likely was trying to convince you that's what you needed to do with me."

Celeste's nerves tensed, making her stomach hurt nearly as badly as her hip. She glared at him. "No, I read that in a book."

"It's hardly fair," Logan whispered and turned toward the kitchen. "Charles got his full two weeks, and I get a Sunday and two half days."

"Fair?" Celeste's voice rose as she spoke to Logan's back. She assumed he was leaving the room to get her a drink—at least, she hoped that was why. "Is getting heat stroke fair?" She spoke up even louder to make sure he could hear. "Is being bucked off a temperamental horse fair? This is not about you, Logan. Nor is it about Charles. I'll tell you what's not fair: this whole ridiculous plan of mine to court two men at once. I should have never subjected you or Charles to such nonsense. No good has come from it. I believe it has ruined you, Logan Jones." She sat up in a huff, slowly moved her legs to the floor, and then hugged herself. *You are not the man I fell in love with.*

Chapter 26

TRYING TO CONTAIN THE PRESSURE mounting inside him, Logan stomped into the kitchen to get Celeste some water. Nothing he did was turning out as he'd planned. And now this. He finally saw that perhaps buying Celeste lots of gifts wasn't the answer, and that spending quality time with her was what she wanted. But now she didn't even want very much of that.

From where Logan stood at the sink, he couldn't see her face, only her back. Her shoulders were shaking. Was she crying? He didn't dare ask. He'd already made a mess of things. The least he could do was hurry back with her drink.

Her shoulders stilled and squared up as he walked into the room. She turned around and looked at him, wiping her eye. "I'd like you to take me home now."

"When will I see you next?" He held out the glass of water.

"I can't say at the moment." She took it and drank half of it.

"You can't say?" Logan repeated, still struggling with the unfairness of this all. "Fine. I'll go get the buggy hitched up. We'll take Bootstrap."

"Thank you," Celeste said as she rose slowly from the couch.

They rode in silence the entire way from the Circle J to the McCurdy place. Logan didn't like that he had time to mull over all his stupid mistakes. Celeste didn't seem to want to talk. Every time he brought up so much as the weather or that bird flying by, she simply nodded her response.

When they made it to Celeste's house, he helped her out of the buggy and walked her to the door. She seemed to be managing her pain okay, as far as getting bucked from a horse was concerned. But her silence was unnatural. Was she feeling pain in other ways?

Still, he had to ask. There were still twelve more days left in his turn with her. "When will I see you again?"

"I don't know." She wiped her eye.

Logan felt numb. "I'm sorry, Celeste." He had not intended to make her cry.

"And I am sorry, Logan. Sorry for taking a wonderful, caring man and turning him into someone I don't know." She said it all over her shoulder, then walked into the house. The door shut in Logan's face.

U

Logan drove his buggy over the rutted road to the McCurdy place. It had been three days since he'd seen Celeste. He imagined it to be plenty of time for her to feel better. The moment he arrived, he jumped out of the buggy, ran to the door, and knocked, not even bothering to shout a hello to Lucas, who was out in the barnyard. Staying away the past few days to give Celeste time for her bruises to heal had been torture. All he cared to see right now was *her*.

"Logan." Kate sounded surprised when she opened the door. "Um, good morning."

"I'm here to see Celeste. I still have nine days left of my turn. Uh, you know, of courting her," Logan added when Kate appeared hesitant to let him in.

"I'm afraid Celeste is not up to seeing anyone today. With all she's been through, her body has been weakened, and she's caught a nasty cold. I've consigned her to bed to ensure it doesn't turn into something worse, like pneumonia." Kate placed her hand on his arm.

Was that meant to be reassuring or to block him from coming inside? Logan bristled.

"I'm sorry, Logan, but I'm sure you'll understand. I'm hoping she'll be up to visitors in a few days—a week at most."

"A week?" Logan spurted out, seeing his time with Celeste slip through his fingers like a slippery fish, unable to grab hold of anything.

Inside the house, a door creaked open. Celeste poked her head out of the back bedroom. Though her hair was messy and her eyes puffy, Logan's heart sped when he caught sight of her.

"Celeste!"

"Logan." Celeste gasped. "I thought I'd not see you again after what I said the other night."

"It'll take more than that to keep me away," Logan said, thinking about how he'd already stayed away for three precious days.

Celeste offered him a weak smile. "That's awfully sweet, Logan, but I really don't feel well."

"You need to see a doctor! I could send a wire to Denver and get the best one there is out here in no time. Money is no object."

"Logan, I already have the best doctor there is taking care of me." Celeste nodded at her ma.

"Oh yeah," Logan muttered. How could he have forgotten about Kate?

"Thank you, dear," Kate said to Celeste. She turned to Logan. "Her condition is not that serious, nothing that some good bedrest and some lemon and honey can't take care of in a few days."

"Or a week," Logan said through gritted teeth. "At the most, you said."

"Yes, I feel that is safe to say." Kate nodded.

"Logan, I really wish I did, but seriously, I don't feel up to company right now. Sorry." Celeste chewed on her lip.

Kate wagged her hand at Celeste. "Now, back to bed, and I'll see Logan gets safely on his way."

"You don't need to bother, Kate. I can see myself back to my buggy just fine." Logan turned away, then spun back around as Celeste slipped from sight into the bedroom. "I'll check back in a day or so, if that's okay—just in case she heals up fast."

"I'd give her at least four days. I'm saying that as her doctor. As a friend, I'd like to say I'm sorry. I realize this was supposed to be your time with Celeste. Maybe she'll extend her time with you, given the circumstances. In either case, Logan, like I said, I'm sorry."

Not as sorry as I am. Logan blew out a breath. "I'll stop back in four days. Goodbye, Kate."

Logan dragged himself back to his buggy. He jerked the reins and made Prince turn it around abruptly, then headed for town to pick up his mail. He may as well do something since he had already left the ranch in the hands of Mr. Crandall for the day. The postal service had not yet found a replacement for him, so everyone on the outskirts of town had to fetch their own mail, same as him.

"Serves them right," he spouted off to no one and drove away from the McCurdy place.

The road felt longer and bumpier than usual. If he was going to be by himself, he would have preferred being atop a horse.

Once in town, he lumbered into the new post office.

The postmaster looked up from the papers on his desk. "Good morning. What can I do for you?"

Logan didn't even know the name of the small man with a big moustache who sat behind the desk. Nor did he care to. He was an outsider—moved there from Steam Boat Springs after the postal service hired him on. Even though Logan no longer needed the money, it still grated on his nerves that *he* didn't get the job. The people of Craig deserved to have a postmaster who knew them. They also deserved a mail carrier for the RFD routes.

"Morning," Logan mumbled, none too happy about anything that had to do with mail at the moment. "The name's Logan Jones. I'm here to pick up my mail."

"Oh, yes, the fellow with all the packages. I hope you brought your wagon today."

"I got a buggy," Logan responded with loathing, thinking about that blasted buggy—the best money could buy. He'd bought it for Celeste. He was darn well going to get some use out of it, so it may as well be for hauling mail-order items he no longer needed. If Celeste wanted no gifts, he certainly wasn't going to give them to her—he sensed she was already upset with him enough as it was. Though he couldn't understand why. This courting business was more difficult than he'd ever imagined.

The postmaster wore a coy smile. "You must have yourself quite the sweetheart to be ordering all those lovely gifts for her."

"How do you know what's in those boxes?" Logan snapped.

The postmaster held up his hands. "Sorry. I didn't mean nothing by it. That big hat box is a sure giveaway as to what's inside. I just assumed the others held more of the same."

Logan flicked his wrist at him. "It's all right." He swore his nerves were paper thin ever since Celeste slammed that door in his face three days ago. "And I didn't mean to get angry with you. How about you give me my stuff, and I'll get outta your hair."

The postmaster slipped into the back room of the new post office and returned carrying the large hat box piled with five smaller boxes. Logan took them without a word, carried them outside, and plopped them onto the buggy's seat, leaving himself barely enough room to sit down. He flicked the reins on Prince's back and headed for home, his heart feeling as weighed down as the buggy.

When he arrived at the Circle J, he hoped Lewis Crandall would be in shouting distance so he could have the man unload the buggy, then unhitch it and take care of Prince. Neither Lewis nor any other ranch hand was anywhere to be seen. In fact, the wagon full of hay he'd asked Lewis to unload into the loft sat untouched next to the barn. Logan set to the task of taking care of the buggy himself, finding it bothersome as well that Mrs. Crandall was not inside the house as he carried in the packages. He imagined she should be cooking something for supper by now. When he got to brushing Prince down, he must have been too rough with the brush, for the stallion reared up on his back legs. His hoof came down, grazing the rounded toe of Logan's fancy new shoe, the one that was built up by an inch. "G—" He slapped his hand over his mouth. Sure, it hurt like Hades, but he'd never taken the Lord's name in vain before. What was wrong with him?

Logan limped worse than ever but walked out of the barn anyway, inserted two fingers in his mouth and whistled. Bootstrap came running from inside the corral attached to the barn.

"Nice to know someone still listens to me." He patted his horse and led him inside to saddle him up. "I need you to help me find Lewis Crandall. When I'm paying someone to do a job, I expect it done!"

Hoping some of the other hands might know something, he rode Bootstrap to the bunkhouse first, keeping his eyes out for Lewis. As he approached the slant-roofed bunkhouse, he got to thinking the wooden-slat structure was plenty sufficient. When he'd taken over the Circle J that was one of the first things he'd wanted to change—it had always worried him. He'd wanted to build a new one, a bigger one, out of bricks, with a high-pitched A-frame roof so come winter the snow could slide right off, rather than the hands needing to shovel it after a deep snowstorm to stop the roof from sagging. Maybe it'd been a good thing he'd been too preoccupied with Celeste to start construction on a new one. This one was fine. It had been for years. A new one would cut in to the ranch's profits.

Stubby, one of the new ranch hands, darted from the bunkhouse and ran toward Logan. "There's somethin' I need to tell ya, boss," Stubby hollered as he got in ear-shot of Logan.

"Not now." Logan held out his hand, palm forward. "I need to find Lewis first."

"That's what I was gunna tell ya. He up and left really quick-like this mornin'. Took his wife with him. Said somethin' about helpin' his boy out—his son that got a nice piece of land from his wife's folks over near Hayden. You hear about that?"

"No. My employee's kids are no concern to me. What concerns me is that I left Lewis in charge while I was gone. Now he's gone." Logan realized he could have said that bit nicer, but gosh darn it, he didn't feel like it at the moment.

"Don't worry none. Lewis put me in charge. I've done my best. Sorry. Can't do nothin' about your supper though. Other than that, I'd say things are runnin' smooth."

"Smooth?" Logan rolled his eyes. "There's a wagon of hay sitting by the barn waiting to be unloaded while the man apparently in charge of my ranch is lounging around the bunkhouse in the middle of the day. I wouldn't call that smooth."

"I can explain, boss." Stubby's face twitched. "I done ripped a healthy hole in my pants to where my backside was feelin' a breeze. I just got done changin' them and was ready to head out to check on the herd over in the north forty when I saw you. As for the hay, I didn't know nothin' about that. But I'll get right on it."

"Don't worry about the hay. I'll take care of that." Logan nodded his goodbye and figured he'd go and take his frustrations out on pitching hay.

U

After two days of cooking for himself, Logan stood at the sink ready to scrub the scrambled eggs stuck to the frying pan when he looked out the window and spotted smoke coming from the chimney of the cottage where he was letting the Crandalls stay. Abandoning the dishes, he rushed outside and walked toward the cottage, grateful at least for his new shoes. Sure, their round toes looked out of place on a ranch, and his ankles were exposed to manure and more, but he barely struggled with walking anymore. When he got past these two weeks with Celeste, he'd see about having a custom set of cowboy boots made while Charles had his turn. It would be Logan's luck that Celeste would be in perfect health that whole time. Logan clenched his fists at the unfairness of it all. To have all this money but be unable to control things more as they fell apart around him gave him the urge to punch something.

"Ah, Logan, I was just coming to speak with you," Lewis said as he stepped out of the cottage. "I wanted to apologize for my sudden—"

"Where have you been for two days?" Logan interrupted, not caring what Lewis had to say but wanting the first word. He was the boss, and he wanted his employees to know that. "You left without a word. You didn't even bother taking care of that hay like I asked you to."

"Didn't Stubby tell you?" Lewis Crandall's voice rose in pitch with each word.

"It's not Stubby's place to tell me; it's yours. If you need time off, you have to ask me and give me at least a day's notice." Logan inclined his head to make sure Lewis knew he was serious. After all, what Logan was asking was not unreasonable in the least. "And to make sure you remember the rules of this ranch I'm going to have to cut your pay for the next month. Understood?"

"But, sir, I can explain."

"Don't bother. Rules are rules. Besides, your pay cut is only temporary." Logan turned and walked away.

"There was an emergency," Lewis hollered at Logan's back. "My son, he got in a wagon accident and was hurt bad. I had to help his neighbor pull the wagon out of a ravine, then get my injured son back to his wife and new baby, where my wife patched him up. I wanted to talk to you, but you were gone. A decision had to be made then and there. I made the one I was sure you would have made—I left the moment I got word and went to help. My son's life was more important than loading that blasted hay into your loft."

Logan stopped. Lewis was right; Logan would have done the same thing . . . if he had a son. His throat tightened. He hoped Crandall's son was doing okay. Should he ask? Should he go back on the punishment he'd dished out? He took a deep breath, ready to turn around and talk to Lewis.

No. If he was going to run an efficient ranch, he needed to be firm with his employees. "Like I said, the pay cut is only temporary. Good day, Mr. Crandall," Logan said and continued to walk away, not so sure he liked being the boss. But the ranch was his now. So was the money. He needed to keep the ranch profitable and prove to his dead father that he wasn't a failure, that he was worthwhile.

Chapter 27

CELESTE HEARD A RIDER APPROACH. She turned away from the wagon she was helping Ma load and leaned to see who came down the road.

Logan clicked his heels into Prince's flanks the moment their gazes met. Celeste caught her breath. He looked so nice in his freshly ironed white shirt and dark-blue denim trousers. It'd been five days since he'd been here, since she'd last seen him. He'd stayed away a day longer than he'd told her ma he would. Celeste was afraid her rudeness from the last two times she'd seen him had scared him away. Then again, five days ago, she wasn't so sure she wanted to see him again. Logan had come across as a little too selfish for her taste. However, lying in bed four days in a row had given her plenty of time to think about Logan's behavior and imagine things through his eyes. He had been dealt a bit of bad luck as it came to spending time with her, especially when compared to Charles's uninterrupted time.

"Oh dear," Celeste said to herself, knowing yet again she'd be unavailable to Logan. Perhaps she could tell Logan to start again with his two weeks to court her the moment she got back from helping Ma deliver Mrs. Drake's twins.

She took her eyes off him, stuffing the traveling bag containing several days' worth of her and Ma's clothing into the wagon and then giving it a punch to make it fit between the extra blankets and Ma's medical bag. If she was frustrated, she could only imagine what this news would do to Logan. But he, of all people, should be understanding of the circumstances.

She looked back up at Logan as he approached. A smile formed as she recalled a favorite story her ma had shared about Logan. He had "fetched" Ma to deliver her first baby out West. Not only did Logan deliver the message, but he rode with her out to the homestead to make sure she got there safely. He spent the night because of the late hour of their arrival but never complained one ounce. Rather, he spent his time comforting the nervous Mr. Castillo while Ma helped Mrs. Castillo through a long labor. Logan wanted to stay the next day to help, but Ma had said everything was under control and insisted he head back home without her, telling him, "Sometimes the birthing process can take several days."

Logan dismounted and, with reins in hand, walked toward her. "Celeste, you're doing better!" The delight in his voice stood out like a rosebush in a field of sagebrush.

His enthusiasm ignited that warm, comfortable feeling inside her heart that only Logan seemed to create. Could it be that her old Logan was back and all his disturbing behavior was behind him, behavior possibly stemming from the awkward situation created by indecision and a poor plan? Well, she didn't need to subject Logan or Charles to another month of this madness. She didn't need any more time to decide. When she got right down to it, she never actually did. Her heart already knew. She loved Logan.

She'd tell Logan and Charles the madness was over first thing when she got back from the Drakes'. She'd made her decision. There was no need to take another month.

"I didn't bother with the buggy today. I thought a simple visit would be best, you barely recovering from an illness and all. I waited a whole extra day on top of what your ma recommended."

"Oh. Thank you," Celeste said hesitantly.

"Should you be working so hard so soon after being sick? You know, loading a wagon for . . ." He glanced at her ma.

"Yes, for me," Ma responded. "I've received word that Mrs. Drake is having pains, so we're heading out there right now before she goes into hard labor. Normally, we'd go on horseback, but given the circumstances and the need for extra supplies—"

"We?" Logan interrupted.

"Yes, Celeste is coming with me. I need her help."

"But you've been sick." Logan rushed his focus onto Celeste.

"I'm feeling fine, honestly. I have been for a whole day now."

"A whole day?" Logan's expression drooped. "You mean I could have come out here yesterday? I waited for nothing? And now you're leaving?" He paused and clenched his fists. "For how long?"

"We could be gone a week." Ma shrugged. "It's possible Mrs. Drake is having twins and will need some extra help. She has no family close."

"Couldn't you take Patrick or Rob?" Logan's fists clenched tighter. "Darn it all, why take Celeste? I—I mean she's been sick, after all. That wouldn't be very smart."

Ma stepped back and stared at Logan. "Seriously, Rob or Patrick? Mrs. Drake is *not* a ewe struggling with her first birth."

"Excuse me!" Celeste glared at Logan. "My mother *is* smart and knows exactly who and what she needs when it comes to delivering babies. And if she says she's going to need me, then I'm going to be there for her. I thought you'd understand."

"Well, you thought wrong." Logan kicked the dirt with his round-toed shoe. "Darn it all, Celeste. I've tried to be patient. I've tried to be understanding when you got sick and couldn't give me my fair share of your time. But when it gets right down to it, I've been dealt a rotten hand. It just ain't fair." He removed his skimmer hat that looked a lot like Charles's and raked a hand through his hair. "Charles, on the other hand . . . I don't want to talk about Charles. How about I hire some woman to ride out to the Drakes with your ma so you can stay here? With me. So I can have the last four days of my time with you fair and square. I'll pay a pretty penny."

"First of all . . ." Celeste stomped to where she stood face to face with Logan. "There's no time to find someone else. Babies don't wait for such things." She took a deep breath. "Second of all, I want to go." *And I want to get away from here, from you, Logan.*

"Will I see you first thing when you get back? You could send Rob or Patrick over to fetch me."

"I don't know." Celeste wiped her eye. She'd promised herself weeks ago she was through pretending, but here she was again, pretending she was okay with this sudden change in Logan. *I won't do this.* "Maybe never—maybe I'll never see you again. I don't know you anymore. You're turning into someone, rather some*thing*, I don't care for."

"But—but—"

"No . . . I'm not interested in courting you anymore. I shall tell Charles the same. So do not worry that I am giving either you or him an unfair advantage over the other."

"But—"

"Goodbye, Logan Jones." Celeste climbed into the wagon. "Come on, Ma. We need to go."

Chapter 28

A week and a half had passed since Celeste told him goodbye. It would be Charles's time if she'd stuck to her plan. Logan would rather have kept up with her harebrained plan and taken turns with her every two weeks than not see her at all. He hated going into town now, but here he was, picking up more mail-order items he didn't need but had ordered nonetheless a few weeks ago. With his buggy loaded higher than ever, he headed for the Circle J. He caught a glimpse of the mercantile on his way out of town. Maybe he should drop these packages off there and give them to Lavender to sell at her store. He certainly didn't need a woman's hat, jewelry, or perfume.

Slowing the buggy down, he had second thoughts.

Heck, I paid good money for this. Why should I give it away?

I won't. They're mine.

He'd take them home and put them all in one of those empty bedrooms of his, just because he could. Rich people bought things they didn't need all the time. Why shouldn't he? He was one of them now.

"Hey, you!"

Those words caught Logan off guard, and he stopped Prince completely. He turned to see who'd said them.

Charles sat at the checker table outside the mercantile, staring at Logan. "You've stopped by to rub salt in my wound, have you?" He stood quickly, tossing the board and its checkers onto the ground. "Or you're here to fight it out like a man, are you, to honorably determine who gets Celeste? Well, I'm up to that." With hands fisted and raised, he stomped toward Logan.

Logan climbed out of the buggy, laughing. He could easily take Charles in a fistfight, if he so chose to waste his time. He lumbered toward him. "Charles, Charles, I see Celeste has delivered you the bad news."

"A day ago." Charles frowned. "First thing when she got back from the Drakes. So . . . you're here to gloat, are you?"

"Not hardly. And put your hands down." Logan grabbed Charles's fists and pushed him back into his chair. "I'm not here to fight you, neither. Though the way I'm feeling, maybe it wouldn't be a bad idea after all. If you hadn't come to Craig, I wouldn't be in this mess."

"What are you talking about?" Charles glared at him.

"Did Celeste not tell you?"

"Tell me what?" Charles gritted his teeth. "All she told me was to leave her alone; she was through with me." He punched his fist into his open palm. "And I had a whole two weeks planned out with her. For nothing!" He punched his hand again. "And my Oldsmobile is arriving tomorrow. Paid a fellow in Steam Boat Springs a handsome sum to get it from the train and drive it out to me. What am I going to do now?"

"Same thing as me." Logan pointed to the boxes filling his buggy. "Take all Celeste's gifts and shove 'em in an empty room. I've got space in my barn, if you want to park your fancy automobile there. At a price." He laughed. "If you can even get it out to my ranch. The roads out that way—and to the McCurdy place—will chew up those flimsy tires like they're made of jerky."

"Are you saying Celeste told you goodbye for good too?"

"That's exactly what I'm saying." Logan lifted his skimmer hat at Charles. "So if you'll excuse me, I'll be getting back to my ranch now. And you, you can get back to New York—or wherever it is you're from." He placed his hat back on his head, wondering why he wore the blasted thing anyway. He'd always hated those hats, liking his beat-up old cowboy hat better. Looking down at his round-toed shoes, feeling the same about them, he shuffled back to his buggy.

"I can't go back to New York," Charles said to Logan's back. "I bought a house here. I have a mortgage. I'm not as rich as you. I can't just walk away."

"Can I help it you were a fool?" Logan said, climbing into his buggy and not offering Charles so much as a glance.

The ride back to the Circle J felt excruciatingly long. He much preferred being on top of a horse—Bootstrap, if the truth be told. Still, he always took Prince when riding into town. Why, though? Why did he need to keep up his image? Celeste wouldn't take notice of him. Even if she were to catch sight of him by some miracle, she preferred his homely old horse over his prize stallion, for some reason. Just as Logan did.

His stomach grumbled as he commanded Prince to make the turn off the main road onto the one leading to the Circle J. He glanced at the sun hanging in the sky above the western horizon. It was well past supper time, and he wondered what Mrs. Crandall was making tonight. He couldn't wait to sit down to her cooking. He had to admit that was a nice thing about being rich, having someone to cook for you. Heck, he didn't need a wife, least not to cook and clean for him.

That pang returned to his chest, the empty cavern created when all hope of being with Celeste was lost. Mrs. Crandall's cooking and cleaning could never fill that. After kissing Celeste, he thought he'd found heaven. Now his heart felt as though it was in hell. Why had he ever let himself hope to find a wife in Celeste? Before she came home from school, he'd managed to accept the reality of being a bachelor quite admirably.

"But I got money now," he said to Prince. The horse didn't even so much as flick his ear, let alone turn his head to acknowledge Logan. He kept talking anyway. "I can buy myself a wife. Heck, my good friend Ron sent away for a mail-order bride, and things worked out nicely for him, so why can't I do the same? I'm sure there'd be plenty a lady who'd look past my bum leg, given I buy them anything they want."

But what kind of company would they be? Nothing like Celeste.

His mind wandered back to the first time he'd met Celeste. He was thirteen, and she was five. She asked him what was wrong with his leg. Kate had scolded her for being rude, but her inquiry hadn't been rude at all. He sensed Celeste as a little girl had sincerely wanted to know because she was concerned for him. So he'd told her the truth. It had been the easiest explanation of his being born that way that he'd ever given anyone. And ever since then, Celeste had never once made him feel inferior because of his bum leg. He truly sensed that she never viewed him as having a deformed leg; she only saw him for who he really was.

The pang in his chest intensified to where he doubled over in pain. "Just take me on home," he said and flicked his reins. Then he realized he wasn't talking to Bootstrap. He couldn't just let go of the reins and let his old friend take over. Forcing himself back upright, he drove Prince toward the ranch as fast as he dared take the flimsy buggy across the rutted road.

When Logan pulled up in front of the ranch house, he expected the ranch hand on duty to come take the buggy away and tend to it and Prince. He looked this way and that, searching for his help as he climbed down. There was not a soul to be seen in the yard. He marched toward the house, determined to have a word with Mr. Crandall. What kind of foreman was he? He'd make sure to dock his pay for this. Again. That last episode should have been enough to set Crandall straight. But apparently it wasn't.

Logan burst through the front door. "Mrs. Crandall, where's your husband?" The house sounded as quiet as the yard. "Mrs. Crandall?" He walked toward the kitchen. Strange, usually he could smell a beef roast cooking or at least a pot of stew. Only the faint scent of the lye soap Mrs. Crandall had made yesterday could be smelled. It was not appetizing in the least.

"Mrs. Crandall," he yelled this time.

He walked through the entire house, looking in every room. The place was clean. She'd obviously been here today, doing a more thorough job than usual, he had to admit. But none of that mattered right now. He wanted to know where her husband was and where his supper was.

He stormed outside, heading for the cottage where the Crandalls stayed. When he rounded the side of the cottage, he spotted a wagon parked out in front of the place. It was loaded to the brim with belongings.

"What's going on here?" he asked of Mrs. Crandall, who had just stepped out of the cottage with a load of bedding in her arms.

"We're moving out," Mrs. Crandall said, as if it were the most natural thing to say.

"Who said you could?" Logan demanded.

"It's a free country." Mrs. Crandall's jaw was set as firm as the look in her eyes.

Mr. Crandall walked out of the cottage a step behind his wife. He carried a kitchen chair. He stared at it rather than give Logan even so much as a glance. "We don't need no permission from the likes of you."

"The likes of me?" Logan repeated, dumbfounded.

"Why should we give you such consideration when you've given my poor Lewis none?" Mrs. Crandall glared at him. "He's given you his all, but you've given him naught but a tongue lashing every day. He was nigh onto a breakdown, so I told him to leave this accursed ranch 'cause I was ready to go with him." She turned her back to Logan and marched her armload to the wagon.

"B-but," Logan stammered, feeling as though his world was caving in, exposing his behavior, letting him see the kind of person he was becoming: a brute. He couldn't believe he'd treated these nice folks so unfairly. "You're right." He hadn't meant to come across so unfeeling. "I'm sorry. Don't go. You can't go. I need you."

"Too late. We've already been hired on somewhere else." Mr. Crandall walked past him. "We start tomorrow. Just found out yesterday. We would have told you then, but you weren't around. Julia's done cleaned your house from top to bottom today, so it'll last you 'til you find someone else. As for the rest of the ranch, Ollie's temporarily in charge. You go talk to him. Maybe he'd be willing to step into my job—despite what I've told him about you being as bad as your brother to work for." Crandall continued walking. Over his shoulder, he muttered, "You should have never fired Tom like you did. He's the only one ornery enough to put up with an ornery landowner like you."

Logan froze. *Ornery?* He'd never, ever considered himself as such. But apparently he'd become that too. Rooted there, dumbstruck, his mind spun through the past several weeks. Maybe ornery was putting it mildly. "I'll double each of your salaries if the two of you stay on."

Crandall turned, faced Logan, and looked him in the eye. "No amount of money could make me stay on here. Even as just the blacksmith. Not even with your *free* cottage for me and my wife."

Mrs. Crandall dropped her load in the wagon and approached Logan. She stopped three feet away. "When you asked me to come be your housekeeper, I jumped at the chance. Though I didn't know you all that well, I knew *of* you. Logan Jones, 'the nicest man this side of Denver,' folks would refer to you as. Why wouldn't I want to move out of a cramped apartment above the telegraph office and come live on the Circle J along with my husband so he wouldn't have to ride so far to work every day? The horrible days of Stanley Jones were in the past. The Circle J would be a wonderful place to live now that his little brother was in charge." She took a step closer to him. "But you've proved me wrong." She pointed a wobbly finger at him. "You're no different from your brother."

Crandall motioned for his wife to step away from Logan.

She hurried over and climbed into the wagon. "You'll find the cottage as clean as the ranch house."

Crandall flicked the reins, moved the wagon forward, and looked at Logan. "Money can't buy everything, Mr. Jones."

Logan, still rooted to that same spot at the front of the cottage, stood helplessly watching his foreman and housekeeper drive away. Their words had rung true, and he knew it.

A horrible fear ignited within him. He was becoming the person he'd sworn he'd never be.

He was becoming his brother.

He dropped to the ground, wishing it would open up and swallow him whole. No wonder Celeste wanted nothing more to do with him. He didn't blame her one bit. If he didn't change his ways, *no one* would want anything to do with him.

Chapter 29

CELESTE TOOK A RARE BREAK from her chores, grabbed the book that had been taking forever to read, and went outside to enjoy it under the cottonwood tree south of the barn. It being early September, the weather had cooled down to where she found being outside rather pleasant, especially in the shade. After passing out that day at the Circle J, she'd been careful to avoid too much sun. She'd been careful to avoid numerous other activities too—anything that reminded her of those three or so weeks in July when her foolishness resulted in breaking three hearts. She passed by Ma in the side yard, hanging out the freshly scrubbed laundry.

"Going to do some reading, I see." Ma pinned Pa's dress shirt to the line.

"Yes, in the shade of the big tree. And it's about time, I must say."

"Definitely." Ma ceased hanging laundry and gazed at Celeste. "It's about time you forgave yourself and quit moping about. Maybe even find another fellow to set your eyes and heart on. It could help you move past this."

"Mother!" Celeste didn't care to hear this lecture. "Please, Pa has tried to tell me the same thing. I don't care to be courted by anyone right now—maybe never again. The idea of being a spinster does not sound all that bad." The moment she spoke the word *spinster* her heart bound up. It was a lie, and she knew it. She'd missed seeing Logan the past several weeks, the old Logan. She'd even missed seeing Charles.

Ma abandoned the basket of wet laundry, walked over, and draped an arm around Celeste's shoulder. "Let's not throw the baby out with the bathwater." She fell in step with Celeste. "Instead, let's see if we need to do some more scrubbing."

Celeste had never heard the second half of that idiom. She tilted her head and glanced at Ma out of the corner of her eye. "Huh?"

"We need to remove all the layers of dirt, you may say, reasons behind the *why* you came up with your idea of allowing two men to court you at once. Then perhaps we can understand your motives, and then maybe you can forgive yourself so you can move on."

"Oh." Celeste had to admit Ma's thinking made some sense. At least, it brought a measure of hope. "All right. But how might I do that?"

"Let's start with your feelings for Logan." Ma removed her arm from Celeste's shoulder and held her hands out in a gesture of trying to understand. "When you first returned from school, it was easy to see that you had your heart set on Logan. What happened to those feelings?"

"I'm not sure." Celeste chewed on her knuckle. "I do believe they were always there, even when I was with Charles."

"Why, then, did you feel the need to have Charles court you, at the same time, no less?" Ma shook her head slowly.

"I couldn't decide if Logan was right for me. Even though in here," she placed a hand on her heart, "I felt good. When Charles showed up again, I figured I'd see how I felt about him to make sure I wasn't making a mistake choosing Logan."

Ma stopped when she reached the shade of the cottonwood and motioned for Celeste to take the old chaise Pa had made years ago. He'd placed it here by the tree just for her when she'd returned from school so she could have a peaceful place to read.

"This is my opinion here, but I swear you and Logan were a match made in heaven. What on earth made you feel that Logan was not right for you?"

Celeste lowered herself onto the chair and stretched her legs upon it. She took a moment to answer, somewhat embarrassed by her reason. "There were a few things about him that I found annoying, and I didn't much care for them."

"Oh, really now?" Ma smiled. "Only a few. I would count yourself fortunate indeed to find a man who only had a few things that annoyed you. I'm not going to ask you to divulge what those traits were but—"

"That is good, because I don't intend to tell you," Celeste cut in, realizing how insignificant Logan's lack of affection was. She'd just needed to give him more time. Their kiss had proven that. But there was a bigger issue now, and it was just as well that she'd ended their relationship: the issue of him having too much money—or rather, the flaunting of that money—and what wealth was doing to Logan. It was turning him selfish. A few weeks ago, when she'd gone into town with Pa, she'd seen something else about Logan she didn't care for at all. Something she could never live with. From a distance, she had seen Logan raise his fists and shout insults at Charles. He was turning into Stanley.

"But," Ma continued, "you need to know that you'll never find a perfect man. There's always going to be something about him that bothers you. And there will be things about you that bother him. But your love for each other helps you put those things in perspective and learn to either accept them or work around them."

"You're saying there are things about Pa that bother you?" Celeste opened her book but stared up at her ma. "I thought if anyone had a perfect marriage it was you two."

"Well, thank you." Ma gave her an appreciative nod. "It is nice to know our hard work has made our marriage look easy."

"Seriously now, what on earth has Pa ever done to annoy you?"

"It doesn't happen all that often, but just yesterday, Pa told me he'd done something very foolish. Something I had warned him against weeks earlier because it was risky. Apparently he proceeded without my knowledge."

"Now you have my curiosity piqued."

"I suppose in this case I can share your pa's poor choice, for I'm sure you will find out about it soon enough. As I tell you this, please do not fear that I think poorly of Charles Weathersby. I realize that he is merely a victim like almost every other person in Craig."

"Do tell." Celeste slapped her book shut and stared at her ma.

"Pa came to me yesterday, like a puppy dog with his tail between his legs caught doing wrong, and told me that he lost the five hundred Grandma had sent us."

"Mother, no!" Celeste knew part of that money was to be for her wedding—if and when she were to have one. She didn't care one whit about that right now. That paled in comparison to the new wagon Ma had hoped they could purchase after they put most of it in savings.

"Yes. It seems your pa invested the money in the company Charles worked for, with the promise of making it all back plus an additional five hundred dollars by the first of November. Yesterday, Charles came out in his new automobile to see your pa. Apparently, Charles had been going door to door in town the day before, telling all the people who had invested with him that his boss had been thrown in jail for fraud. He told them, and your pa, that the government was seizing all of his boss's assets, splitting them up, and paying off the investors as best they can."

"Oh, poor Charles." Celeste let the book fall from her hands and onto the dirt.

"Poor Charles? What about your poor pa?" Ma picked up the book and handed it to Celeste. "He doubts he'll ever see a cent of that money. I fear the same."

"At least Charles had the decency to face all those people. Another man might have simply skipped out of town in the night."

"True." Ma tilted her head and met Celeste's eyes with a look of concern in her own. "Are you considering rekindling your affection for the man?"

"Give yourself no worries there. Even if I still had feelings for Charles, which I do not, I would dare not face him after all the hurt I have caused him." She hung her head as she considered Logan. She opened her book and pretended to read. "The same applies for Logan."

Ma said something about hoping her daughter had settled her feelings and was ready to move on, but Celeste wasn't really listening. The ache in her heart got in the way.

Chapter 30

LOGAN RODE OUT TO THE north forty of his property to check up on his men rounding up twenty head to be moved to Steam Boat Springs for market. He lifted his cowboy hat and wiped the sweat from his brow. "How's it coming?" he asked his newly hired hand, Ben.

"We've picked twenty of your best," Ben said, motioning to the cattle. "We're just waiting for your word, and we'll drive them out. We'll have them to Steam Boat and the rail yard in two days' time. And we'll be back in one more."

"That's nice to hear." Logan smiled as he nodded to Ben and the others. "Good work. Get movin' now."

Ben whistled to the other men, and they got the cattle moving.

Logan waved them on, thinking how normally this would have been the foreman's job. He, however, found himself liking his ranch a whole lot better now that he was out working alongside all the hands rather than from a distance. And men under his employ seemed a lot more content and willing to work harder now that he was doing so.

Though he was saddened by the way the Crandalls left his employ, it had been a gift from heaven at a time he needed it most. He'd hit rock bottom. Losing Celeste had been only part of it. Turning into Stanley and scaring the spit right out of himself had been the clincher. The Crandalls leaving had been the slap in the face he had needed to get his life back on track.

Fortunately, he'd only let money ruin him for a few weeks. "Hopefully, that ain't long enough to make my stupidity permanent," he said to Bootstrap as he patted his horse's neck.

Bootstrap neighed and shook his head.

"That's nice to know, my ole pal." Logan patted him again. "You know what else is nice to know?"

Bootstrap's ears twitched in response.

"That I don't have to keep all this money to myself. Sitting all alone in that big house trying to buy happiness didn't work, did it now?"

Bootstrap neighed.

"Heck, I bought myself the most expensive horse money could buy. And what did that make me do with my best friend?" Logan rubbed Bootstrap's neck with affection. It was a far cry from giving affection to Celeste, but it would have to do. "I put you out to pasture like Celeste has done to me. But I deserved it. You didn't." He rode several yards in silence and then added, "That was just plain stupid. But I ain't stupid no more. I don't sit alone in that house and wonder why I'm not happy. I get out and work—help those who are helping me. And if I'm going to spend money, I'm going to spend it on other people." A stab of pain tore through his heart. "Not to buy their affection, mind you, or to make myself look better than another. No siree. But because if somebody needs something and they can't afford to buy it for themselves, I got plenty to share."

As he approached the ranch house, ready to head on in to make himself a spot of something to eat, he noticed a man coming down the lane toward the ranch house. On foot.

"Come on, Bootstrap. What kind of fool comes all the way out here on foot?" Logan nicked his heels into his horse and took off. "Unless he's in some sort of trouble?"

The man's face came into view. *Charles?* Logan was tempted to turn Bootstrap around and hightail it out of there. The man's pathetic, long face made him stop. It was obvious Charles wasn't here to rub salt into the wound of their friendship—Celeste was out of both of their lives. It could be only one reason Charles was here. He needed help.

Logan rode quickly to him. "Morning, Charles," he said, pulling Bootstrap to a stop as he met Charles at the edge of the yard. "Hopefully you come in peace."

"That I do."

"That's good. We've had enough bad feelings between us to last a lifetime. We don't need anymore."

"Right you are, good fellow." Charles tipped his hat. "And thank you kindly for the warm greeting, for I feared quite the opposite. I swear it's the only one I've received all week. But then, you're the only one I didn't cheat out of money. Only a gal."

Celeste was much more than "only a gal." Logan dismounted and took a deep breath to soothe the ache his memories inflicted. He turned to face Charles. "What are you gibbering about?" He took a good look at his one-time friend, blinking once or twice as he took in the man's disheveled appearance. "Charles, you look awful."

"I feel awful."

"Come inside, sit down, and take a load off your feet." Logan motioned for him to follow him into the house.

"Thank you." Charles fell in step with him. "Mostly for not throwing me out on my ear for wanting to beat the pulp out of you a month ago." He hung his head. "Among other things."

Logan invited Charles to sit in the most comfortable spot in the great room and then hobbled into the kitchen to fix them both something to eat and drink. When he returned, Charles had his feet propped up on the foot stool and was reclined into the cushions of Logan's favorite chair.

Charles dropped his feet to the floor and sat up, accepting the food Logan offered him. "You really are a good fellow," he said with his eyes focused on the cold roast beef sandwich. "I'm not using that term loosely here. I mean it." He took a bite of his sandwich. After he swallowed, he asked, "What changed?"

Logan gave him a sidewise glance, not exactly sure how to answer.

"When you first came into your inheritance, you were quite the cad."

"Cad?" Logan could imagine what that meant. "You mean self-absorbed and greedy?"

"Something like that, sure." Charles smiled and nodded at Logan. "Was it having Celeste telling you she was through with you? I know that certainly turned my world upside down."

"She was the start of it. But, actually, it was when I realized I was headed down the same road as my brother, Stanley. He was the one who used to own the Circle J."

"Where is he now?"

"Dead. Got hanged for shooting Lavender's husband in the back. Over money." Logan shuddered.

"I do believe I've heard his name mentioned here and there around town."

"Nothing good, I presume."

"No, quite the opposite."

"Yep. That's why I had to change. I like folks too much, and I was getting to where I didn't like them. Probably because I couldn't make them do what I wanted. I thought if I threw enough money at people, I could get them to like me or at least bow and scrape to me just like my brother did. And he died a lonely man. No one shed a tear when he died. They all came out to see him hang. I even heard a few of them cheer. No, I didn't want to go down that road. I only hope that I've turned myself around quick enough that I haven't lost any more friends other than Celeste." Logan's heart twisted, and so did his expression as he glanced at Charles. "And you."

"I don't think you're too late there." Charles offered a feeble smile.

"So tell me, what brings you out this way, on foot, no less?" Logan sensed the man was in trouble. "Something tells me you didn't come just to chew the fat with an old friend you didn't even know was still your friend."

"You are correct there." Charles took another bite of his sandwich and held up his finger for Logan to give him a minute to chew and swallow. Then he stared at the floor. "I need help. Actually, I need money. Lots of money."

"I thought you were rolling in money, what with that big investment company you're working for."

"That's the problem. My boss was nothing but a con artist. He took the money he and I brought in from new investors to pay the past investors, until everything fell apart a few weeks ago and the law was onto him. I should have known there could never be enough money generated by selling stamps."

"You mean postal reply coupons. I could have told you that," Logan said, thinking back at how uncomfortable he'd felt when Charles had explained the process. "There's only a set amount of coupons out there. Even if your boss was making money at the beginning, selling those coupons at a profit, no way in Hades could he have made all the money he pretended to make."

"I don't think he ever sold a single coupon," Charles admitted with a grumble. "He was scamming even me from the very beginning. But I was so all-fired anxious to get rich quick that I only saw what I wanted to see." He wrung his hands together. "Now I've gone and lost all the money that the good people of Craig have entrusted with me. How can I face them? I've told them there's a chance the government will get some money from liquidating my boss's assets, but I doubt any of it will trickle down to them."

"And how do I play into all this?" Logan asked.

"I know it would be asking a lot, and I wouldn't blame you one bit if you said no, but I have to ask. I was wondering if you could lend me the amount of money I owe the people of Craig so I could pay them back, at least their investments. My word, some of these fine folks gave me every extra dollar they owned because they trusted me." Charles clapped his hands to his face and bowed his head.

"I have a question," Logan said. "Perhaps it's more of a curiosity. I'm guessing most men in your situation would have just skipped town. Why didn't you when you found out the bad news?"

Charles set down his sandwich and blinked hard, as if emotions inside him were stirring. "Because I like this town. I never felt so welcomed at a place in all my life. I'm wanting to put down roots here even though I no longer have myself a house or a gal. But nonetheless, I want to stay."

"Um." Logan's brain churned, realizing Charles was the "good fellow" he'd first thought of him as. He wanted to help, but throwing money at things was not always the best solution to a problem. "How much you figure it is, the total amount you're owing everyone?"

"Two thousand, six hundred seventy-five dollars." Charles said each number slowly, like each inflicted pain with its mention.

"That all?" Logan thought about Stanley's gambling debts he'd noticed on the books as he'd gone through the ranch's finances last week. They had added up to well over six thousand dollars, and Stanley's trip to South America last winter had been almost as much. If the ranch could absorb such losses and still function, surely it could afford to help out these people in need. "I think I can scrape up that much. It might take me a day or two, or three or four."

Charles's smile lines no longer drooped but came to life as he grinned from cheek to cheek. "Thank you!" He jumped out of his chair and rushed to Logan. "My good fellow," he added as he reached out to shake hands.

"Hold on." Logan held up his hand. "I wouldn't be flat-out giving it to you. It'd be a loan. Coming into a large sum of money without a lick of work ain't necessarily good for any person. Believe me, I know."

"A loan would be dandy. It's more than I'd expected." Charles chewed on a corner of his lip. "But as you know, I'm unemployed at the moment."

"How good can you ride a horse?" Logan asked, an idea forming.

"Not at all." Charles winced. "That's why I bought myself a car. So I daresay there aren't many places in northwest Colorado that would hire me on. Especially not after what I've done. And even if good fortune came my way and I found a job, say, washing dishes at Sunny's Place, it'd take forever and a day to pay you back. But I promise I'll do it. Somehow."

Logan shook Charles's hand and then motioned for him to sit back down. "Finish your dinner. And don't fret about paying me back until you get a job." Logan's idea of hiring Charles himself might not work after all. But that didn't matter; he had more money than he'd ever use. It's not like he played poker or had an itch to travel the world like his brother. It'd do his heart good, though, to see Charles and the hard-working folks of Craig recover from this little fiasco.

Charles picked up his sandwich as his eyes opened wide. "Did I hear you correctly?"

"Yep." Logan had to admit it was the first time having loads of money made him feel good—in a positive way, not in a power-filled way. "Now we just need to find you a job."

Charles's eyes looked a bit glassy with moisture. "Thank you, Mr. Logan Jones."

"You're welcome, Mr. Charles Weathersby." Logan was moved at the thought of having yet another friend in the town of Craig. "And I wouldn't worry yourself too much. With your smile and two good legs, you're sure to find yourself a gal in no time." Logan hobbled over and plopped onto the sofa adjacent to Charles. He patted his bum leg. "With me, it might take a little bit longer. But that don't matter. Maybe I'll never find myself a wife. If it requires that I have to wear those darn elevator shoes and pretend I'm someone I'm not, then I know I won't."

Charles finished off his sandwich and wiped the crumbs from his lips with the back of his hand. "I've got to be honest with you, my dear friend, though it pains me to do so."

"Yeah?" Logan leaned forward, his eyes connecting with Charles's as his gut anticipated more bad news.

"You never needed to pretend to be someone you were not."

"What do you mean?"

"I'm talking about Celeste here," Charles explained. "She liked you the way you were, even when you were poor as a church mouse. Even more so, I'm sure of it."

"Well, it's too bad she don't see me that way anymore. I can't go back to being poor, even if I *have* stopped myself from turning into my brother."

"No, but don't worry. I could see it in her eyes and hear it in her voice when she spoke of you."

"You talked about me when the two of you were together?" Logan hardly ever recalled hearing Charles's name come up in their conversation. But then again, he'd only had a few days with Celeste before she called it quits.

"All—the—time." Charles's eyes bore into him. "Celeste liked me just fine, as a friend. But you, my good fellow, she loved."

Those words reached inside Logan and ignited a fire. For good or bad, he was unsure. "Loved," Logan stated. "That means in the past. I'm sure she wants nothing to do with me anymore. She made that quite clear the last time we were together."

"That's when you were being a cad." Charles moved his plate off his lap and lifted his feet onto the ottoman. "But you've changed. You're back to the good fellow I first met, the one who welcomed a bedraggled stranger to your town the first day he was here—and made me feel like a million bucks."

"I hope I have," Logan admitted. And dare he hope Charles was right about Celeste?

"I'd say I was slitting my own throat here, but not really. I never had a chance with Celeste. I know that now. But you . . . you need to give Celeste the opportunity to see the new Logan Jones, or rather, the old Logan Jones."

"You're saying I should go pay her a visit, even though she said I shouldn't?" Logan wanted to hear it from someone besides his own thoughts screaming at him to do so.

"That's exactly what I'm saying." Charles stood and dusted the crumbs off his trousers. "Now, I'd better get going. I've got to find myself a job. And a cheap place to live. And learn to actually *work* again for a living."

"Are you willing to *learn* to ride a horse?" Logan asked, seeing this as the best solution for Charles to find employment and pay back the loan—not that Logan needed another ranch hand or the money, but because Charles needed to feel worthwhile. No one needed feelings of worthlessness rattling around in his head or his heart. And no one knew that better than Logan did.

Chapter 31

CELESTE SETTLED INTO THE OLD chaise lounge chair set amongst the cottonwoods. No sooner had she opened her book than the sound of a horse plodding along caused her to close it and lean forward to see who approached. Pa rode down the lane. Sighing her disappointment, she reopened her book and chided herself silently for being saddened it was only Pa. Who else would it be visiting them? Certainly not Logan delivering the mail. Those days were gone.

Pa veered off the road and brought his horse under the shade of the cottonwood tree. "Afternoon, Celeste. Sure is a pleasant one to read a book." He glanced overhead at the blue sky and then at the trembling leaves of the aspens in the distance that hinted fall was on its way.

"Yes, it is." Celeste tilted her head as she looked at Pa. "Is there something you want to tell me? You could have wished me a good afternoon from the road."

"You always were a perceptive child." Pa rubbed his chin. "That's good. I'm hoping you can take what I'm going to tell you and do what you need to with it."

"Is there something wrong?" Celeste brought her feet down at the side of the chair and sat up straight. "Bad news you've encountered in town, perhaps?"

"More like good news." Pa pulled a piece of paper from his shirt pocket. "I got our five hundred dollars back from Charles. This here's the deposit slip. I decided to put it in the bank. I plan on showing it to your ma. 'Twill make her happy."

"That's wonderful, Pa," Celeste said but somehow didn't feel it. "Now Ma can get her wagon."

"Yeah, 'tis quite amazing. Though I thought you'd be a wee bit happier." Pa's face grew serious. "There's something I think you should know. It's about how Charles came to have the money to pay back all his investors in town."

"Wasn't it from the liquidation of his boss's assets?"

"Nope." Pa shook his head. "The money came from Logan. He lent Charles the money he needed to pay off all his debts, then hired him on at the Circle J so he could earn the money to repay the loan, plus have a roof over his head in the bunkhouse."

"What are you saying, Pa?" Celeste believed she already knew.

"I admit it saddened me when I saw hints and then heard the rumors that Logan was falling into Stanley's footsteps. But I've a dandy thing to tell you." Pa smiled his crooked smile. "Logan's back to his old self. Only better. Imagine a soul as giving and loving as our original Logan once was but with scads of money he has little need of. What would a person like that do?"

"Help people," Celeste said, knowing exactly what the old Logan, the Logan who had captured her heart, would do with such a resource.

"Celeste, dear." Pa's expression grew serious. "I've never really told you what to do, because of course, you've always made your mind up by yourself. But right now I'm going to at least try to tell you what I think you should do. 'Tis the happiness of two peoples' lives, who are dear to me, at stake." He cleared his throat. "Give Logan another chance."

Celeste had thought of little else since she'd broken things off with him over a month ago, trying to figure out a way she could make things work with a man who was seduced by money and power. She could never think of a suitable solution. But this news was an answer to prayer. Unfortunately, she'd dealt rather harshly with Logan. "I fear he shall never wish to hear from me again. The words I lashed him with as we parted surely have left a mark."

"Celeste, 'tis Logan we're talking about. The old Logan, the man who wouldn't know how to hold a grudge even if his life depended on it."

"You are right," Celeste said softly and more to herself than to Pa. Dare she hope? "Even if he held no grudge, there's a good chance I have extinguished any feelings he once had for me."

"There is only one way to find out." Pa turned his horse back toward the lane. "Ask him," he said and then rode toward the corral.

Celeste settled back into her chair and opened her book to read. The words appeared as blurs on the page. Her mind refused to focus on them but focused instead on Logan. She had to know for herself if it was true, that Logan was his old self. Her heart nearly burst at the prospect. She didn't need to evaluate her feelings to know where her heart lay.

She closed her book with a snap and stood. Perhaps it wasn't too late to saddle a horse and head over to the Circle J ranch. By herself.

And stop being miserable so she could get on with her life.

The sound of horse hooves plodding through the rocky dirt told her another rider headed down the lane. She stepped past the tree enough to get a good look. Her heart sped. She recognized the horse, even from that distance. Bootstrap!

"Oh my word!" Celeste rushed her hand to her hair in an attempt to bring the wayward strands into the bun at the back of her head. She stepped back into the cover of the tree, realizing her dress was dirty from weeding that morning. And her face? She feared it, too, might be smudged with dirt.

Bootstrap drew closer and thus Logan. She could not make a run for the house so as to clean up without him seeing her. He might wonder if she was running away from him. That was one impression she cared not to inflict upon him again. Or ever. She stopped and stood firm, awaiting his arrival. She would apologize, ask his forgiveness, and then wait to see if he truly was the old Logan who'd captured her heart those many years ago as a child.

His eyes connected with hers while he was a good twenty yards away. She couldn't move her gaze elsewhere. He kept his eyes locked on hers as he pulled Bootstrap to a stop a few feet in front of her. *He's back to riding Bootstrap!* She took courage.

"Celeste." He spoke her name softly, with reverence it seemed. "What are you doing standing there?" He smiled with that particular grin Celeste adored, lifting one side of his mouth more than the other. "It looks like you're waiting for the mail."

"I always did enjoy that." Celeste reached back to those memories with fondness. She couldn't hold back her own version of a lopsided smile. "Even though there was never so much as a postcard in that mail for me."

"Well, you're in luck today." Logan dismounted and immediately dug into his saddlebag. "I've gone back to delivering mail to the RFD routes now and again."

"Why?"

"Because even the new mail carriers need a day off from time to time." He retrieved a handful of letters and held them out for Celeste to take. "And I always did enjoy this job. It gives me a chance to talk to folks a heck of a lot more than running a ranch."

Celeste took the mail from his hand, accidently touching his fingers. The press of his calloused skin sent a tingly sensation up her arm. "Yes, that makes sense." The feeling spread through her body, and she recognized her old Logan.

"My but you look beautiful today, Celeste." He gazed at her.

Celeste felt her face flush with warmth, especially as she stared at him, standing a mere two feet away from her. He wore a new cowboy hat, not an expensive one, but the basic kind that the mercantile stocked on its shelves. The same with his cowboy boots and his trousers and shirt. His clean-shaven face was lit with his usual smile and twinkling eyes. What caught her eye the most, however, was his hair. It reached down almost to the top of his collar and curled up at the ends. "You don't look so bad yourself, Mr. Logan Jones." She couldn't keep the tease from her voice.

A blush of pink appeared on Logan's cheeks, making him all the more handsome. He pointed to the top letter in the stack she held. "Like I was telling you, there's actually something in the mail for you today."

She moved her shaking thumb to one side so she could read the writing on the envelope. It was addressed to her, Celeste McCurdy. The left-hand corner simply held the name Logan Jones. There was no stamp in the right-hand corner. "So you're sending me a letter for free, cheating the postal service out of a two-penny stamp, are you now?" she teased outwardly. Inwardly, she was touched and could hardly wait to see what that envelope held inside.

"Good point," Logan said. "I'll make sure I give Harold—he's the new postmaster—two cents when I get back. Nice man, good as they come. You'll want to meet him next time you're in town." He pointed to the letter again. "I wrote that in case you weren't here when I came today." Pausing, he swallowed hard. "Or you were here and you wanted nothing to do with me. I was hoping written words might get you to at least read my apology and give me a second chance. But—" His voice broke, and he sounded on the verge of tears. "But you are here, talking to me like nothing changed. I hope that means what I think it means."

Celeste set the other letters on the chaise, holding onto the letter from Logan. "Would you mind if I read this now? Or would you rather I read it in private?"

"No. I mean yes." He rubbed the side of his head. "Go ahead, read it. I'm making such a mess of talking right now. I think it'd be best if you read what I'm trying to say."

Celeste opened the envelope, pulled out a single sheet of paper, and flattened it so she could read. It held lines of neatly written cursive. Strangely, she was touched by yet another simple but endearing quality this man possessed. With anticipation, she read.

> *Dearest Celeste,*
> *I wish to apologize for my inexcusable behavior while courting you and the weeks that followed, most of which you were probably*

unaware. I won't go into detail on those matters, as you already have enough ammunition to use against me. Just let it be known that I behaved poorly toward your friend Charles Weathersby and toward everyone who came in contact with me during those dreadful weeks after I received my inheritance.

One good thing, however, did come from me sinking so low as a man. I recognized I was headed down the same path that my brother, Stanley, took in life. A path I vowed I'd never go down. Yet there I was, a good stride or two in. Needless to say, I hightailed it out of there.

But I fear some damage has already been done. And done to the person who means more to me than anyone else on God's green earth. You, dear Celeste. I'll understand if you choose not to give me another chance. But my heart demands that I ask you for one. You see, I love you Celeste, more than these words on this page can ever say. Please, give me another chance to court you and show you properly how I feel about you. My efforts might not be perfect, because I'm not perfect. But I'll be better at it this time because I've learned what's important.

It certainly isn't money.

It's you.

Love,

Logan

Celeste folded the letter and stuffed it into its envelope, letting its contents settle inside her as well. "That was beautiful, Logan." She could feel its sincerity, almost like he was the one wrapping his arms around her at the moment rather than the splendor of his prose. Funny how she once thought he lacked expression of his feelings. If he were to take the entire length of their courtship to bring himself to take her into his arms and kiss her as passionately as she wanted to kiss him at that moment, she could wait.

"You really mean that?" Logan stepped closer as Celeste nodded. "So . . . does that mean you accept my apology and you'll give me another chance?"

"Yes," Celeste responded, fully aware of his broad shoulders, thick arms, and narrow waist standing merely a foot away from her now. She had to change the subject to divert her thoughts. To throw herself into his arms would not be prudent. Bringing the knuckle of her forefinger to her mouth, she chewed on it while she scrambled for a different topic to discuss.

"You know, you are adorable when you do that," Logan said, pointing to the knuckle in her mouth.

She quickly pulled her hand around to her back and held onto it with her other hand. "I heard that you helped Charles. That was very admirable, loaning him the money to pay back all his investors, then giving him a job on your ranch. Charles doesn't even know how to ride a horse." Gracious, she was making a mess of getting her mind off wanting Logan.

"Aw, I had some extra money kicking around. Seemed like a good thing to do at the time. Same with giving Charles the job of foreman at my ranch. I taught him how to ride first—probably the hardest thing I've done on the ranch since I took over." Logan chuckled.

"You did that?" Celeste's voice squeaked.

"Heck, I needed a foreman, not another ranch hand. I figure I'll have to teach him nearly everything he needs to know for the job. But the way I see it, that could be a good thing. I'll have the type of foreman I want."

"You are too modest, Logan." Celeste inched closer to him. "I daresay I like you much better this way than . . ." Her heart could barely contain her feelings for him as it was, and here he kept piling on more and more for her to adore.

". . . a month ago when you told me goodbye?" Logan finished for her.

"Yes." She gazed up at him, at the light shining from his eyes like they were a window to his soul. Oh, how she desired for his arms to wrap around her and tell her he was hers, to have and to hold, for the rest of her life. "Concerning that, I'm so sorry," she murmured. "And all the pain I have caused you. Will you ever be able to forgive *me* for my selfish idea to let you and Charles court me at the same time?" She just needed to hear a yes, and the rest of her day, her month and the year would be complete. Whatever pace he cared to take their courtship was fine with her.

U

Logan gazed into Celeste's eyes, a treat he feared he'd never partake of again, and she was asking for *his* forgiveness? "Excuse me? You think you have caused me pain? I must have too much wax in my ears, 'cause that can't be right."

Celeste quietly laughed in a most delightful fashion. Logan could have listened to it all day. "You always did have a way of saying things to put me at ease," she said

"Really?"

"Yes." Celeste's face was mere inches away as he lowered his head, keeping his eyes locked with hers. "You make me feel at ease . . . now—now that you are back to being the Logan I used to know."

"Uh . . ." The right words wouldn't come. "Enough talking."

He stepped forward and wrapped his arms around her, pulling her close and lowering his mouth to hers. Her lips felt soft as rose petals as they invited him to linger, pressing against his as they parted, beckoning him closer. A heavenly sounding gasp escaped her throat, setting his heart on fire. He'd never dreamed a kiss could be so wonderful. It was even sweeter than the last one, being fueled by love rather than a passion for what he wanted. Hesitantly, he ended the kiss as her lips pulled away. He gazed at her face, so close to his he could see gold specks amidst the green of her eyes. She was his gold, more valuable than any form of money could ever be.

"Marry me, Celeste." The words spilled from his mouth without forethought. "I don't want to chance losing you to anyone else."

"There would be no chance of that," she said softly as the gold in her eyes seemed to sparkle. "Yes, Logan Jones, I would love to marry you." She reached her hand around to the back of his neck, ran her fingers through the ends of his hair, and pulled them and his head back down to meet hers. They kissed again, longer and harder this time, both love and passion fueling the fire that burned wildly within him. He'd never felt so needed and cherished in his life.

Celeste's Apple Pie

Filling

 6 apples, Granny Smith variety is best (one quart of drained, bottled apples
  can be substituted)

 ¾ cup sugar

 ¼ cup cornstarch

 ½ teaspoon cinnamon

 ⅛ to ¼ teaspoon nutmeg (according to taste)

 1 tablespoon melted butter

 ¼ cup orange juice

Mix above ingredients together and pour into prepared pie crust.

Pie Crust

 2 cups all-purpose flour

 ⅔ cup lard

 2 tablespoons butter

 1 teaspoon salt

 4 to 6 tablespoons cold water

In large bowl, mix flour and salt. Cut in butter and lard until mixture resembles coarse crumbs. Add water 1 tablespoon at a time, mixing lightly with fork after each addition, until dough is just moist enough to hold together.

On lightly floured surface, with floured rolling pin, roll half the dough into a twelve-inch round. Roll dough round gently onto rolling pin, then ease into pie plate. Add filling. Roll out remaining dough, place on top of filling after wetting edges where top and bottom crusts meet, crimp edges together, then brush with an egg wash (a beaten egg applied with a pastry brush). Bake in a 350-degree oven for one hour.

Author's Note

THIS BOOK IS A WORK of fiction, but the Ponzi scheme mentioned in these pages is based on historical fact. The Securities Exchange Company and Charles Ponzi actually existed and served to scam numerous investors out of money similar to how it played out in this novel. Please forgive me, as an author, for setting this story ten years earlier than when Charles Ponzi's scheme went into action. It was necessary to keep the dates accurate with the preceding books in this series and to keep my main characters at a believable age to fall in love with each other. Charles Ponzi was, however, alive and working various other shady deals in 1910, and the U.S. postal reply coupons were in effect at that time. So this story *could* have happened as written.

U

About the Author

CAROLYN GREW UP IN A small town in rural Utah. In elementary school she discovered her love of creative writing, and in high school she put this to work on the school newspaper staff with her own column, *Carolyn's Corner*. She minored in journalism in college but soon abandoned writing for her love of plants and a degree in botany when a professor squashed her desire to write, "preparing her for the real world." Years later, after reading a disappointing book in her neighborhood book club, she decided she could write a better book than that, and she set herself to the task. Rediscovering her love of writing, Carolyn has since written twelve published books, including the four previous Western historical romance novels in her Craig, Colorado, series. *Where Her Heart Lies* is the fifth and final book in the series.

When she is not writing, Carolyn loves to garden, remodel houses, and spend time with her seven grandchildren. She also loves the color yellow, the smells of Mother Nature, and the sound of thunder. She dislikes shopping, social events, and milk chocolate. Yes, she realizes she's unique.